MINE

Lulu,
thanks for
your support. I
hope you enjoy the
book!! 2017

RB

MINE

RYENN GINGER

iUniverse®

MINE

This is a work of fiction. All of the characters, names, incidents, organizations, and dialogue in this novel are either the products of the author's imagination or are used fictitiously.

iUniverse books may be ordered through booksellers or by contacting:

iUniverse
1663 Liberty Drive
Bloomington, IN 47403
www.iuniverse.com
1-800-Authors (1-800-288-4677)

Because of the dynamic nature of the Internet, any web addresses or links contained in this book may have changed since publication and may no longer be valid. The views expressed in this work are solely those of the author and do not necessarily reflect the views of the publisher, and the publisher hereby disclaims any responsibility for them.

Any people depicted in stock imagery provided by Thinkstock are models, and such images are being used for illustrative purposes only.
Certain stock imagery © Thinkstock.

ISBN: 978-1-5320-1727-8 (sc)
ISBN: 978-1-5320-1729-2 (hc)
ISBN: 978-1-5320-1728-5 (e)

Print information available on the last page.

iUniverse rev. date: 02/27/2017

PROLOGUE

I WISH I could say my life has been easy. It's been nothing like that. Instead I felt love when I was a child but then paid the ultimate price: betrayal. People say they will always be there for you; but he never was. Not when it really counted. And I did the only thing I was able to do at the time. Run.

No one was going to be there to hold my hand. No one was going to be there to tell me everything was going to be all right... that I would get through it. NO ONE. It was the price I paid, I guess. I didn't know it would haunt me forever and that it would become my mission in life to find what was truly MINE!!

So many things can change over the course of hours, minutes or even seconds. What you once believed would last forever, can be taken from you in the blink of an eye. Not just once, but twice.

People always says they will do what is right for their children. I just hope that one day mine will understand. What I did was the hardest thing I ever had to do in my life.

As for him, he will never know. I did what I felt was right at that point in time. Who knew it would turn out like this that everything could disintegrate like a sandcastle?

As I lie here staring up from under my helmet, into those crystal blue eyes, I wonder if he even know it's me. But when he finds out......
Well, who knows what will happen......

— *Elizabeth Domenica DiAmmaro*

ONE

LIZZY'S EARLIEST MEMORY was as a five year old, running in her grandparents' back yard. Her grandfather would call her over to pick string beans from the garden and they would pick and eat them right there. Life was so easy back then. Just play, enjoy, love. You were a child and nobody expected much.

Her imagination was vivid. Pretending to be a wizard, she would stand in the window of her parents' family room singing a song until the rain stopped. She genuinely believed it was because of the song and her parents never said otherwise. They just smiled.

She would also stand for hours trying to figure out why the pictures of the ocean on the basement wall moved. It was a long time before she realized they were fish tanks with frames around them.

Then came the teenage years.

She was not what you would call a troublemaker, but neither was she an angel. Like every teenager, Lizzy pushed the limits; wanting to see how far she could go.

At sixteen, she met Nick, the LOVE of her life (he still was in a lot of ways). They did everything together and it drove her father nuts. Her dad always said Nick was bad news and would not amount to anything.

When she came home with her first tattoo, Lizzy hid it because she knew it would get her in shit. She had it put on the hip, just for her and no one else. It was a cute tattoo, though. A little star in a diaper, with a soother in its mouth. She always referred to it as her inner child just busting to get free.

Lizzy's second tattoo was a little more obvious: a bright white daisy on her forearm. Her mom noticed right away, her dad about a week later. She could tell they were not impressed.

Nick was tall, about six feet and lean with a rock hard body. The kind most guys would workout years for, but never achieve. She loved to run her fingers through his sandy blond hair. There was something about the feel of that slight bit of curl hugging her hand as she combed through his hair. She would get lost in his crystal blue eyes. No matter what they might be doing, those eyes just drew her in.

When he held her in his arms, she felt safe, like nothing could hurt her. It was a feeling she wanted to last forever... Lizzy should have known better.

They were like most people at that age, hanging out in parks and drive-ins, enjoying each other's company. Laughing and cracking jokes with friends... having the occasional adult beverage.

Lizzy would always stay out past curfew *because* it would drive her parents nuts and always joked that she was part angel her halo was just hanging on her tail.

One of her favorite summer pastimes was camping. Lizzy's parents believed those trips were with a friend's parents and the girls. They never knew the guys would camp out at the next site beside them. As soon as the parents fall asleep, the girls would sneak over to the guys' tents.

Sex was a big part of those weekends. As long as they were back in their tent before the adults woke up, they were fine. And they *made* sure never to get caught.

It was their private time, when they could lie there and be with each other. The world outside the tent forgotten, they would plan their futures: where they would like to go, what they would love to see.

Lizzy dreamed of going to see the places her parents had been born in Italy. How, one day, she would actually do it and no one could stop her. Nick always replied that they would meet there and run away together. When you are sixteen, you know it probably won't happen, but you still enjoy the dream.

Nick liked to do some extra credit stuff for shop class. Parents really should read the fine print, though, before telling their kids to take shop as an elective in school. He learned about the inner workings of cars. In fact, he learned well enough to know how to steal them, too.

He wouldn't cause any damage, just take them for a quick ride and then park them the opposite way in the driveway. It was a game he played even after graduating high school. That all changed when the car he tried to take was an unmarked police cruiser. He had pranked the same neighborhood too many times and the cops laid a trap.

At 22 years old, he was off to jail for six months. Who knew so much could change in such a short time? Her father was so happy Nick was gone that he wanted to celebrate.

"Now that the good-for-nothing boy is gone," he said, "you can smarten up and get your life back on track."

"I'll wait for him just to piss you off!" Lizzy screamed at her father as she ran up the stairs. "Just you watch!" It was one of the last conversations she had with the man.

Nick had been in jail for about a month when everything changed. Lizzy found out she was pregnant, and wanted to tell Nick, but wasn't allowed to talk to him. Nobody would give her the number at the prison or tell even tell her where he was. In the end, she had no choice but to tell her parents.

Mom would not even look her way. All she could do was shake her head and mumble, "Elizabeth, how could you?".

Dad… Well he said to get out and never come back.

Not the reaction she was hoping for at all. But, with just the clothes on her back Lizzy headed for the door. As she hesitantly reached for the door knob, she hoped for a 'Stop.' Or 'Don't go. We can work through this.' Instead, the reflection of her parents in the glass said it all. Mom had her head down and was crying. Dad just glared the anger radiating from him.

Seeing her five foot three inch self in the glass she paused. Her dark brown hair that hung past her shoulders with a slight curl, the hazel of her eyes as they darkened in dis-belief. A narrow waist, full chest and slightly rounded hips; she knew her features would be changing with the months to come. Placing her hand on her belly, whispering, "Don't worry little one. It's just you and me now."

Nick didn't know she was pregnant with his child. His father was an alcoholic and would just tell her to get lost. Lizzy had no other family except for one cousin who she only ever spoke with via email.

She had a fifty dollars in her pocket and that was it. She resolved to make it last as long as she could.

The first few weeks were spent with different friends here and there, but she never stayed very long in one place. Her parents had said what they had to and there was no going back for Lizzy or her unborn child, so she had to keep moving.

One of those nights, she stopped by her friend Jan's house. Although Jan wasn't there her mother still invited Lizzy in. Jan's parents had company over and she felt bad, but really needed someone to talk to. Jan's father was in the office just finishing a business meeting with one of his suppliers and her mother had been in the parlor with a group of women, talking over coffee.

Jans mother introduced her to a woman Mrs. Ciresco and they began chatting. The two older women had just met that night and Lizzy became the buffer between them. It seemed that Jan's mom really didn't want to entertain the woman as she kept excusing herself to the kitchen.

During one of those absences, the woman and Lizzy began talking and Mrs. Ciresco told her they were looking for someone to help out in her gardens over the summer, complete with room and board. Afraid the offer might be taken back, Lizzy quickly accepted but did not tell Mrs. Ciresco about the pregnancy. For a few months, at least, she would not need to worry about where to stay or what she was going to eat.

When Jan's mom came back, Lizzy excitedly told her she was going to work for the Cirescos, but asked her not to tell Jan or anyone. Jan did not need to be put in the middle of this, she thought, and Nick did not need to find out about the pregnancy from someone else.

As the office door opened, a tall dark haired man exited with Jan's father. Arrogance radiated from him. The dark suit and stiff demeanor made him look unapproachable. How the sweet lady she had just met was married to this man, they seemed nothing alike. As he walked closer to him, she could see the stiff set in his jaw and intolerance in his eyes.

It was only as he neared his wife that his features softened as the corners of his mouth slide up.

His wife filled him in, with a glaring expression, Lizzy knew that his Mrs. Ciresco got whatever she wanted. In hindsight, Lizzy should have asked more questions, but that was something she would learn the hard way.

As she left Jan's house, Lizzy had a strange feeling. She should have paid more attention to her gut, but if she had, then she would not have grown into the woman she'd become, by virtue of having gone through all the things that the decision had led to.

"Do you need to stop somewhere to get your things?" Mrs. Ciresco asked as they all got into their car.

Lizzy told Mrs. Ciresco her parents asked her to leave after an argument, not because she was a bad kid, they just didn't agree with her life or boyfriend choices. Her benefactor was very nice and said not to worry. They would fix the problem in the morning. She would take Lizzy shopping to buy a few things. She seemed very nice and just wanted to help out in any way she could. It was the beginning of what Lizzy thought would be a nice friendship.

As they were driving, Mrs. Ciresco seemed so happy to have Lizzy coming with them. She told the young waif she would love their place on the outskirts of Toronto, in a little town called King City. It was quiet and quaint, she said, and they had lots of gardens and green space where Lizzy would be free to enjoy and wander the grounds, and generally make herself feel at home.

When they exited the 400 Highway and turned onto King Rd, Lizzy thought they were in the middle of nowhere with all the trees and forests.

She had become so used to seeing the CN Tower from her window, she hadforgotten how pretty everything could be.

Mr. Ciresco turned the car left onto Jane St. and went further north until they turned to face a beautiful stone and iron gate at the foot of a long driveway. It was like nothing Lizzy had ever seen and she still could not see the house.

Her new friend had not been kidding when she said the grounds were big. They were like a few hundred acres big. Wow, Lizzy thought, she was going to enjoy the next few months because, after this, who knew where she would end up.

They continued up the long, winding driveway and after a few minutes finally reached the most beautiful mansion — because house just would not cover it — she had ever seen. It was stunning: the clean light grey brick and stone facade, oversized windows giving you the view of the gardens, and the gardens with lush flowers everywhere… there was so much to take in and so much to see. Lizzy figured it would take the whole summer to find her way around without getting lost.

Inside, Mrs. Ciresco showed Lizzy to a room the size of all the bedrooms at her parents' house put together. With rich canopy bed sitting in the middle of the room. Red velvet comforter covering the king sized bed and soft pillows decorating the top. In the corner was a chair and small table facing towards the window. The walls were a soft caramel colored with black accented sheer drapes. Antique dressers and tapestry decorated the rest of the room. Mrs. Ciresco let her know their room was down the hall if she needed anything and gave Lizzy a pair of pajamas to sleep in.

The only question she could think of was where to find the bathroom. She did not expect for it to be in the same room. The thing was massive. You could throw a party in the bathroom alone.

Once her benefactor took her leave, Lizzy took one of the nicest showers ever in her life before putting her head on the pillow to fall into a dream-filled sleep. She dreamt of being able to raise her child in such surroundings and it never having a worry. That would be nice.

Lizzy slept for what felt like days and was fully rested when she awoke. She was surprised to find her clothes folded neatly on the chair in the corner of the room never having heard the maid come into the room.

Lizzy laid in bed staring at the room, unable to bring herself to believe this was not part of a dream; that, even for a short time, she could enjoy this.

MINE

After dragging herself out of bed (because it was so comfortable), Lizzy made her way to the windows, opened the curtains and just stared at the view. In the distance was the forest with all its lush trees: maples and oaks nestled between evergreens. The trees must have been there for centuries because of their sheer size.

You didn't see that growing up in Toronto. Sure there were trees, but nowhere near the size of these. When Lizzy noticed see the roman shaped pool with its deck and gardens surrounding it, she thought spending the summer working here would definitely be one to enjoy.

Terring herself from the view and managing to get dressed. Lizzy wondered if it looked that good from inside, how would it look like from outside? The only problem was, she had been so tired when they reached the estate last night, she was not quite sure how to make her way around.

Deciding to exit the bedroom and listen for some noise: children, TV, anything that would give her an idea which way to go. Lizzy was so happy to see someone walking down the halls she almost ran them over in her excitement.

"I'm sorry. Can you please show me the way to where Mrs. or Mr. Ciresco are please? I would like to thank them for last night and begin working as soon as possible." If gardening was the only way to pay them back, she planned on being the best gardener they'd ever had.

"They are in the kitchen," he said. "Right this way, miss."

Thanking the gentleman as he kindly showed the way to the kitchen. It took so long to get there, she would never have found it without his help.

Mrs. Ciresco was so happy to see Lizzy she jumped out of her chair.

"Did you sleep well dear?" she asked graciously. "Can I get you anything? Cook will make you whatever you like for breakfast." She looked so happy to be doing something for me it was strange.

"Thank you," Lizzy replied, "just some toast would be nice. I don't normally eat breakfast, but I'm a little queasy this morning." Not wanting to let them know about the morning sickness.

"After you eat something," Mrs. Ciresco added, "we'll head to the store and buy you a few things you'll be needing."

7

"That would be great. But please, take it out of my pay. You've been so nice to me already, I wouldn't feel right."

"OK, I'll take it out of your wages, but you are going to be treated like a member of the family and are to eat your meals with us or no deal."

"That would be great," Lizzy stammered. "Thank you... for everything."

After breakfast, Mrs. Ciresco took her new charge to the stores. While she made sure Lizzy had everything she could need, the young girl made sure to get things which were loose and stretchy so they would last a while — who knew how long the pregnancy would take to show. Mrs. Ciresco bought dresses, pants, shorts, t-shirts, undergarments, shoes, soaps and shampoos. It was like she was having more fun than Lizzy and probably spent all the money Lizzy would earn over the whole summer. And wow, she didn't blink twice.

On the way back to the estate, she told Lizzy about Mr. Ciresco and herself. How they'd moved here from Italy when they were newly married but went back and forth among their homes in Rio, London and Paris, and how they travelled the world for Mr. Ciresco's business dealings. He was an importer/exporter with holdings all over the globe. She loved Canada the best, so they spent a lot of time there.

She was a lovely woman in her late thirties, with shoulder length, chestnut-brown hair, a slender build and green eyes. Her eyes, though, they held a sadness Lizzy couldn't understand. Mrs. Ciresco met her husband when she was 21 and they married only a few months later. He was the love of her life and they had never been apart. Even though she told their story with a lost look in her eyes. Her parents did not want them to get married (to which she totally related), so they eloped and ran away to Canada and settled here. His parents were extremely wealthy so he was able to work from anywhere in the world.

Lizzy asked her about children and Mrs. Ciresco drew quiet. No matter how much as she was interested, though, she did not press the subject. It was her boss's private business.

As they returned to the estate, the grounds were busy with workers. The butler came out to help with the bags and Mrs. Ciresco directed him to take them to Lizzy's room. Then, she quickly took the young lady by the arm for a tour of the grounds. As the move brought back her smile, Lizzy let her lead on.

Even though she thought the view was stunning from the bedroom window, Lizzy discovered the grounds were a thousand times better up close. The air *smelled* clean. You could actually hear birds chirping in the trees. And I mean birds, not cooing pigeons, actual birds greeting the day with their songs. Even the colors on their feathers were breathtaking. As they walked the grounds, Lizzy discovered paths and surrounded by butterfly gardens, as well as walkways etched in stone with shrubs and daisies (which are still her favorite).

Mrs. Ciresco took her to a little garden on the side of the pool that was breathtaking. Each plant complemented one another gorgeously, but was still beautiful on its own.

"This will be the garden you are to tend," Mrs. Ciresco told her. "It won't take you long each day, and the rest of the day is yours to do with as you please, but I would like if you could keep me company."

"It's so pretty, but are you sure this is all you would like me to do?" Lizzy asked. "There isn't more?"

"This is all, this garden is very special to me and I like it looked after constantly. The other gardeners are wonderful, but this one deserves so much more. I began planting it when we first bought the house just a few years after we were married. We tried for years to have children, but were never so blessed. Each time we tried, though, I would come out and tend to this garden. It's always been my own special place."

"I'm sorry you were unable to have kids," Lizzy said softly. "You would be a wonderful mother. I can see that in just the short amount of time we've spent together." Her heart truly went out to the woman; *that* was the sadness in her eyes — the longing for a child. She instinctively reached down and felt that much closer to the hope in her belly.

As the weeks went by, Lizzy grew closer and closer to Mrs. Ciresco and no longer thought about her parents turning their backs on her. She did, however, think of Nick often knowing he would be out in just a few more months.

It was almost the end of July as Lizzy celebrated her 22nd birthday. The weeks had just flown by and Lizzy thought she would miss all this when she left.

A few times over the summer, Mrs. Ciresco commented on how pale her new gardener was looking and suggested she see her doctor. Lizzy knew what was wrong, but was due for a checkup anyway, so she agreed.

Sitting in the doctor's office, all Lizzy could do was imagine what it would be like. Mrs. Ciresco had become like a second mother. In fact, Lizzy thought Mrs. Ciresco enjoyed it as much as she.

The doctor came in the office with his portable ultrasound machine wanting to check everything out. Lizzy had told him about the pregnancy right away and he agreed not to tell the Ciresco's. You could tell he wasn't impressed with the young, unwed mother, though. Oh well, at least she was not his kid.

As he placed the cold jelly on her belly and began to move it around, she felt excited. This would be the first time Lizzy would see her baby and Nick wasn't there to share it. He didn't even know there was a child on the way. A deep sadness washed over Lizzy, but there was nothing to be done about it and she knew it.

Now, when you're getting an ultrasound done and the doctor says OOOOOOHHHHH, you probably have a reason to be surprised as well, right? Well, let's just say Lizzy was surprised. He told her the baby was happy and healthy, but then he proceeded to inform her there wasn't just one baby — let's try triplets. At which point, she passed out.

As Lizzy slowly came to, everything the doctor had said came flooding back.

"WHAT DO YOU MEAN I'M PREGNANT WITH TRIPLETS?"

"That's what the ultrasound showed," he said, "three babies. And that would be why you're so pale. You need to eat more because they are taking all your nutrients."

He went on to tell her a whole bunch of stuff, but after the word triplets, he kind of lost her. One baby she could deal with. Three. OMG. It was a whole different story. She was 22 years old — no parents to help; a boyfriend in jail who did not even know she was pregnant, and she was about to have not one, not two, but, yes, three babies. That's right, she hit the baby lottery. *WOW!* was all that was going through her mind.

When she walked out of the office, Mrs. Ciresco rushed over. Lizzy wondered if she really looked that bad. *Hello!! Triplets!* Yes, she looked that bad.

Mrs. Ciresco was genuinely concerned, you could tell by the way she was fussing, and Lizzy thought she had to tell her; she deserved to know the truth. She knew Lizzy was not well and cared enough to bring her to the doctor but she did not push for answers, so Lizzy figured it could wait until they at least got home.

There, Mrs. Ciresco did everything a mother would: she saw Lizzy to her room and ordered up some soup and ginger ale. It felt nice.

"Elizabeth, let me know if you need anything," she said. "Just buzz down and I'll be right here." You could hear the concern in her voice, as if she didn't want to leave until she knew the girl was going to be all right.

"Mrs. Ciresco," Lizzy began, "please don't leave. I'd like to talk to you about something… I'll understand if you don't want me to stay after what I have to say, and I appreciate all the kindness you and Mr. Ciresco have shown me…"

"Elizabeth," she said and walked over to sit at the side of her bed. She slipped her hand into Lizzy's and gave it a small squeeze. "Whatever it is, it will be fine. Now please tell me and don't worry."

Lizzy told her about Nick and her parents. The day she found out she was pregnant, how she was about 18 weeks along, now, and today the doctor said she was going to have triplets. Lizzy confessed how scared and alone she felt and how Mrs. Ciresco had shown more kindness without knowing than her parents had when they found out.

She couldn't hide the pregnancy any longer. She was definitely showing (ya, three kids showing). She explained how Nick didn't know and how there was no way of telling him because she did not know where he was. Towards the end of the conversation, Lizzy proceeded to cry her heart out. The crying was a long time overdue.

After she confessed everything, Mrs. Ciresco just sat there stroking the top of her hand with her thumb; not judging, simply crying with the young girl like the pain was her own. She stood up, leaned over and brushed the hair off Lizzy's forehead and placed a kiss there.

"Get some sleep Elizabeth and everything will be all right," she said. "I promise you. Don't ask any questions, just relax. It's what is best for you and your babies right now."

She turned around and slowly walked towards the door. Just before leaving, Mrs. Ciresco turned slightly and Lizzy mustered up a thank you. She smiled, closed the lights and shut the door. That's what a mother is supposed to do, not turn her back on her daughter. Comfort her when she needs it. And with that, Lizzy slowly closed her eyes and rested knowing that for tonight, at least, someone was looking after her. It felt nice.

TWO

As SHE SLOWLY shut the door and left Elizabeth resting in the room, Mrs. Ciresco knew what she wanted to do. She made her way to the study to find her husband.

Finding this girl and bringing her to the house had been a blessing. It allowed her to finally feel like a mother; something she had been denied all these years. She enjoyed having a girl in the house, being able to spend time with her and spoil her. Elizabeth was just what she needed to feel fulfilled. And now to find out that the child was pregnant. And, not just with one child, but triplets. The girl would never be able to give them the life she and her husband could. Their prayers, and possibly Elizabeth's, may have been answered.

She knew her husband would be hard at work in his office. The hours of slaving away and immersing himself in his work. This would bring them back together, give them a family. Well, her, at least. She lost her family years before and this would help ease the hurt she still faced every day because of it. First, however, she had to present him with the idea. But, she usually got what she wanted.

As she neared the study, she could feel her heart race. Deep down she was nervous. It was a big step, but one she was ready for. Elizabeth had made her ready to ask this question. It was one she had been wanting to ask for a long time. Finally the timing was right.

Placing one hand on the handle, her other palm resting flat on the door's surface, she just needed a deep breath to relax. Feeling herself slowly turning the knob, she knew she was ready. Their lives were about to change.

"Darling, do you mind if I come in and talk to you for a moment?" she asked Mr. Ciresco. "I have something I would like to discuss with you— something that could affect both our futures."

Intrigued by his wife's request, Mr. Ciresco put his work down to listen. It wasn't often she made requests like this. By the look on her face, he knew it was important.

"As you know," she began, "I have grown quite fond of our dear Elizabeth and....."

"Yes, dear I know. And, I know how you've longed for a child. But she already has parents and we are but a temporary substitute."

"Yes," she countered. "But, as *you* know, I took Elizabeth to the doctor's today. It seems the girl is pregnant. And at such a tender age, you know she will never be able to look after the child properly. I was suggesting asking her how she feels about adoption. We would make wonderful parents and give the children a life she would never..."

"First you said child and now you're saying children. What exactly are you talking about?"

"Well, yes," she paused. "I did say children. Triplets to be exact. That's why she's been so weak and pale all the time. She won't be able to raise them as she would like to.

"I haven't mentioned it to her, but how do you feel about adoption?"

"Three babies are a lot to deal with," he said, "are you sure this is what you want? Do you really think she would give her kids up for adoption?

"There are many factors to Consider," Mr. Ciresco continued. "We travel so much. Where would they go to school, and where would we stay. You know our business, we are constantly on the move because of work. This will mean major changes."

Seeing how eager his wife was — and how his reaction seemed to dampen her spirits— he wasn't sure which way to go. "Talk to her," he said, "and then we'll go from there."

MINE

"Thank you," she said with relief. "I will mention it to her in the next few days and see what happens. I will let her get used to the fact of triplets and all the work they will involve first."

As she left the office, she knew what she had to do. No matter the cost, she was going to be mother to those babies. Something like this doesn't happen every day, and she was going to use it to her advantage.

THREE

THAT NIGHT, LIZZY did not sleep much. One baby, ok. Two, wow. Three, HOLY CRAP! *What am I going to do?* was all that kept going through her head. Pregnant at 22 with triplets and their father in jail. Lizzy wondered what she had gotten herself into while she rubbed her belly, knowing it was now her and three kids was overwhelming. *But,* she thought positively, *I can do this. No matter what, I would do this.*

In the morning, she got up, showered, dressed and made her way to the kitchen where she found Mr. and Mrs. Ciresco sitting at the table. They both looked up and smiled when she entered.

Lizzy was startled as she could not remember the last time someone seemed happy to see her. She missed Nick terribly at that moment, wanting him to share this... but he didn't even know, and still would not for at least two more months. Wow!

"How are you doing this morning?" Mrs. Ciresco began. "What can I get cook to make you?"

"Nothing right now please," Lizzy answered. "The nausea is gone for the moment and I'd like to keep it that way."

"Well today," Mrs. Ciresco said, "we are going to get you some new clothes. You will need them in the coming weeks. I also scheduled you another doctor's appointment so we can determine your exact due date and what the obstetrician thinks the best route is for you."

"Mr. and Mrs. Ciresco," Lizzy pleaded, "I appreciate all you have done and *are doing* for me; but can I ask you why? No one has *ever* been this nice to me. Why me?"

Mrs. Ciresco looked across the table to her husband. He nodded, got up and left the two of them alone to talk.

"I don't have a child anymore," she began, "let alone a daughter. That is what you feel like to me. You have given me a feeling I never thought I would have again. And, for that, I am truly grateful. My husband and I have been blessed with wealth, but no one to share it with. Having you with us, gives us the chance to do something good."

"But," Lizzy said, "my job will be done when the season comes to an end. I will miss you and hope we can remain friends after. But…"

"We have discussed that," she cut in. "Mr. Ciresco and I think it's in your best interest to remain with us. We can help look after you during your pregnancy, and make sure all your needs are meet."

"And what would you like in return. As much as you say this is your way of being good, I've learned no one does anything nice except for their own purpose. As I said, I appreciate all you've done but… what is it you want from me, Mrs. Ciresco?"

Having a feeling deep down, already fearing the answer, her hand slowly slid down to cup her swollen abdomen.

"Since you are being so direct with me," she said, "I will do the same. Mr. Ciresco and I would like to adopt your children."

"WHAT!"

"Hear me out first, please. You're 22, pregnant with triplets and your boyfriend is serving time. Correct me if I'm wrong: You can barely look after yourself, let alone three babies. And when this Nick comes out, are you sure he will be thrilled with being a daddy? He, himself, is still a child. Think very carefully Elizabeth. I offer you a chance to keep your youth. A chance to finish school and make something of yourself. Your children will want for nothing, ever. They will have everything their hearts desire, every whim answered. The best education money can buy. Can you do that for them?"

After the soliloquy, Lizzy sat at the table dumbfounded. First, for the gaul this woman had to openly say she wants her children, and second, for stating the obvious: Lizzy could never give the children what the Cirescos could. She pushed the chair away from the table, not really knowing where to go, knowing only she needed to escape. At a loss, she attempted to walk away from the conversation.

"Elizabeth, take a walk through the gardens and think about what I've said. Before you say no and leave the estate, really consider what is best for your babies. Please."

With that she was out of the house. Lizzy must have wandered the grounds for hours until she discovered a nice shady patch of grass under the tree near the pond. So much weighing on her thoughts, she plopped down and began to cry. Mrs. Ciresco was right and she knew it. Lizzy could never give the kids this life and they could. *Am I being selfish in wanting to keep my kids?* She thought. *What kind of life could I give them? Going on welfare, living in squalor. They deserve better. Hell, I deserve better.*

But, what did the Cirescos do? He was always working and very secretive. She just seemed to flutter from one thing to the next. She did not know these people, but neither do most parents who give their kids up for adoption. At least, she had the opportunity to live and spend time with these people they treated her like their own daughter — not the hired help she was.

Living without her children wasn't an option, though. She would never forgive herself, Lizzy knew. If she ever did see Nick again, she knew she could not look him in the face. The worst was he would never get to know his own kids. There had to be a way of keeping them in her life — there just had to be.

If the Ciresco's wanted to adopt her children, Lizzy would ensure it was on her terms. Yes, it was selfish; she was pretty much an orphan herself as her parents did not want anything to do with her, but what did she have to lose?

As she made her way back to the house, Lizzy envisioned the kids running around here, driving the maid and butler nuts. It was true, they would have everything they could ever need or want. She wandered through the house until finding Mrs. Ciresco.

"May I speak with you please?" Lizzy asked. "Mr. Ciresco, as well? I would like to say this only once if possible." Her nerves were going nuts and her nausea was back full force.

"I'll call him," she said while walking to the buzzer on the wall. Within moments Mr. Ciresco was entering the room.

"I've thought a lot about your offer," Lizzy began. "Please let me finish before you judge or question. I do believe you both can give my children a better life than I could ever imagine… And I am truly grateful for the offer, but I couldn't live with not knowing my children. I don't have a family anymore and they're all I have.

"What I suggest is," she continued, "if you are willing to adopt my children, I come with them. You adopt me, as well."

Pausing a moment to let the idea take root in their minds, Lizzy went on, "I'll change my name so there is no trace of my old life. I will be your daughter and you can raise my children. That way, I can see them grow up and live without guilt. My children will call you mom and dad, and know me only as their big sister.

"At the same time," she added, "you'll have the knowledge they will always be in the best of hands — I would never let anything happen to them — and they would carry your name. There would be no need for the adoption process because no one would be the wiser. Only the three of us and the current staff here would know. The opportunity would allow me to finish school and know that as I lead my life I would always be a part of theirs. This is something I could live with without regrets.

"Can you say the same?" Lizzy finished. "I will go to my room and give you time to consider my offer." It took everything in her not to cry as she delivered her speech. Nick would never see her again or know of his children, but they would be safe, loved and have everything. There was nothing more for which she could ask.

On the way to her room, she could not keep from continually second guessing her decision, but she wanted her kids to have the best. They did not choose to be born to an unwed, 22-year old mother who had been disowned by her own family; or to a father who was serving time (even if it was only for a few months). They deserved the best and this was an opportunity to give it to them. Lizzy would be damned if she did not take it. As long as this all played out in the children's' favor, nothing else was important.

She knew her kids would be happy growing up in these surroundings, as well as healthy and looked after. What more could any parent want? And, if the Cirescos agreed she would be on the journey with them. She would be there to see them crawl and take their first steps; watch them run around and play tag. Be there when they graduated high school and found their first loves. She would see it all. So what if they believed her their sister and not their mother. They would at least be in each other's lives forever.

But what to change her name to? Something both fitting and that would let no one know it was her. There had to be something fitting. This was going to be fun, she thought. It couldn't be something too close to Elizabeth, just in case. And her middle name was completely out of the question, no one was going to call her Domenica. I'm sure the Cirescos would like it but, um, no... There had to be something.

Then she remembered her Nona use to call her Mimma. After considering it for a bit, she thought it kind of sounds like momma, but nobody would really clue in. And on top of that, it *was* a variation on Domenica that would allow her to hold on to a piece of her old self. It might just work. Mimma Ciresco. That would be it. And every time her kids would say it to her it would feel like momma and no one would ever have to know.

It felt like hours had gone by since speaking with the Ciresco's. When they finally asked her to join them she was actually frightened. What if they didn't like the offer? What if they still only wanted the kids and not her? There were so many what ifs she was making herself sick.

She took a minute to pull herself back together. This was, after all, her choice. She had presented them with an offer. Lizzy eased out of the room and headed for the stairs, following a route she had travelled quickly many times in the past few months. Today; it felt like an eternity would pass before she reached her destination. As Lizzy reached the parlor door and rested her hands on the handle, she knew she could do this.

She slowly entered the parlor to find Mrs. Ciresco standing there... smiling at her? Ok, now she was confused and worried at the same time. Mr. Ciresco was sitting on the wing chair, sloshing around some port in a tumbler. All she could hear was the ice cubes knocking around the sides of the glass. Her anxiety level rose considerably.

"Elizabeth," he began, "Mrs. Ciresco and I have talked extensively about your proposal. We would like to make some adjustments to your offer."

He sat so calmly as he spoke. All the while, her knees were knocking together faster than she ever thought they could.

"Sir," Lizzy blurted out, "I can't separate myself and my children. Even though they aren't born yet, I am connected to them..."

"Yes, Elizabeth," he continued before she could go on. "We realize you're all a package deal. Please, just hear us out first. And please have a seat, you look completely flustered."

He motioned for Lizzy to sit in the wing chair adjacent to his own. It was definitely not her first choice, but she was not about to refuse. Lizzy was sure they would hear her knees going if this took much longer.

"Mrs. Ciresco and I have thought about your offer," he said. "But we do have a few conditions. First, we will need to change your name, as you so mentioned prior.

"Second," Mr. Ciresco continued, "once the babies are born, we will leave this house for one of our other homes for the season. Somewhere we haven't been for a while so people will believe all of you are our children.

"When we return here it will be with new staff," he went on. "We expect you to behave like you were raised by us. That means a lot of training on your part. You *will* be part of the kids' lives on a daily basis, but you are expected to receive an education and work in the family business when the time comes. No one besides the three of us in will know the truth. You will have no contact with your previous family and are expected to welcome and greet all my business partners as my daughter. All of whom will show you the upmost respect. Can you abide by our terms?"

"So," Lizzy asked, "when the kids are born, we leave the house, I groom myself to work for your family company and I get to be in my children's lives forever? I know I can live with that."

"From now on though, Elizabeth, you're to call us mom and dad so we don't raise any suspicions. We will leave for the cottage in the morning so there's no need to start until we are on the road. The staff there were all hired over the past season and will not question anything.

"So, welcome to the family, daughter," he smiled. "Now, all that is up to you is to choose a new name for yourself."

"I gave it some thought while I was upstairs," she smiled. "I would like if you called me Mimma... Mimma Ciresco."

"Very good, I will have your knew ID's drawn up shortly and then there will never be a problem. How's your Italian?"

"Manageable, but it could use some work," Lizzy said. She knew the odd word, not the best words, but the odd word.

"We will have a tutor at the cottage waiting for you to begin your Italian lessons," he laughed. "If you are to truly be my child, you must learn my language. Now, go get cook to make you something to eat, tomorrow will be a busy day."

"Yes, Sir... I mean, Dad." Wow, that sounded weird, but it was for the good of her children, and she could do anything for them.

As she left the room, Lizzy heard Mr. and Mrs. Ciresco talking about something, but could not make out anything clearly. She was going to see her children grow up and that was the most important thing, she thought, so she shrugged it off.

*   *   *

"Thank you darling," Mrs. Ciresco said. "You've made me a mother. I don't know if anything will ever make me happier than I am at this moment."

"You're welcome. Just make sure our Mimma learns everything befitting of our home. We wouldn't want any accidents to happen. Now go and enjoy our daughter, and I'll join you later."

As the words came out of his mouth, he knew what the future held. But, he would live up to his proposal. She would see her children grow up, and she would work in the family business. Lots of training would go into her. Who else but the children's mother to protect them. She would get the best training in the world and, when the time was right, she would learn the truth of the family business. But, for now, his only concern was her and the children's health was good.

He was going to make sure she was well educated. Anyone who knew him knew he praised education. She would have to work twice as hard, to ensure no one ever questioned her parentage.

He walked over to the bar and refilled his glass of port, taking a cigar out of his humidor. "The family she has always wanted," he thought. "And the best person to protect them."

As Mr. Ciresco made his way to the terrace, he knew what the future would hold. The rest of them would have to wait and see.

His wife's happiness was all that mattered. He'd seen her despair over not being able to have a child. A part of her life had always been missing. She was so young when they'd met. He stole her away from another. But he never really gave her a choice. When he saw her for the first time, he knew he wanted her — and he always got what he wanted. He promised her the world and gave it to her, not caring what she left behind. He had given her an option when they first met and she traded one life for another.

She left with him to protect the other. He knew that part of her heart was never truly with him. He was just better at hiding it than her other partner. Hopefully, with having children to call her own, she would have her life whole again. Her happiness meant the world and he would do whatever it took to make it happen.

FOUR

IN THE MORNING, everything seemed to move very quickly. Before Lizzy knew it, they were packed and on their way up to the cottage. On the way, she overheard the Cirescos say it was on Lake Rosseau. That was where you found the most expensive cottages and where stars were rumored to have their summer homes. Most people who lived here did their best to spend their holidays elsewhere, but the stars came to Canada to get away. LOL. I guess it is the same no matter what country you live in.

It was a roughly two hour drive from the Ciresco's home. But it was a nice drive. Lizzy remembered taking day trips to the beach up north with her parents as a child, so she was familiar with the route. Once you passed Orillia, you were driving through the country. It was very pretty. So many trees. You did not see much of those growing up in Toronto. Sure there were parks and forest, but not this close together.

For the first time since she found out she was pregnant, Lizzy was beginning to relax. She knew things were going to be all right and a feeling of peace came over her. In the seat beside her, Mrs. Ciresco was talking about something, but she was not really paying much attention. So many thoughts were going on in her head, Mrs. Ciresco's words were not even sinking in. They might have been important, but Lizzy just could not focus on her. She was so relaxed and peaceful; concentrating on the conversation was not part of it.

When they finally made it to the cottage, the car pulled up a long, tree-lined driveway. It was so beautiful. The cottage was still nowhere to be seen, but the surrounding gardens were amazing. As they rounded the drive and pulled up to the front of the building, Lizzy realized this cottage was bigger than their house. If this was where she was supposed to relax and take care of herself and the children, it was not going to be a problem.

She still had to get used to calling them mom and dad, and Lizzy had to do it fast because these people were all new staff and didn't know who she was. She wondered how they would react to a pregnant 22-year old. It was going to be fun. She could only guess what her new parents were going to tell their staff as it was not every day the wealthy had a child who came home pregnant. Oh well.

"Now, Mimma, from this moment on you are to refer to us as mom and dad. I know that it will be hard for you at first, but we must keep up appearances."

"Yes, Dad, I understand." Wow, that sounded strange.

He gave Lizzy a sideways glance and smirked. She had a feeling this was going to be an interesting summer.

Mom made an appointment at the local gynecologist's office as they needed to know how far along Lizzy was and when to expect the babies.

The fact her children would not be calling Lizzy mom would be hard, but she kept reminding herself they were going to get the best life possible.

Settling into the new surroundings, Lizzy was shown to her room. She was pleasantly surprised when she opened the closet to put my few belongings away and found it already filled with everything she could even think she might need. Mom and Dad must have ordered things and had them sent over. She would have to thank them as soon as she found them in this new maze of a house. Lizzy believed it might take the rest of the pregnancy just to figure out where the stairs were.

She wandered the halls not knowing which way to go. Up. Down. Left. Right. There were turns everywhere as if the house were hiding something in its sheer size. After the long drive, the biggest hidden prize, though, would be the bathroom. With three kids resting on her bladder, Lizzy was in no mood to play hide and seek. It had to be around here somewhere.

So many doors, which one to choose…? In desperation, she decided to just open them all. After finally finding it though, she learned there was one in her bedroom through the closet.

Next, Lizzy decided to continue exploring the house. Some of the rooms still had sheets covering the furniture because they were not used very often. The curtains were slightly translucent and you could see streams of sunlight in the dust floating through the air. It held such beauty.

Upon discovering all the important places — the family room, bathrooms and kitchen — she concluded the cottage was just plain beautiful.

Tired from the exploration, Lizzy found a throw and cuddled up on the couch. Mom did tell her to relax after all, she thought. In truth, the drive and excitement of the day had completely worn her out.

As she nestled down in the couch and closed her eyes, Lizzy guessed Dad didn't see her when he entered the room. Although she could hear him on his cell, she could not understand any of the conversation. It was one of the few times she wished her Italian was better because his tone said he wasn't happy with whomever he was speaking.

She had been more tired than she realized as the staff had to track her down for dinner. Mom had been beside herself with worry. Apparently they had been searching the house for 20 minutes.

Lizzy apologized for making everyone worry and Mom just smiled and told her to let someone know next time she took a nap.

That settled, the Cirescos — Dad, Mom and Lizzy — sat down to their first family dinner. Dad seemed to have a lot on his mind and did not talk much throughout the meal. You could tell something was bothering him and Mom did not press the matter. She just sat there and moved food around on her plate. Lizzy, on the other hand, was famished and devoured everything in front of her. It probably did not help that she had slept through lunch.

"Mimma," Mom asked, "would you like to take a walk around the grounds with me after supper?"

"Sure, that would be nice."

"Wonderful, I can show you where everything is. That way, no one will know you've never been here before."

"That would be nice. Thank you, Mom. By the way, what *do* the staff think?" Lizzy knew it was the million dollar question, but it had to be asked.

"*That* we will discuss on our walk. For now, finish eating."

Dinner went by rather quickly. Dad just sat there without saying much, but you could see he was thinking about something. Mom went on and on about how much Lizzy would enjoy the rest of the summer relaxing. At least she had that part right. Relaxing was one thing to which Lizzy was looking forward.

At the end of the meal, Lizzy and her new mother excused themselves from the table and made their way out the patio doors. The terrace was stunning. In fact, everything in the place was; it was as if you opened up a copy of *Architectural Digest* and BAM! this was the featured house.

The walk through the gardens was soothing. She could see herself walking through it on a daily basis. But knowing Mr. Ciresco, uh, Dad, her time was going to be more for studying than anything else. Lizzy hoped she could get some of the classes to be out here, sure learning could be much better outside than stuck in any office. After all, she had always been more of a visual person.

They had been walking for quite a while and since there was no around, Lizzy believed it was a good time to ask the question again.

"Can you tell me what the staff believe? I don't want to step on any toes or lead people the wrong way."

"They all believe you are our daughter who became pregnant while away at college," Mrs. Ciresco said. "You had to drop out, but are going to continue your studies at home with tutors. You shouldn't worry, after the baby is born the staff will be dismissed and new ones will be hired. These were only hired on a four month contract."

"Mr... I mean Dad has thought of everything, hasn't he?"

"He does like to keep his life private. All his employees sign non-disclosure documents before being hired. What happens here, stays here."

And that was the end of a very short conversation. She was unwilling to tell Lizzy anything else.

Although she understood, it did not mean Lizzy stopped wanting to learn more. All in good time, she thought. Nick used to say everything eventually comes out. Secrets only keep for so long. She hoped he would be wrong this time.

FIVE

As the pregnancy progressed, so did Lizzy's Italian. By the end of summer, her vocabulary had grown as much as her waist line. Nouns, verbs, adjectives, pronouns; would it ever end. Dad kept saying, "If you are truly to pull off being my daughter, people would expect you to be nothing less than fluent in the language." At this rate she would not only be fluent, you would swear Lizzy was born in Italy.

Mom went with her to all the doctor appointments and made sure she had the best care. The doctor put the due date to be around November, but because of Lizzy's age, and the fact there were three babies, he said she would probably deliver early. The children would most likely make their grand appearance in October.

Truth be told, the timing was just fine by Lizzy. She was already using the bathroom every two minutes and it was only the beginning of September. Her body felt bruised from the inside out. It definitely was not fun when your ribs were a punching bag for three young boxers. Wow, these babies wanted her to feel everything.

Lizzy was really looking forward to meeting the little ones. She could not wait to find out if they were boys, girls or both. Mrs. Ciresco, aka Mom, wanted it to be a surprise, and really what was a few more weeks at that point. The babies were healthy and so was she. That was what mattered.

Every now and then, though, she wondered about Nick. If he was thinking about her? If he wondered why she never called? Lizzy knew he would be mad about not knowing about the babies; but believed she was doing what was right by them. At least, that was what she kept telling herself.

Mom and Dad were right: Nick and she would never have been able to look after them properly by themselves. He was only 23 and there was so much of life left to discover. Thankfully, Lizzy thought, she would be able to discover life with her kids along for the ride.

Nick would be getting out of jail in another month. He wouldn't go to Lizzy's parents because her friends would have told him she had been kicked out. No one except her real parents knew she was pregnant so there was no worry about him finding out. She would just be the girl that every now and then someone wonders about:

"What ever happened to Elizabeth?"

"She just got up and left one day."

No one would come looking for her. Lizzy's parents had made it clear she was a disappointment. She was alone with her new family now and it would be that way forever.

September turned into October. Thanksgiving came and with it the waiting game. Mom decided it was best if we moved back to civilization before the babies came just in case there were complications — she believed the doctors were much better down by Toronto. When she saw the first snowfall was more than three centimeters, she knew it wouldn't be long before the snow was feet deep and she wanted no part of it.

Once the babies were born, she wanted to go back home. Lizzy assumed home was Italy, but if she learned anything living with her new parents it was to assume nothing because, truly, she did not get any of it.

Dad, was always sequestered in his study and she only ever saw him at dinner. If he wasn't at the table, Mom would march right up to his office and scream something to him. Within seconds he would come out and not go back again until the next morning — or at least until we retired for the night.

He entertained a lot of friends and business partners from around the world. She never met them, but he did tell them he had a daughter who was away at school and would return home for the holidays. Mom was never at those meetings, either. He would simply say she was on bed rest for the duration of the pregnancy and didn't want to see anyone.

All the men knew better than to upset a pregnant women. They just didn't know it was Mimma who was pregnant. That was the Ciresco's little secret.

It was late October when early one morning — the day she was leaving Lake Rosseau to head home, actually — Lizzy didn't feel well.

Maybe it was the stress of the move...who knows? She just wanted to lay down and rest. The butler was almost finished loading the car when Mom woke her up on the couch. She had warned being tired was part of the pregnancy, so that was all she had thought of it.

But, as they drove down through Orillia and made their way onto the 400, she realized it was more.

"Um, Mom," Lizzy groaned. "Could we make a detour?"

She seemed to know before the words were even out of Lizzy's mouth. Before she knew it, they were at the hospital, Lizzy was in a wheel chair being with Mom by her side just repeating,"Oh my God, oh my God, the babies are coming."

News flash, everyone knew they were coming. just no one realized it would be so fast.

The entire experience moved in slow motion. Up the elevator, down the hall, parked in a doorway. Thrown on the bed, Lizzy's legs put in stirrups and, seeing the position, realizing they were not for her benefit. The nurse paged the doctor and Dad was kicked out of the room. Mom was to be there, but Dad, um, that was way too up close and personal.

She remembered all of a sudden having all this pain and pressure. Lizzy looked at the nurse who looked at Mom. Mom looked back at Lizzy and she screamed her head off as the doctor walked through the door. Screamed probably put it mildly. Didn't they have drugs for this sort of thing.

The doctor became all too personal with Lizzy's anatomy as he said she was crowning. If that was a nice way of saying the babies were coming, she was not buying it. He kept saying stop yelling and push, all she could think was, "I'm squeezing a watermelon out of a lemon and you want me to not scream."

She thought he was nuts, but as another contraction ripped through her body, Lizzy took his advice, shut up and pushed. And wouldn't you know it: out came baby very quickly. The best description of how it felt would be like a gushy plop. Now, to do it two more times. She did not even hear whether it was a boy or a girl because the nurse was off to the corner while another baby was set to make its appearance in the next moment.

At first the doctor did not seem too impressed with Lizzy's age or pregnancy. When he realized triplets were in there, it became an interesting day. While baby number one was getting all prettied up, baby number two came out even faster than the first. She guessed the first just stretched the way.

She must have been delirious at this point because Lizzy thought the doctor said girl, but really couldn't tell you. And then baby number three was so quick even the doctor was surprised. One push and plop, out it came. As she lay there recuperating, Mom looked over and said Lizzy had given birth to two daughters and one son. All were healthy and looked great. They were seven weeks early and still big babies.

The nurse brought the children over one at a time for Lizzy to hold and then asked if we had names picked out. Names? Shit, we never discussed names. Lizzy asked for a few moments alone with her mom while they looked over the kids.

"I know we never discussed what the babies' names would be," she began, "but would you mind if I named them? It will be my legacy to them."

Mom just sat there for a moment. She and Dad must have already discussed names because she had that look on her face.

"Well, your father and I thought we would give them simple names like: Tori, Anna and Tiano. Did you have another idea?"

Lizzy thought about it for a minute. She knew people by each of those names, but they were short forms. This may work.

"Can we call Tori, Victoria; Anna, Julianna, and Tiano, Christiano? That way they have both your names and my names in them."

She smiled. Mom must have liked the idea because she leaned down, gave me a hug and kissed Lizzy's forehead. When the nurse came back, they told her the names and Lizzy was taken to her children. While in the hospital, for all intents and purposes the children were Lizzy's. She knew Dad would have the paperwork changed later, but for now she was going to be listed as their mother; father unknown. The best way to get around that situation.

So. Lizzy was now the proud mother of three healthy, beautiful children. Victoria, Julianna and Christiano and those would always be their names to her. Mom went out to talk to Dad and bring him in giving Lizzy a minutes alone with her children.

As she lay there on the bed, her children in her arms, all Lizzy could do was smile at them. They were perfect. Perfect little fingers. Perfect little toes. And, perfect little noses. The beautiful pink glow of their cheeks and the purity of the innocents.

She leaned down and whispered to them: "The three of you are my pride and joy. I will look after you always and forever. You will always have me in your lives. Hopefully one day you will learn the truth and forgive me, but I am doing this for you. You will always be mine and nothing, not heaven nor earth, could ever change that.

"Victoria, Julianna and Christiano, you are my pride, my joy and my sole reason for living. You may call them Mom and Dad, but mine you will always be. I'm your momma, and you will call me Mimma. To me, it will be like hearing you call me momma and no one will know it was why I truly chose the name."

As she hugged them close, Mom and Dad came into the room. They were both so happy and proud looking upon our children. Lizzy knew she made the right choice. They may be their parents once she left the hospital, but the four of them would always be there for each other. Still, maybe one day they would know the truth.

*   *   *

Soon after Lizzy and the children were discharged, the family of six made its way back to their home close to the city. As they entered the house, she realized there was an entirely new staff. No one knew she had been pregnant. No one knew the children were actually Lizzy's. All they knew was Mr. and Mrs. Ciresco were heading home with their four children, and there was much to get ready.

*   *   *

As the weeks went on, life slowly began to work itself out. Once her strength returned, Dad insisted she take up martial arts. He said "Every child of his would be able to defend themselves in any situation." And, "It was not up for debate."

So as vigorously as she learned Italian (because there was no English used in the house in order to improve my accent), she was pushed into martial arts.

Her own private sensei was brought to the house. He taught Lizzy the arts of judo, jujitsu, wushu and capoeira. Sensei said once she had knowledge of all four, the MMAs would come into play. For that she would train at the dojo.

Sensei was there all day, every day. She really enjoyed capoeira as it was more like a dance than martial arts and she could see its usefulness. Wushu was very calming, but as Lizzy increased her sash level, weapons became involved. She really enjoyed the graceful movements, and its fluidity was amazing. Between business studies (because Dad wanted her to have a firm understanding of how business works) and her tactical training, there was barely had any time to herself.

What time she did manage was spent with Tori, Anna and Tiano. Watching them grow and change every day was amazing.

*   *   *

As the years went on they may not have been calling her mom, but Lizzy knew the life the Cirescos gave them was better than she could have imagined. Every single day, as their personalities came out, she could see something of Nick in them. Anna, with her eyes, Tori with her determination and Tiano with his playfulness. They would never know their father, but he was in them nevertheless.

As they got older, the children ran to Lizzy with every problem — which she loved. It was always Mimma this and Mimma that; Mimma, Tiano took my doll; or Mimma, Tori made a mess in my room, or Mimma, Anna won't let me watch TV. She loved every minute of it.

Mom and Dad doted on their every whim, but Dad still worked a lot and had tons of business meetings. Once Lizzy finished college, he started taking her along on those meetings in Rio, Rome, Paris — to name a few place those meetings took us — and introducing his daughter to his business associates.

Mr. Gonzolez of Rio was very welcoming when they met. He had a nephew about Lizzy's age so they got along very well. However, he kept asking her about our suppliers, questions to which she really did not know the answers. He did not press, but it was weird.

Lizzy became quick friends with his nephew, so was thrown when one day, out of the blue, Dad said she was not to have any more contact with him. He explained it was part of business: sometimes friendships just didn't survive. Lizzy guessed he was right, but part of her still felt she was missing something. At the time, she just chalked it up to an overactive imagination, but she should have known there was more to it.

*   *   *

There was a lot of activity going on around the house as everyone got ready for the start of the children's first school year. The babies were going to be going off in a few weeks as they were going to be five soon. You would have thought we were preparing for the end of the world with the amount of clothes Mom was buying. She wanted to make sure they had everything they could possibly need — and then some. She hadn't been joking, when she said they would be spoiled all those years ago.

Later that week, Dad and Lizzy had a business meeting up north. It would be just the two of them going as the triplets needed to get into a routine before school started. She didn't mind it was going to be a nice break. A few meetings and they would be back home amidst the chaos again. Seventy-two hours of relative peace sounded great.

Dad had Lizzy drive up in her car and him in another so she could go explore when he was busy. It was fine by her. In fact, she wanted to see what her little red Cougar could do on the highway anyway and if he was there she wouldn't be allowed to have any fun. Lizzy and her five-speed were going to become closely acquainted on this trip. Gotta love it.

Dad gave her the directions and told Lizzy to start heading up with him right behind after speaking with Mom for a few minutes.

As she gave the kids a big hug goodbye and told them their big sister loved them, she knew something was wrong. Lizzy didn't listen to her gut, though. She just pulled out of the driveway and proceeded to the highway. As much as she wanted to see what the car could do, she wasn't speeding. She kept checking the rear view mirror wondering when Dad was going to be behind her. Oh well, he would catch up.

Once on the highway, Lizzy decided to see what her little Cougar could do and opened it up a little. Boy did it respond. All it needed was slight movements of the steering wheel and it shifted seamlessly though the gears. This car was meant to be driven.

When she checked the mirrors again there was still no Dad, but she noticed the same car had been on her tail for the past 20 minutes. So, Lizzy being Lizzy, she decided to have some fun: She changed a few lanes, accelerated here and there, checked the mirror again and, yep, the car was still there.

Whomever was in the car either thought her car was someone he knew or was a teenager being an ass. Oh well, she thought, not her problem. As she neared the merge onto Highway 11, she looked in the mirror and saw the car wasn't behind her any longer. Lizzy felt strangely relieved until she saw it was now in front of her. This guy was really starting to tick her off.

She was getting hungry so Lizzy decided to pull off the highway to grab a burger, fries and a root beer and give "buddy" a chance to get a little further ahead. It was a nice little break in the long journey.

As she left the restaurant, though, there was the car sitting there like it was waiting for her.

She did not remember much of what happened after that: Lots of screaming and yelling… The sounds of sirens... Someone yelling, "She's bleeding"… Then everything went black.

The next thing Lizzy knew, she was waking up in a hospital room hooked up to all these different monitors with beeping all around.

The nurse saw her open her eyes and buzzed for the doctor. She said her mom had just gone to get a coffee. Lizzy didn't know what was happening, only that every part of her hurt. The darkness swept over again. It was hours later when she came to because it was dark out and there was a different nurse with her.

She babbled something about Lizzy's mom being back in the morning and asked if she hurt anywhere. Did everywhere count? Apparently, she had been hit by a car in the restaurant parking lot. She was lucky to have suffered only a concussion and some internal bleeding. Although she was stabilized, Lizzy would be in the hospital for another week.

Another week, she thought. That had to mean she was already there for a week. Oi, this was too much to handle.

When the sun came up the next morning, she was still awake. She guessed after a week of sleeping she wasn't so tired anymore. Mom came in soon after.

"Mimma, how are you?"

"Besides the fact I was hit by a moving object?" she groaned. "I'm great." At least her sarcasm was still intact.

"I've been here every day. I didn't tell the triplets what happened because I didn't want them to see you like this. They think you went on a business trip."

"Sort of true," she grimaced. "I was on my way to one. How did this happen? There was a car....it followed me from home......I remember turning off the highway to grab something to eat, thinking maybe I was imagining it......but when I got out of the restaurant... it was there. Waiting for me. The next thing I remember is sirens and then here. What happened?"

Mom filled her in on what the police told her, but she seemed distant when she was talking. The doctors told her Lizzy would be in for a few more days. She arranged for her cougar to be put in the parking garage at the hospital so Lizzy could drive home when she was finally released. With the kids starting school in two days, she wasn't sure if she would be able to get back up. Things were a bit crazy.

She leaned down and gave her a quick kiss on the forehead, gave Lizzy her purse and car keys, and said she would see her soon. Something was off in Mom's tone, but when Lizzy considered the amount of pain killers they must have pumped her full of over the last several days, she wasn't sure if she didn't dream the whole thing.

When she left, Lizzy slipped back into a peaceful sleep dreaming of when her babies were born; their first smiles and giggles, when they learned to walk and how soon after they were running. Those memories got her through the next few days alone in the hospital. Those memories would make anyone happy for a lifetime.

SIX

MOM DIDN'T COME to visit in the days to follow. She *had* said she would be busy, but Lizzy had hoped. Even a phone call would have been nice. But there had been nothing.

She tried to call home a few times herself, but the butler always said they just stepped out or they were with company. Frustrating, yes. Annoying, yes. Lizzy just wanted to talk to her kids, that would make her feel better.

The doctor came to visit and said Lizzy could go home the following day. He added, though, she would still need to relax for the next couple of weeks and should go see her family doctor in a few days just to get looked over. He gave Lizzy his business card and said to call his office if she had any questions. But, that's what they say to everyone, isn't it? It's part of the required discharge procedure.

Lizzy tried calling home a few more times to let them know she would be home tomorrow. Not even the butler answered this time.

You know those warning bells that go off when something's not right. Let's just say her were going into overdrive. She needed to leave this place now, but no one would let her out. She even got dressed and tried to leave in a group of people, but nurse cranky over by the desk spotted her.

Sixteen more hours and Lizzy would either be free or crazy. One way or the other, she was going to be out of this place. But what to do for 16 hours? She had no computer; the TV had nothing but re-runs so nothing good was on, and there were no books to read. It was going to be a long day. At least she had some of her own clothes thanks to Mom.

Maybe a warm shower and clean clothes, she thought, and she would feel like herself again.

As she got into the shower, Lizzy caught a glimpse of her reflection in the mirror. It wasn't a pretty sight. There were black bruises all over her stomach from the needles they gave her each day. Her eyes were sunken in and she had a few lovely new scars. Nothing that could not be hidden over time but, still, the one on her back was pretty big.

There was no way in hell she was going to live with the reminder of what had happened. Lizzy figured that when it healed in a few months, another tattoo would cover it nicely. So she needed to start picking out what she wanted. She just had to find a way incorporate it into the work already on her back.

Lizzy thought to herself, Turnabout *is a bitch. And I get better at being a bitch every year.* Someone used her for a points marker and when she found out who it was, they were not going to like it.

She sat in the hospital the rest of the day plotting and planning what she would do to the person. Lizzy always had a wicked streak, now with the training Dad had given her, let's just say, that person was really going to regret it.

This was intentional. It was thought out. Whomever did this was going to rue the day. Whatever it had been worth to them, her payback would be worse.

Her body would heal, her mind would heal, and the scars would fade. The memory, however, would not. If there was one thing she had taken from her old life and this one it was: Fuck with her and you really won't be able to prepare for what you get in return.

What she did to Nick… If they ever ran into each other again, Lizzy knew he would never forgive her. And if he knew what she did, he would never let up. But to ease her mind, all she had to do was remember the outcome: The kids had the promise of a great life. If he knew what they received, there was no way he could deny they got the better end of the stick.

Nick had looked after Lizzy and made sure she never got hurt. Although she hurt him in a way he would hopefully never know, she believed one day he might come to understand.

But, he would never stand for someone doing something physical to another person. It didn't matter who you were, where you lived, physical violence just wasn't tolerated. So, when Lizzy took her revenge, she would take it knowing Nick would be with her in her heart. He would always be with her.

Lizzy thought he had to be happy by now. Sure, the first few months when he got out would have been hard, but it had been almost six years. He would have met someone new and moved on with his life. Still, he would always be her first and only love, and his image in her kids would keep Lizzy's love for him strong.

*　　*　　*

NICK

He could still see her. Sitting there under the tree. That sheepish grin on her face. She always had a way of getting him to smile. She tolerated his crap and still cared about him. There wasn't a day that went by Nick didn't still think about her.

The first thing he did when he was released was go to her house. But, she wasn't there.

Her mother answered the door and said, "Because of you she is gone and never coming back. Because of you, if her father never sees her again it will be too soon."

Obviously something big happened when he went in to serve time. What was it?

By talking to mutual friends, he worked out Lizzy left within a month of his going in. But not one person had heard from her. Her cell phone had been disconnected. All her email accounts were closed. She literally just vanished. No one had seen or heard from her, or knew anyone who had. It was so not Lizzy's character.

No matter how much of a fuck up he was, she saw the good in him. She was on the honor role, valedictorian; hell, she even graduated school a year early and was going to college. Lizzy, just didn't run off and leave everything. Her father was an asshole, everyone knew that. But, run away from something? That wasn't her style at all.

She did have another side to her, though. She was rebellious. Nick was with her when she got her first couple of tattoos. A cute little star just on the inside of her left hip and a daisy on her forearm. Her dad always kept the house so cold you needed a sweater so her parents never saw them. He didn't think her parents even knew. If they did, they never said anything.

Nick even asked his father about Lizzy when he got out, but he was so drunk most of the time, he couldn't tell you which way was up, down, left or right. He said Lizzy came by to ask where the jail was, but he was so knackered he couldn't remember. And she never came back to ask again.

Six years of searching and nothing. She disappeared into thin air. Nick even went so far as to go to the police to file a missing persons report. But because she left willingly there was really nothing they could do. If something turned up, though, they would let him know.

No matter how many times Ty and Nick went over it, it didn't make sense. Poor Ty, Nick thought he must have driven him nuts. When they were in prison together, Lizzy was all he ever talked about. Now that they were out, she was still all he talked about.

When they got out of jail Ty and Nick decided they were going to straighten themselves out. They both went to college and became private investigators. What better way to track down someone you love? They were making great money at it, too. Still, Nick kept hoping one of the cases they took would lead him to Lizzy. But nothing ever did.

"How do you just vanish?" Nick asked Ty yet again. "I don't get it?"

"Nick," he pleaded, "come on. We've been over this. She doesn't want to be found, or we would have found her by now. You've been everywhere, checked every lead. She's gone man."

"She's not gone," he insisted "She is out there somewhere. I know it. Don't ask me how I know. Deep down, I just know it."

"You've been saying it for years, but you've still got nothing."

"You're going to eat those words Ty. Mark my words. One day you're going to eat them."

"Ya, ya, ya..."

* * *

MIMMA

Lizzy was finally able to leave the hospital; not that nurse cranky made it easy. You can trust there was no love lost between either of them. That nurse really needed a holiday. Lizzy thought to tell her supervisor to give her a break, but somehow she did not think a holiday would have made a difference.

Lizzy's bag was packed as soon as she had the release forms. Purse and keys in hand, she ran out of there before they could change their minds. Unfortunately, she really did not know where there was because she did not even know to what hospital she had been taken. *Oh, well,* she thought. *Thank god for GPS. Just punch in home and away I go.*

It took her a while to find the car in the parking lot. She always knew there was a good reason to have an alarm on it. Lizzy was sorry for annoying the people in the area, but she had no idea where her Cougar was. Once she found it, though, she was happy. It was time for some real music. Lizzy grabbed a CD from the glove box, opened the sun roof and away she went.

Once she entered home into the GPS, Lizzy realized there was at least an hour drive in front of her. Once she found the closest coffee shop, though, all would be right again in the world. She needed coffee, real coffee. The hospital coffee was crap, but this cup she would thoroughly enjoy.

Lizzy raised the cup to her lips and smelled the goodness. Crap it was hot! OK, she would give the coffee a few minutes to cool down and try that again. Her quest for coffee had taken Lizzy 15 minutes out of the way, but it was well worth it. The bruising and her seatbelt were not the best of friends right then so Lizzy adjusted her seat while waiting. On top of that, she *was* feeling a little stiff, but like hell she was going to tell anyone. As soon as the doctor said she could go she was gone.

As she merged back onto the highway for the first time since the accident, yes she was a little nervous. Lizzy constantly checked her mirrors, but everything seemed normal. That was definitely a good thing. She picked up her cup and enjoyed the liquid gold as it coursed down her throat. It had to be the most wonderful cup of coffee she'd had that year.

Lizzy just cruised along, listened to her music, drank her coffee and thought about how happy she was going to be when she reached home. She was going to give those kids the biggest hug of their lives. Lizzy was so glad she was a part of their lives and did not want to miss any of it for anything.

She was so happy when she turned off the highway; there were only a few more minutes before Lizzy was home. But then she got that feeling again. Something was wrong and she could feel it. She didn't like it and had to get home as fast as possible. Something bad always happened when she got that feeling.

As she raced down the street towards the house, Lizzy was thankful there were no cops. She pushed the button to open the gates and made her way up the drive. Those bells going off in her head were blaring tenfold by the time she got to the door. Where were all the cars? Was *everyone* out for the day?

As she quickly looked around, nothing seemed out of the ordinary. Maybe the kids had started school and Mom was shopping. She tried the door and it was locked. Panic began to set in. Why was the door locked? Where was the butler? The door was never locked! What the hell was going on? Damn! Where were her keys? Where the hell were her... the car!

Lizzy ran back to the car and tore through the glove box. She always had a backup set stashed there. She had asked the butler for a set just in case there was ever an emergency. HELLO!! EMERGENCY!!!

She yanked the keys out from the bottom of the glove box and rushed back to the front door. When jumping over the flower bed on the way, she tripped on a rock. *That was going to leave a scar — what the Hell one more!?!* She was half expecting someone to be waiting at the door with all the commotion, but knew deep down there would not be.

Lizzy jammed the keys into the lock, muttering to herself "Come on, come on... Open already." The tumblers finally caught. Who put a latch on the door? Fuck! A few good shoves... her shoulder was going to hate her after this, but why the hell was there a latch? What the fuck is going on?

After a few good shoves, it gave and the door was open, but her shoulder was a completely different story.

"MOM, DAD??" What the hell? "TORI, ANNA, TIANO… WHERE ARE YOU? I'M BACK!"

Nothing. There was no answer… not from anyone. Not even the staff. Lizzy began to panic. Where were her kids? Where was the staff? WHERE THE HELL WAS EVERYONE?

She ran around the house from room to room, up the stairs to the second floor, down to the basement. Nothing. *Outside*, she thought, *I have to check outside.* Lizzy raced through the kitchen and out the back door. She covered the entire grounds. No one. There was no one anywhere. She had to have missed something. Think Lizzy, think!!!!

Lizzy checked all the rooms again, terrified something terrible had happened. One good thing she had inherited from her real parents was the ability to rationalize in a panic situation. She went around the house again more thoroughly. One room at a time.

First, she checked the kitchen: when she opened the fridge it was empty. The pantry, too. She ran down to Dad's office: his desk was bare; the computer gone. She rummaged through the desk drawers, but it was the same thing: empty. She noticed the picture on the wall was crooked and made her way over. Surprise, an open and empty safe. Something was wrong, seriously wrong. Mom had known. That's why they never answered the phone; why she didn't come back to visit.

She ran up to their room and found all the closets and drawers were empty. It was the same with the kids' rooms. *MY KIDS!!*, she thought. Everything was gone: their clothes, their toys, their pictures from the house.

Lizzy leaned against the wall and slid to the floor. Her kids were gone. All traces of them. Her family had been torn away and she had no idea where to start looking. The Cirescos had planned this. They would regret it.

She did not know how long she sat there. Hours, minutes, it did not matter? The most important things in her life had been taken and she wanted them back. At 22, Lizzy was young, naive and stupid. She put her trust in complete strangers who took advantage of a scared girl. She had been smart enough to include her in the equation with her kids, but dumb enough to trust the wrong people.

As Lizzy regained her composure, she wiped the tears and snot from her face and got up off the floor. Everything in the house was gone. Everything that ever mattered to her was gone. She made her way to her room. It was the only room that had not been touched. They knew she was going to come home. They wanted Lizzy to see she held no value to them.

She grabbed only what was needed: some clothes, soap, shampoo and other basic necessities. Nick always told her to keep a special place for stuff she never wanted anyone to have. Thank goodness she had listened and cut a small hole into the bottom of the box spring under her bed.

It was where she kept an old purse with both her passports (because she had kept her real one) and about $40,000 in cash. While she spent lots of money on the kids, very little was spent on herself. She always kept some of her pay aside, just in case.

Lizzy's laptop was with her at the hospital so all her contacts and files were safe. But, who was she kidding? Where was she going to go, or start? The Cirescos had the resources to be anywhere in the world. If she was reckless, $40Gs wouldn't keep her going for very long. She had to be smart.

Lizzy could not go to any of their friends because she did not know any of their addresses and everyone always came here to see Dad. Except those from out of the country. Out of the country... Out of the country? She could feel the wheels beginning to turn.

That was it. The one person who could *maybe* help her find them. She was sure he was not going to like seeing her, especially with how they left things; but he might be the only one who could help.

She gathered what was needed, grabbed the few pictures she had of her and the kids, and left the house without looking back. Each child had left a stuffed animal on her bed before Lizzy left to go on the business trip. She brought those with her, as well. She took comfort in having at least a small piece of them with her.

As Lizzy stepped from the house, she glanced down and saw a copy of the paper. She did not know what possessed her to pick it up, but she did. Upon taking a closer look, she saw it was folded open to the Obituaries.

She couldn't believe her eyes. Right there, the first one on the page:

Ciresco, Mimma- Passed away on August 21. She was taken from her family during a hit and run. She will be missed by her mom and dad, and three younger siblings. May she rest in peace. She will be forever in our thoughts.

Holy crap! What a load of crap. They told everyone she was dead. Maybe that's what they thought or that's what they wanted. The kids, *her kids,* were told she was dead. What they must be going through. She was their world and they didn't even know she was alive.

This was planned. But, for how long? This had to be why Dad took so long that day. He wasn't coming up north. There was no business trip. That's why she was being followed. So much more began to make sense. They needed her help while the kids were small. They educated her so they would feel like they paid for the kids. They insisted Lizzy learn martial arts so she could defend herself; so whatever "happened" would look like an accident.

As the enormity of their machinations slowly sunk in, Lizzy didn't want to believe it. They had never wanted her; only her children. This had been planned from the beginning. Every aspect of the last six years, every outing, every trip — everything leading up to this point — had a greater purpose. They had the means, the money and the resources...

How could she ever have believed they would want her? Her own parents didn't want her after they found out Lizzy was pregnant. Probably even before that. The Cirescos used her until they didn't need her any more. The only thing they hadn't planned for was her surviving.

But, Mom knew Lizzy was alive. Didn't she tell him? The date in the obituary was the day after the accident. Maybe she couldn't go through with it. Maybe she thought Lizzy would just leave things alone. Well, Lizzy could thank Mom for not telling him because if she had, he probably would not have stopped until she was dead. But, if they thought they could just do this and she wouldn't do anything, they were dead wrong.

Mom, I may spare, she thought. *But Dad, he was going to get another thing entirely. And I wasn't going to be nice by any means.*

The world may have thought Mimma Ciresco was dead; the Cirescos had another thing coming. Getting to Brazil and finding Mr. Gonzolez, would be the first step in finding the Ciresco's. Lizzy just hoped he could help, or would be willing to.

Taking the paper with her, she knew she had to get out of the house and quick. Just in case anyone came back. They didn't need to know she was there. But where to go? There was a cheesy motel not too far, one that didn't really ask any questions. She decided to go there for the night, get situated and then go to Brazil.

Thank heavens for her original passport. Lizzy had updated it two years ago so it was still good. A dead Mimma Ciresco leaving the country wouldn't really look good, but the fully alive Elizabeth Domenica DiAmmaro would be just fine. She could slip back and forth between both identities and no one would know.

She left the house and made her way to the motel. There was so much to do in so little time. The age old saying was as true today as ever. Since the motel wasn't far away, it didn't take long to get checked in. The first thing Lizzy did was take a long hot bath. She was still sore and aching from the accident, and ramming herself into the door really didn't help her shoulder at all.

She quickly ran the hot water and eased into the tub. The bruises stung slightly as she hit the water, but her muscles needed the relief. Lizzy let the buoyant warmth take her away and before she knew it, she was crying as waves of emotion washed over. She couldn't keep bottled up a moment longer.

As reality set in, she knew there would be no going back. From that moment on, every decision would revolve around getting her children back. It didn't matter what had to be done, Lizzy's children were going to be with her... one way or another and God help anyone who was dumb enough to get in her way.

Revenge wasn't a strong enough a word for what she wanted; Lizzy needed vengeance. To her, there was a world of difference between the two. Revenge necessitated an end, vengeance would go on until she was completely satisfied. Her devilish side that had been locked up for all these years was crying for release and a release it would get. She always said she was part angel, part devil with a halo was around her tail. The more she thought about it, her halo was getting more and more tarnished.

After finally dragging herself out of the bath, Lizzy wrapped a cheap motel towel around her and went to work. No one needed to know any more than necessary. She booted up her laptop and booked the first flight to Mexico — which left in five hours. Once there she figured it would be easier to travel. Next, she created a new email account, pulled out a contact from her other list and sent off an email. *Hopefully Alexsandro would be able to help.*

> *Dear Alexsandro, it's Mimma. I need your help and don't know where else to go. I'm not dead, no matter what you've heard. If you haven't, I'll explain when I get there. I'm flying into Puerto Vallarta and grabbing a few different flights from there to get to Rio. My flight leaves in five hours. Getting a new laptop and destroying this one after I have everything uploaded. Message me at this account for privacy, and please don't tell anyone you've had any contact with me.*
>
> *Again I'll tell you everything when I see you. I need your uncle's help and have nowhere else to go.*
>
> *ttys*
>
> *Mimma*

She hoped it would work and he got the message. Alexsandro and his uncle were the only ones to who she could go. This could backfire and blow up in her face, but she had to try. Lizzy quickly got dressed, threw her few belongings into a carry-on and left for the airport. It was only 30 minutes away, so she had plenty of time to pick up a new laptop and get them to transfer the files over.

* * *

NICK

"Fuck," he groaned as the chair went flying across the room. "What else can happen?"

"Nick," Ty said, "calm the fuck down and get over yourself. So we lost him, he won't get far and you know it. He's a little punk and will turn up in a day or two."

"That's not the problem. It's been six years, and still no one has seen or heard from her. It pisses me off. Where the hell did she go!"

"Enough already, Nick," His partner and best friend told him. "I hate to tell you, but give it up. If Lizzy wanted to be found she would have been. From how you've described her over and over again, she's a smart girl. When she's ready, you'll see her and not before then. So enough already. After work, we are going for a drink. Got it?"

He was glad he was there for Nick. But, looking for Lizzy for the last six years, when she did turn up, she was going to get it from him after Nick was done with her.

"We have another case coming in from up north," Ty brought up. "A doctor who needs some help. He's looking for a patient that left the hospital three days ago. It seems when he was reading the paper he saw her name in the obituaries. But the date of her death doesn't match up with the day of her release from the hospital. The paper said she died in a hit and run 12 days before she was released fully alive from the hospital. She even drove herself home.

"He wants answers," Ty said. "He thinks the girl might be in trouble. She's 28 years old, 5'3", dark hair, blonde highlights, golden brown eyes, with a tattoo of a daisy on her left forearm. He's sending over a picture. Apparently she was hurt pretty badly in the hit and run, but recovered enough from her injuries to be released. He said he would email a picture of the patient shortly. Her name was Mimma Ciresco."

Nick just stood there, that description? The tattoo? It couldn't be? After all these years, could it? Take away the blond highlights and leave the dark hair, eye color and the tattoo, that was Lizzy. He would know that description anywhere. Even the height was right. He couldn't stop staring at Ty. This was Lizzy. He knew it. It had to be. But why was she calling herself Mimma?

"Ty, the description sounds just like....."

"Don't even say it Nick, the girl's name is Mimma Ciresco. She came from a very wealthy family. But for some reason someone apparently doesn't want her around. It's not Lizzy. When we get the picture, you'll see it. I know it and you know it. It's just another case, OK."

It didn't matter what Ty said, Nick knew it was going to be Lizzy's picture coming through on the email. Deep down, he knew and he would be one step closer to finding her. He paced the office in anticipation knowing it was driving Ty nuts. He was a great friend and the best business partner. No one else would put up with his shit. Hell, Nick wouldn't even put up with his shit. With all the attempts to look for Lizzy that didn't pan out, it was amazing Ty still tolerated him.

When he heard the chirp of the email on his handheld, part of him didn't want to open it. He just wanted to keep believing it was going to be Lizzy. The longer he waited the worse he was. When Ty told him to come over to his computer, he knew it was her. The look on his partner's face gave it away.

He made his way to the desk as Ty turned the monitor around. Staring back was Lizzy. She was bruised up a lot, he guessed the picture was taken right after the accident, but it was her. By the look in her eyes he could tell someone had hurt her. From the look of the pictures, someone had hurt her a lot. By the way the obituary was written, he knew it was intentional. But why post she had died when she was alive.

Nick looked at Ty. It was the lead he had been waiting for. If the doctor saw the obituary, she probably did as well. And if she knew she was in trouble, she would run.

He was so close to finding her, he wasn't going to lose her now.

Looking at each other, Ty and he knew they had their work cut out. But, he was going to find her. The worst part was, according to the address the doctor gave, she had been living 20 minutes from him the entire time he had been searching. Ty realized it as well. Nick grabbed his car keys and made his way towards the door, Ty right behind.

"You've waited this long, Nick. Don't think I'm going to miss out on the fun now."

"Let's just hope were not chasing a ghost right now. I just found her and I'll be damned if I'm going to lose her. If she were dead, I would have felt it. She's not and I'm getting her back."

He slammed the office door shut and got into the car. Ty programmed the address into the GPS and they were off. He only hoped they were not too late. Nick gunned the accelerator as he made his way onto the highway. To hell with the speed limit, he was going to get there and it wasn't going to take 20 minutes. He just hoped the cops had other people to keep them busy for the time being.

They exited the highway and were only minutes away. Nick was so close… this was where she had been all this time and he never knew. *Why hadn't Lizzy ever tried to contact me?* he thought. *What the hell was going on?*

"You're not going to like this Nick," Ty said. "I sent the name Ciresco out to some of our contacts. Let's just say the guy doesn't play nice. He is said to be connected right up to the top. No one can pin anything on him. This doesn't look good."

Hearing that just made him drive that much faster. *What were you into Lizzy? What happened to you?*

As they rounded the corner and came up to the drive, he saw the iron gate was left wide open… If this person was into bad shit, that meant something bad was going on. As they approached the front of the house, the door was wide open. He threw the car in park, flew out the door and slid across the hood gun drawn. As Nick made his way inside, Ty was right on his heels.

It was quiet, way too quiet. Everything was empty. Whoever had been here took everything. The furniture was all covered. They left and weren't coming back anytime soon. "Fuck, we are so close," Nick said in exasperation. "I'm going to check upstairs, Ty keep looking around here."

There was nothing. All the bedrooms were empty — except one. And it looked like someone had been through it not too long ago. There were no signs of struggle or blood; that was all good. It meant she was alive when she left. But where had she gone?

He went through all the drawers and closets. She took only what she needed. When he looked under the bed, he had to smirk. She had done at least one thing he taught her. Hide what is important to you; and her hiding spot remained the same — the box spring. Same old Lizzy.

"Nick," Ty called out, "no one is here. Everything is emptied and gone."

"Same upstairs," Nick called back. "She was here, though, and left on her own. She had enough time to grab some things of importance and get out.

"If they truly think she is dead," he pointed out, "they won't be looking for her for a bit. I think she's safe for now, but where the hell did she go?"

They knew their work was going to be cut out for them. The next step was to check all the borders, airports and train stations. What was worse, they would have to check under both Lizzy Micelli and Mimma Ciresco, and still hope those were her only two identities.

As Nick drove, Ty made the calls. He hoped she was still in the country, but his gut said she was long gone. She wasn't going to run from whatever or whoever was behind this. Lizzy might have done what her parents asked, but outside of that she was a completely different person. That was the person he fell in love with. When he found her, though, Nick was not sure if he would kill or hug her depending on how far, and how long, she made him look. The worst part was she probably did not even know he was looking.

She could be with someone else at this point, but he just had to see her one more time and make sure she was safe. Whatever she wanted to do with her life after that was up to her. At least then, maybe he could move on.

Oh, hell, who was he kidding? He would kill the fucker because Lizzy was his.

"I found her!" Ty exclaimed, "Or her trail."

"Where is she?"

"She left for Mexico three days ago on a flight to Puerto Vallarta. But the trail goes cold from there. She got off when the plane landed and didn't book anything else."

"Ok, book…"

"Done," Ty cut him off. "We leave at 6:30 tomorrow morning. Go home, take a shower and get your shit together. Pack light, I think we'll have a lot of travelling to do."

SEVEN

THE FLIGHT TO Mexico wasn't that bad. It had actually given Lizzy some time to relax a bit and sleep. She was safe — at least for 3 hours. She looked out of the small window and stared into the clouds. What was she going to say to Mr. Gonzolez? Would he even help? He only met her the one time even though his nephew and she remained friends. If he couldn't help, Lizzy did not know anyone else who could.

She was surprised and happy when she exited the plane in Mexico. There waiting in the airport was Alexsandro. Lizzy was so happy to see him, she must have started to cry. Before realizing it, his arms wrapped around and she was blubbering like a baby. He took her bag, passed it to someone and just held her.

"Mia bella, what's wrong. I got your email, but, I don't understand?"

"They wanted me dead," Lizzy blurted out. "Mr. and Mrs. Ciresco wanted me dead. What's not to understand?"

"Your parents? But why?"

"Alexsandro, there is so much to tell you, to explain. I don't even know where to begin. And if you and your uncle can't help me, I..............I......"

"Don't worry," he consoled her softly. "Relax for now. You can explain everything when we land in Brazil. I'm here to make your journey much shorter. Let's go. You can eat and rest on my plane. Just know all will be well again."

Alexsandro looked at her and knew Lizzy would need his help. For now, though, he just held her and offered the warmth and security he could. His uncle may not be so kind, but looking at her, he knew she needed it.

"You didn't have to pick me up, I was more than prepared to make the trek to Brazil and see you."

"Yes, but I am not at the city home right now, so you would not have found anyone there. Plus, my plane will allow for a lot more discretion and judging by your email, I think we are going to need it."

"Thanks Alexsandro, I knew you would understand."

"And for the thousandth time," he smirked at Lizzy, "Sandro. Just call me Sandro, all right."

Sandro always knew how to make her smile. That slight upturn of his lip would send women swooning. He had matured so much since the last time she had seen him. And the years had been very good. This part of the trip was going to be easy.

"Um..... where's the plane? And why are we leaving the airport?"

"My plane?," he smirked again, "I left it docked in the marina. That way we can take off and land right on the property. I hope you're OK with the water."

"Oh... yea... fine. No problem." Lizzy was going to be sick. Water and she weren't exactly the best of friends. There are fish in the water and the closer to land she remained the happier she was. She didn't even like flying, but at least an airplane landed on the ground. The idea of landing on water was whole other set of problems.

The marina was just a quick walk from the airport and they were there before Lizzy realized. Sandro wasn't joking about the water thing either. There sitting in the marina was a seaplane. And it wasn't that big either.

"You want me to get into that? With you? Have you completely lost your marbles? That holds what? The two of us and a bag, maybe?" This was the smallest plane she had ever seen. *OMG!!!!!!!!!!!!!!* was all she could think.

"You'll be fine," Sandro said. "I've been flying for years."

"But that's a tin can with wings and floater thingy's."

"They're called pontoons, and it's perfectly safe. Now get on would you, already."

"You do know that I'm putting my life in your hands, right."

"Like it was any safer in yours. And how exactly where you planning on getting to Brazil from here anyway??"

"Hey, I never said that I had everything thought out........"

"Ya, that's what I thought, Mimma. You'll never change."

That was where Sandro was wrong. She had changed more than he knew. When she told him the whole story, Lizzy feared he may not ever want to see her again. For the moment, though, he was her only friend and the only chance at finding her children. Ya, just wait till he found out they were her children… that she was a mother. Wow, that conversation was going to go downhill fast, and that was putting it mildly.

"Fine, I'll get on your little plane. But, please take it easy on me. I had enough problems getting on a bigger one. This is like a form of torture."

"You'll be all right. I'm here with you and I'll make sure nothing bad happens, OK."

When she saw the trust and caring in Sandro's eyes, Lizzy knew she had made the right decision. He would help. For the first time, she felt like her life was coming together the way it was meant to.

* * *

NICK

"Ty, when we land, we have our work cut out for us. She left Canada using her real name, but everything can change once we land. We don't even know how she left. If Lizzy even thinks she's in trouble, she won't make things easy."

"I know. I'll look into every avenue. Just keep her picture handy, maybe someone will remember her."

"Here's hoping."

Lizzy hadn't made the trip easy for either of them, but Nick needed to know where she went. While he was on the plane he found as much information on the Cirescos as he could. But there was nothing. It was like they didn't exist. What were they into? And where did they go?

Nick's contacts were working around the clock. All he knew was the Cirescos dealt in black-market trading, but he couldn't pin down what product exactly. Lots of little things, but he was missing something.

He would find out what they were up to. Whatever it was though, it wasn't anything good. Something wasn't fitting together. After all these years, why would Lizzy take off? What had happened between her and her parents to make her leave so suddenly? It just wasn't like her. And to vanish with no trace. Then years later pop up using a false name. Whomever wanted her dead obviously thought they did the job — or at least someone wanted them to think so. But, why take everything and leave her things behind?

Nick stared out of the plane window and found himself wondering if Lizzy did the same thing. He pushed his hands through his hair in frustration and looked over towards his friend. He knew Ty could feel his pain. Hell, he couldn't just feel it, the poor bastard had lived it with Nick for the past seven years. He owed Ty big time when all was said and done. Ty would make sure to collect, but Nick would do the exact same thing in his position. They were best friends and would give their lives for one another.

As they flew over the ocean and the pilot prepared the plane to land, Nick could just picture Lizzy clinging onto the seat and breathing deeply. She had always said she didn't like heights. For her to get on a plane was something big. Who knew? She could have flown and gotten used to it over the past few years, but knowing her as he did, she would never get used to it.

Lizzy As the plane touched down, the two looked at each other. Their work was just about to begin. This was definitely going to be one hell of a bumpy ride. Oh, well. who ever said that love was worth fighting for had it right. She was worth fighting for even if he needed a whole damn army for the endeavor.

* * *

LIZZY

How Sandro talked Lizzy into getting on that flimsy tin can with wings she had no idea. The entire flight was spent holding onto the seat for dear life. Flying on a big plane was smooth; this tiny puddle jumper was another experience altogether — one she hoped not to have ever again. As much as Lizzy loved Sandro to death, she truly hoped it wouldn't come to that.

I can do this, she thought. *I can do this.* Nope! She couldn't convince herself no matter how many times it was repeated it in her head. By the look on his face, Lizzy knew Sandro was enjoying every minute of the flight, as well.

"You're really trying to kill me in this small plane aren't you Sandro?"

"Would you relax," he smirked, "we are almost there."

"Ya, easy for you to say. There are things that live in the water down there bigger than either of us. If we go down, I'll probably end up being the appetizer; you would be the main course."

"If you stop talking about it, you would enjoy the flight more," he said seriously. "Now look out your window and enjoy the view. We will be landing in a few minutes and the view of the house is beautiful from up here."

"I think I'll just keep my eyes closed. All you have to do is tell me when we're by the dock so I can begin breathing again."

"You're such a drama queen! you know that, right?"

"You say drama queen, I say self-preservationist. I'm on this plane and will take the ride that best suits my personality. Flying with my eyes closed so as not to see anything works just fine for me."

The less she was able to see, the better Lizzy felt. She hated flying; anything that involved heights for that matter. Add water and you had a recipe for disaster. The two things she hated most of all. The only reason she was able to endure it was because the Cirescos jumped past them to the top of the list. She would do anything for her kids.

It's funny, though. She was such an adrenaline junkie, but Lizzy never got absolutely anything from flying or water. The odd sea-doo ride, as long as she was in control, but that's about it. Even then, she usually chickened out about half way through. One time, she made it all the way through the canal, but by the time they were 100 yards into the lake she was ready to go back. Swimming in open water was out of the question. She would go in with her kids, but only ever up to a certain point.

Lizzy was actually an amazing swimmer, having snorkeled in the ocean on two occasions. The first time was beautiful, she could see the ocean floor and all the fish swimming below. She even swam through a giant tunnel near the shore. The second time, Lizzy put her face in the water and saw hundreds of beautifully colored fish, but no one told her about the tiny little jelly fish. Stings from the ones close to the surface feel like mosquito bites. Mosquito bites she could really have lived without.

The guide in the canoe laughed while Lizzy swam her ass as fast as she could back to the boat, climbed out of the water, and took off her mask and snorkel. She then headed to the bar in the middle of the boat and drank shots of tequila the rest of the day. Her friends laughed but she didn't care. After that, it would taking something big to get Lizzy to willingly swim anywhere with fish again.

She could not even remember how they gotten her on the booze cruise in the first place. She never even liked driving around the lake, much less on it. It just always freaked Lizzy out. Water had its place and she hers. She decided a long time ago if it was not in a clean pool, she was not going in past her waist. And if she couldnot see the bottom, she was not going in at all. Lizzy was sure Sandro was getting a kick out of her phobia, but he could just suck it.

"Ok, Mimma," he finally said. "You can open your eyes, we're here."

"Give me a minute," she replied. "I just need to dislodge my stomach from my throat and tell my brain the rest of me is still in working order."

"Haha, very funny. Come on. If you don't get out now, I'm going to leave you here as shark bait."

"You wouldn't dare," she screeched. "You're such an ass, you know that, right."

"Yeah, yeah, yeah. That's what they all say," he laughed. "Now come on, my uncle is waiting for us up at the house. I had one of my men message ahead so he was in the loop, but he is very curious why his ex-business partner's daughter is on his doorstep. And, he's not too pleased. I love ya Mimma, but you have a lot of explaining to do."

"I know. I just hope you will understand the reasons behind everything I did and not judge me for them." The last thing she needed was for Sandro and his uncle to judge her.

Exiting the plane, she could not have ever been more nervous. The beauty of the house took her breath away. The rolling hills of grass that led up to the house, an abundance of flowers and trees that drew you in further. If you were to look gardens up on the internet, you still would not find anything as picturesque. Someone obviously took pride in their work and it reflected in calm that washed over you as you strolled along.

The cobblestone walkway leading through the trellis was all the invitation you needed, it begged to be entered waiting to reveals its secrets. The soft bouquet from the combination of flowers was heavenly against the distance smell of the salty sea only a short trek behind.

What came next was completely unexpected. As they rounded a corner of the gardens, sounds that were barely noticeable before grew louder. They weren't the sounds of nature as she expected. The closer they were the more she realized the initial impression of the house was meant to delude you. The beauty it showed on the outside slowly faded into the background. This wasn't just a house, it was more like a compound. The noises weren't of the local wildlife, it was of people training and running drills.

Lizzy looked to Sandro hoping for answers, not quite sure what to ask. What was this place? Where did he bring her? As they approached, he was still smiling at her while everyone around showed their respect. They would invariably stop whatever they were doing and stand at attention whenever he got close. Armed and dangerous would be how to describe these men. None of it seemed to fit. Everything looked right, but out of place at the same time.

The closer to the house they walked, the more the flora and fauna returned. It was as if nestled amongst all the beauty was a secret. One she was about to find out. Lizzy wasn't sure she really wanted to know the secret, but realized she asked to be here and there was no choice.

As they say in the movies, "I think I've seen too much." Keeping her guard up and trusting Sandro at the same time, she slipped her hand into his for comfort.

She wasn't sure what the next move would be. The truth, obviously, but Lizzy had no idea what she was about to get into; which right about now seemed like the basis of her life. She made choices hoping for the best outcome, looking for the best in people. But the Cirescos had no good in them. Too bad she had to realize that at the cost of her children.

She hoped Sandro and his uncle would be able to help. Looking around the compound, Lizzy had a feeling they would be able to do that and more.

Sandro led her to the terrace along the patio. A beautiful stainglass door slowly opened and he extended his arm for her to precede him. He gave her hand a quick squeeze, she knew he wouldn't leave. She could trust Sandro, but Lizzy also had a strange feeling she was about to sell a piece of her soul for his help. *It was a small cost to get back what was mine*, she thought.

"Mimma, come in," a familiar voice greeted. "May I offer you a refreshment? And please, call me Tio, I insist."

Holding back the rich cobalt blue curtains, gazing out the window, waiting for her was Sandro's Tio. He looked a little older than the last time she had seen him, but otherwise the same. He was a very distinguished gentleman: greying hair, slender build and an aloof quality about him. Now that she was older, Lizzy was able to appreciate it more. This was a man you didn't want to mess with; a man who would give his life for his family.

"Good afternoon Tio. Thank you for taking the time to see me I know......"

"Mimma, being that your father is one of my *ex*-partners, I am very curious as to why you are here. So let's just get straight to the point, please."

She could feel her face getting flushed, this man was intimidating and he wanted Lizzy to feel it.

"Yes, Tio, you must have a million questions. Although I have answers for them, some may not be ones of which you are aware. Maybe you can also help me with questions I have."

"Let's eat," he said. "We can discuss it over dinner."

"I appreciate that, but I'm not sure I can handle food at the moment. I think you are the only one who can help me at this point…I don't know where else to turn."

Lizzy's eyes welled up with tears; she must have looked like an idiot. After coming all this way her emotions and exhaustion had gotten the best of her.

"Mimma," Tio offered, "come sit, relax and tell me whatever you feel comfortable with. I have no love lost for your father. For you to come all this way, and to travel the way Sandro has told me, means it is of importance. Please, feel free to begin wherever it is you feel you should."

She saw the beautiful, cream colored chaise and felt a need to sit down. Letting the soft warm grey of the room relax her. She felt her friend put a lush blanket over her shoulders for comfort. This was going to be a very long discussion; one that needed to be realized in order to begin the next chapter in her life. When Sandro took the seat beside her and reached for Lizzy's hand, she knew she could do this.

In the corner of the room, stood an exquisite bar. Watching as Tio poured himself and Sandro a drink before taking a seat across form her in the black wing backed leather chair. The harsh color of the chair looked out of place against the peacefulness of the rest of the room, as if it was placed as an afterthought.

"First of all Sandro and Tio, and I say Sandro first, because I feel I have deceived him the most. My real name isn't Mimma Ciresco…"

"What!" they interjected. "Whatever are you talking about?"

"This is a long story," she pushed along. "I hope you understand why I have done what I have; and please don't judge me before you've heard the entire story. It is hard enough for me to have lived through my mistake in trust, but it is even harder reliving it. I believe you are the only people who can help me find the CiTescos and, without you, I don't have another option. My real name is Elizabeth Domenica DiAmmaro, Mimma Ciresco is my alias. As far as the world knows I'm dead."

Slipping the folded item from her bag, Lizzy passed the newspaper clipping to Tio and waited for him to read it. He then passed it to Sandro while he swirled his port around his glass and lit a cigar. As she was sure he had done a thousand times before, she wondered what he was thinking.

"Mimma, Elizabeth," Tio began, "why don't you tell me exactly what is going on, please. And don't leave anything out. It seems someone wants you out of the picture. I don't think I have to guess who that someone is, either. They seem to think they've completed the job, but with you sitting here we know they have failed. So whomever it is isn't going to be happy about it if they find out you're alive. Now who would want you dead? Do you have any ideas?"

"Mr. Ciresco. I believe he's had it planned for a number of years. But, while his plan didn't work, it did leave me in pain for weeks — pain from which I'm still recovering. I think Mrs. Ciresco lied in hopes of saving my life, possibly out of guilt for what she has done."

"Guilt and Mrs. Ciresco," Tio said. "There is more to the story, so please continue."

"Mimma," Sandro added, "I mean Elizabeth, please tell me everything. If I can help, I will."

"Thanks Sandro, without your friendship, I would not have known where else to go. And you can call me Lizzy, all my friends used to when I used that name."

"Lizzy," he smiled that amazing smile of his, "please continue."

As she retold the story of the last seven years, it sounded so crazy. If she had not been the one who had lived it, she would have sworn it sounded like something right out of a book.

Lizzy began by telling them how she met the Ciresco's; she was pregnant but needed the job so much she didn't tell them until weeks after having been hired. She described how Mrs. Ciresco had such a fondness and treated Lizzy as her own daughter. The bargain she made in order to see her children grow up and have a life she could never give them. She emphasized how the deal with the Ciresco's was supposed to allow her to be part of the children's lives.

It had all seemed so perfect, too perfect now that she thought about it. Reliving it all over again — all the pent up emotions, all the happiness and sadness — everything came rushing back. All the elements that tempered her determination to find Sandro and get his help in getting her kids back.

She detailed everything: the lies, the ambition, and the determination to one day find them if it was the last thing she did. Lizzy was surprised when the looks on their faces held no shock after learning her tale. It was as if they knew what the Ciresco's were really like all along. They knew the life she had lived with them was false, and they had never shown their true form. But there was something more, something they were going to tell her. Judging by their reaction to what she had told them, she was not going to like it one bit.

As she came to the end of the sordid tale, Sandro and Tio kept exchanging glances. With no idea of what to make of the whole situation Lizzy sat there. Surprisingly, she wasn't nervous. It felt like she would get some long awaited answers.

As more time passed, there was too much silence. Lizzy's voice faltered as she finally broke through the dense air, "Sandro, say something please."

"So," Tio summarized, "you are not his daughter, they have taken your children and tried to kill you in the process. She obviously developed some feeling towards you because your dear, adopted mother is just as nuts as he is. Did I get that right so far?"

"Yes Tio, that's right." Feeling the tension leave her body, never realizing she had been holding her breath waiting their response.

"So now my dear, what do you need of me?"

"I am asking for your help to get my children back. I want back what is MINE. They may have taken them from me, but I always get what is mine."

"Why not leave well enough alone? You have your life and a chance at a new beginning. They didn't succeed in killing you. The next time you may not be so lucky."

"Lucky," she spat out, "I spent weeks in the hospital recovering only to go home and see my obituary on the front table; my kids and all their stuff gone with no warning. Just taken from me. I want them back and won't stop until I have them. So, if you want to help me, fine. If not, I'll do it myself!!"

As Lizzy spun on her heels to leave the room, Sandro jumped up and held her arm. The next thing she knew he had spun her around and placed her on his lap. He was holding her there like he knew she would run if the answers she sought were not forthcoming.

"Lizzy," Sandro said, "we are going to help you. But there is much you need to know first. You're not even well enough to go after them yet. They aren't the people they led you to believe. And when we tell you what we know, you're not going to like it at all. But, we will help you get your kids back. You just need to be smart about it."

"You're really going to help me?"

"Si, bella. We will help you."

A wave of comfort enveloped Lizzy. She knew Sandro and Tio meant what they said. They would help her see her children again.

All the bottled up emotions, stress and indecision was flushed from her system. They would give Lizzy the answers she sought. They said she wouldn't like those answers, but the kids would be with her again. She tasted the salt on her lips as the warm tears slid down her cheeks. She didn't care, all that mattered was things would one day be right. Tio muttered something to Sandro and the next thing she knew he was carrying her down a hall.

"I can walk, I'm fine."

"For once Lizzy, let someone help you. You don't always have to be strong you know. The devil himself came to pay you a visit this week, and you kicked him right back in the ass. Let yourself get better before you take him on again."

"But, the farther away the Cirescos get, the longer......"

"If you don't get completely better, you won't be any good to your kids. They need you to be strong. Just relax and let us look after you. Tomorrow we will tell you everything you need to know about them."

Never letting her go, he ascended the stairs, making his way around the curved hallway.

Nudging the door open with his foot, light flooded the room. Red curtains were pulled back framing the oversized windows. With doors in the center that opened to a terrace overlooking gardens and the ocean in the distance.

The delicate blankets that covered the bed only offset by the rich material framing the canopy bed standing in the middle of the room.

Nick had been the only person able to make her feel this safe. He helped Lizzy with everything when they were growing up. He was her protector; her companion. Part of her wished she had told him the truth all those years ago, but she knew neither of them would have been ready to deal with one child, let alone three. Lizzy felt she had done what was best at that moment in time, who knew it would bite her in the ass?

As Sandro laid Lizzy down on the plush bed, she didn't want to let go. The warmth of his body felt so good. The closeness was wonderful. She didn't want it to end.

"Sandro… Please don't leave. Just stay with me."

"Lizzy you know that……."

"I know. Don't worry. Your friendship means the world to me. You just make me feel safe and I haven't felt that way in a very long time. Please, just lay down with me. I'm afraid and I have no idea what to do."

Sandro climbed onto the bed beside her. She knew he wouldn't let anything happen and finally let the tiredness wash over. It had been a very, very long time since Lizzy had the feeling someone else was watching over her.

Her eyelids grew heavier by the minute. As she felt his body slide up beside her, his arm coming to rest across her stomach, Lizzy closed her eyes and succumbed to the darkness.

*   *   *

Lizzy woke up in a panic. It took a few moments to adjust to the environment and the man lying in the bed beside her. Then she remembered what transpired: Sandro had stayed through the night. He looked so peaceful resting beside her. She was truly thankful for him because she would have been lost otherwise. It took someone strong to see past all the lies she had told. Knowing he understood, she settled back down and let herself melt into his arms.

He never pushed and they had an unspoken understanding with one another. They understood each other even if no one else did. Lizzy considered herself lucky to be his friend. As sleep consumed her once again, she drifted off into peace and dreamt about her children, their smiles and their laughter. She knew someday, when Sandro finally came to meet them, he would love them as his own.

*   *   *

NICK

"Well," Ty said, "I talked to everyone on shift when Lizzy's plane landed. The good news is a few of them saw her and she still looks pretty much the same. The bad news is she got on a private plane with no flight plan, so there's no trace of her after that. They say she was on the plane in a matter of minutes of landing here. It looked like she knew the people she was with, but that's all. Whoever picked her up just landed at the seaport, greeted her here and they were gone."

Nick wondered out loud, "Who is she involved with that they are able to just come and go like that?"

"First someone wants her dead. Then she gets picked up by people who don't need to register a flight plan. Ty, do they have…"

"Already on it. They are bringing up the security feed as we speak, but they don't think you'll be able to get anything from it."

"Just get a copy, Ty we've come this far, I'm not quitting now."

"Nick, for your sanity I hope that you get the answers you are looking for."

"You have no idea."

Damn, Nick thought, *I couldn't come this far and lose her now.* She was up to something and was being cautious about who she told. He wished he could help. All of this didn't make any sense. There still wasn't any info on the Ciresco's personal life. No pictures, no nothing.

It was as if they did not exist. All he had was information on alleged arms dealing, but there was nothing to grab hold of.

What had Lizzy gotten herself into? At least when she did something, it was all or nothing. He just hoped it doesn't cost her life.

*   *   *

LIZZY

"Lizzy... Lizzy... Get up. Come on sleepy, get up. Lunch is ready."

"Lunch?" she asked her benefactor groggily. "How long have I been asleep?"

"Two days," Sandro informed her. "And restless ones at that. You kept muttering 'Nick,' and saying you're sorry."

"Argh, what else did I say?"

"That I was the most handsome man you had ever seen and we would defeat everything together."

"We *will* defeat everything together, but won't your boyfriend get a little upset if we don't include him? How's he doing anyway?"

"Wonderful, thank you. And Tio still doesn't know so keep pretending you're interested in me and I'll do the same. I know I should tell him, but it's the rest of the guys I really don't want to hear it from."

"Well, if they haven't figured it out by now, I'd say you're doing a pretty good job? So who was your pretend girlfriend when I wasn't around?"

"His sister, so it worked out great. All of his family know the truth, so it is all good."

"Well, I can see why we both get along so well. We're a good set of liars."

Not many people knew Sandro's secret, but those who did would keep it forever. He was a fierce fighter and as loveable as a teddy bear. When they first met, Lizzy knew instantly they would be great friends. When he confided his truth with her, she agreed to help him as much as she could knowing he would be there for her if ever needed — and was he ever needed. He was not Nick by any means, but he was her knight when she needed one. And she would be his when he needed.

"Tio, is waiting for us in the dining hall. There is much to talk about today and lots for you to learn if you're up to it."

"Yes, I'm definitely up to it. And how could you let me sleep for two days."

"Having a woman in bed for that long looked really good for me. And you looked so cute."

"Ha, ha, thanks. You're the best you know that." Lizzy gave Sandro a big hug as he always knew what to say.

"That's what they keep telling me."

"Again with the smart ass comments."

"You love every single one of them, Lizzy."

You know what? He was right.

As she showered and dressed, part of her feared what Tio was going to say. With him wanting her to call him uncle, though, it made Lizzy feel like family. While her own family had kicked her out with her problem, here was a stranger who was willing to help — not like the Cirescos, who only wanted her children, but as a man who valued family above all else.

Whatever he had to say, though, Lizzy knew deep down she would not like it and that it would scare the living crap out of her.

When she entered the dining room, she heard the distant sound of helicopters and planes. She had truly entered another world; a world which was about to become her own.

EIGHT

NICK

WHAT HAD LIZZY gotten herself into? The security cameras showed nothing. There were no distinguishable markings on the plane and no clear view of any of the people on board. She had definitely been familiar with the man who greeted her. You don't embrace someone like that who you don't know — and that wasn't going over too well with Nick at the moment. It should have been him she hugged like that, not the faceless man behind the glasses. Who was he? He should have been happy for Lizzy, but something kept telling Nick he was missing something.

The people at the airport said the plane landed 10 minutes before hers. The faceless man greeted her on the runway and they left together arm in arm. She went willingly, but where? *Where did you go, Lizzy?* he thought. *What are you doing on an another airplane? First of all you hate them, and secondly...* Oh hell, who knew what secondly was. There were so many possibilities he did not have any idea where to start.

They still had no information on the family she stayed with; just the obituary and hospital report. None of it made any sense. Why pretend to be someone you're not? Why have an entirely fake family and persona? Lizzy's real family still wanted nothing to do with her. Still, he had thought for sure her cousin would have heard something from Lizzy at some point, but there was nothing there, either. When he found out what she had been up to Nick had a shitload of questions for Lizzy — and her boyfriend.

* * *

LIZZY

"Good afternoon, Lizzy," Tio welcomed. "I'm glad you're well rested and on your way back to recovery."

"Gracias, Tio. Thank you for helping me. Even just a good night's sleep is important to me at this point."

"Well, we are going to help you get your children back. But first you need to know your enemy. After that, you are going to train very hard to get your strength up before you meet them.

"They are not who you think they are," he explained. "We were in business together until he double crossed me. Actually, he was an enemy years earlier, he just never knew it. Like the saying 'keep your friends close and your enemies closer.' As you can gather from the training grounds you walked through, we are very protected here."

"If you mean the exercises we walked through when I first arrived, yes, I can see that. But, what does that have to do with anything?"

"Everything. You see, your father, well Ciresco, and I did a lot of business together — none of it above board. While I have many true companies, there are also many areas of grey in my business dealings."

"Ok, I get the grey," Lizzy affirmed. "But what type of dealings are we talking about? Drugs? Black market computers?"

"What my Tio is getting at," Sandro interjected, "is he and the Cirescos were into arms dealing."

"Excuse me, what?"

"Arms dealing." He explained, "They bought and sold to the highest bidders around the world. When they had to go somewhere where someone might question the legality of the organization well, those were the meetings *we* were brought to. No one would think you might bring your kids to shady dealings now, correct?"

"So you're telling me they were arms dealers and I never knew. How did I not know? I don't get it."

"You would see just what they wanted you to see. Why do you think they didn't trust anyone but you around the kids. You were their mother and would protect them with your life. All the martial arts they put you in was to ensure they had some form of protection."

"But, I never.....they never..."

"Where is the last place you would suspect someone?" Sandro noted. "In your own house, of course. Why do you think they have homes all over the world? Depending on which country or who they are dealing with, they had to show different facets of their life. If you were going to a poorer country and were selling to people you didn't want to question your power, you would have them perceive you a certain way, would you not."

"Yes, but."

"No buts, Lizzy. Tio and he had a business arrangement that went sour. Because of the people involved when he crossed my uncle, we couldn't go after him. If we had, there would have been too many questions, but everything has its day."

"So, Tio, you are biding your time?"

"Yes," Tio answered. "If you strike your enemy too soon, they are ready and waiting. When you take your time and calculate all the possibilities, they won't have their guard up — it becomes all the easier."

"But, It's been three years.....why so long?"

"They've had time to get comfortable in their surroundings and let things slip. Patience is the virtue, Lizzy. You want your children back, yes? If you rush, you risk losing them forever. If you bide your time, though, and learn you enemy's weaknesses, you will have that much better of a chance at succeeding."

"Wait! How do I wait, he has my children."

"Yes, but he doesn't know you're alive. That is much to your benefit. Study him, his movements and his weaknesses, and you will succeed — with my help, of course."

"Your help will be appreciated," Lizzy noted, "but what I have in mind for him… I want to exact my revenge. I want him to look in my eyes and see he seriously misjudged me."

"You may have that retribution. But first, I will help you learn the skills you will require to achieve it.

"The Ciresco's have made many enemies through the years and many of us have banded together," Tio explained. "We make it harder for them to survive. I will spread word of what they have done to you in order to ensure your children remain safe — and that you get the final turn."

Lizzy knew by the look in his eyes she had his word.

"Tio," she asked eagerly, "what do I have to do? Where do I begin?"

"My army will train you with weapons and stealth. You will learn how to get around on everything from a motorcycle to a dirt bike or car. You must use every bit of your wit and personality in what you do. Are you ready to take this on Lizzy."

"I'm ready for everything you can throw at me, Tio. Getting my children back is worth more than anything."

"Sandro, take Lizzy and get her outfitted with some guns and teach her how to use them. You are to train her like you would any member of the militia. Do not go easy.

"Lizzy," Tio affirmed, "when we're done you will be ready for anything. That I promise."

"Thank you, Tio. Thank you. Sandro, where do we begin."

"Are you sure you're ready little miss Lizzy," Sandro teased.

"Are you taunting me Sandro? You know it will only make me crave winning more."

"That's what I'm counting on, let's go."

Lizzy had a long road ahead, but now she knew Tio would help. When the time finally came and Mr. Ciresco looked her in the eyes, he would know he lost. He would know he lost at the hand of Lizzy DiAmmaro!!

As she left the dining room, Lizzy knew her life was going to change more than she could ever imagine. She didn't care. *Me...* she thought, *my kids and their happiness are what matters. For that I can endure anything.* Knowing Sandro was not going to make this easy was what she needed.

Tio had said to buy new clothes, but these were not what she had expected. Sandro had custom ordered pants and shirts that fit like a second skin. It felt like she was wearing nothing. They flowed with every move as if they were born on her body, hugging every curve and leaving no room for imagination. Still the feeling of being in them was like nothing she had ever felt. The sleek lines, the snugness. These were designed for swiftness and manageability at the same time. She simply loved these clothes.

The gun holsters for which Lizzy was fitted felt the same. Sandro said that to be a great mercenary, her clothes and weapons needed to be an extension of herself. The smaller the target, the harder it was to hit. And with everything being so close, it was easier to access. All she needed to learn was how to fire them with precision and she would be ready.

Sandro's arms training began with light artillery: the glocks were good, as well as easy to manage and handle. The rifles and she, on the other hand, didn't like each other so much: the kickback left her shoulder bruised. Although she knew a rifle would be useful for long range targets, Lizzy's shoulder needed to get on track with that.

* * *

The weeks and months went on and on. Sandro never let up and ran her through the paces day and night. Lizzy was prepared for every scenario possible. When he and Tio said she would be training with their army, they weren't joking. The men would attack and she had to give it right back to them.

Throughout, she could see Tio watching from the terrace and smiling down at her. He was creating the ultimate weapon against his enemy. But with a common enemy, they would both get their vengeance at the same time. Ciresco had no idea what was coming.

* * *

"Lizzy," Tio called down one day. "Sandro, can you come here please."

"Do you know what Tio wants, Sandro?"

"No, but your guess is as good as mine."

Together, they made their way up to the terrace to find Tio sitting in his chair, a look of satisfaction on his face. He was happy with something and wanted to share it with us.

"Lizzy, I see Sandro has been training you well. However, for me to know you are ready I want you to take on my best man. If you win, I know you are ready."

"Ooookay, are you sure."

"Yes. You are to spar with Sandro — no weapons. The first one to submit wins. And, Sandro, there will be no taking it easy on her, she doesn't need that from you."

"Yes, Tio."

"Good, begin. You will not always meet your opposition in a training room. Life gives you many different avenues so take this one. NOW!"

No sooner had Tio said the words and Sandro was on her. He was her friend, but this was nuts. To be successful, Lizzy had to put all emotions aside. His uncle knew that and by matching them against each other, they would have no choice but to succeed.

She had seen Sandro fight, this was going to hurt. He was quick, lethal, and precise. But, she was fighting for her children. *So*, she thought, *sorry, Sandro, I was going to fight for all it was worth.*

She felt him holding back on his attacks. Even then, it hurt when they connected, and she used the pain to drive her on.

Sandro underestimated Lizzy, though. She had moves not used in practice, so that was good. He knew of her earlier training with the Cirescos, but he didn't know the extent of it. When he charged and locked her under his knees to take her down hard, he wasn't counting on Lizzy getting up. One quick move and she took the advantage. Each move brought her one step closer to her children, one day closer to finding where they were.

After about 20 minutes Tio called it. Sandro won of course, but it wasn't for Lizzy's lack of trying. He sent them both to the shower and wanted to speak again at dinner that night. A warm hot shower sounded just about right and she knew Sandro was thinking the same thing.

To show everyone, he threw her over his shoulder and headed for the house. All the guys thought it was funny, but they both knew the truth

— she simply wanted to be carried after spending the last 20 minutes trying to kill each other. And if she smelled half as bad as he did, it was no wonder Tio wanted them showered before he spoke with them.

When Lizzy returned from the shower an hour later — for Sandro's benefit — Tio was already waiting on the terrace. He was staring off over the open waters of the ocean at the view Lizzy had admired since arriving. You could lose yourself in the sea's vast blue wonder. Some days, it was all she wanted to do.

He looked so peaceful just standing there with the wind slightly moving his hair and rustling against his shirt. He was obviously deep in thought and she did not want to disturb him, but he already knew she was there.

"Come here, Bella" he began. "I would like to talk to you about something while Sandro is still getting ready."

"Yes, Tio, anything. You have been so generous in your help to me on my journey."

"I can see the desire in you. I can see that your children will drive you to do great things. They will be with you again, just remember: Timing is everything. What I am going to tell you I haven't told anyone, and I hope it will remain that way. Family is the most important thing to me and I protect mine with everything."

"You have a good heart. Tio, and you wear it on your sleeve. Any member of your family should be proud of you."

"My sole remaining family is Sandro. As far as he knows, he is my nephew but, in truth, he is my son.

"I met the love of my life many years ago and we were wed," he explained. "I kept her hidden from the world in order to keep her safe. And because she knew the line of work I was in, she agreed to be kept so.

"A few years later when we had a child, we went away for a while to keep the pregnancy to ourselves. You see, there were those out there who would do her wrong and I did not want to lose my world."

"You must have loved her very much."

"Yes," he paused retrospectively, "I did. She was my heaven and earth. Soon after Sandro was born, my wife wanted to return home. We told everyone the baby was that of her sick sister and we would take care of him until she was better. Then, one day my wife went to town to do some errands. That's when everything went wrong. My enemies found her in the market and corrupted her to show they could get to me. She eventually left both Sandro and me behind."

"Oh, Tio, I'm so sorry, I had no idea."

"Thank you, Lizzy," he continued with a sadness to his tone. "It was a long time ago. After that, it was even more important to keep my son safe so I never told even him the truth. He knows only that his mother loved him very much and died when he was very young.

"There are those out there whom, if they found out, would do harm to him. In order to keep him safe, I kept the lie going. So, Lizzy, know that *I* know what drives you and I will do anything to help you get your children back."

She could see in Tio's eyes the pain and sorrow behind the story. To have a son and never truly know him as a son was no different than Lizzy's pretending to be her children's sister. *We do what we must to protect those we love*, she thought.

"Tio, he is old enough now. Perhaps you should tell Sandro. He deserves to know the truth. He will understand what you did and respect your choices."

"Lizzy, it's been so many years."

"You have Sandro here with you. He's a grown man now and needs to know the truth. He already grew up thinking of you as a father, tell him. You will feel better and so will he. Isn't it better to spend your time you have together as father and son? No one except for the two of you needs to know."

Lizzy hoped she could make a difference, watching as Tio thought over what she said.

The truth needed to come out. She made the choice to protect her family, just as he had all those years ago with Sandro. Tio had his chance to finally make it right; Lizzy only hoped that one day she would get hers.

There was an unspoken understanding. They both knew the hardships of life and what they would do to survive. There was nothing more important to each than the lives they brought into the world.

We didn't always make the wisest choices. But, hey, we are always learning and sometimes that's the best part of it all. There was no manual for what to do when you screwed up. There are those in life who understand why we do what we do, and those who don't. In the end, there will only be one judge to say if we lived our lives well.

When the door to the terrace opened, Lizzy knew Sandro's life was going to change forever. She immediately went over, wound her arms around him, and told him he was one of the best people to ever come into her life. Looking over her shoulder she could see Tio watching. She placed a kiss upon his cheek and rested her forehead on his. As they looked into each other eyes there was a trust. Nothing could be more special than that.

She excused herself and retired to the library. While she had promised to be there to support both of them, they didn't need an audience for this conversation. Lizzy knew Sandro would see why his uncle did what he did. She also knew it would be a good thing for them.

In the library she looked around to find a book on travel. Not knowing where she was headed, Lizzy thought it would make a good read. There were so many places in the world the Cirescos could be and she had no idea where to begin. Her funds were limited so she would need to work scattered jobs to survive until she found them.

Then, what? Lizzy thought. She would have to support her children. There were a few things she could do, but all of them would have to be out of the public eye. It was going to make it even harder.

There had to be a way to earn money and keep her kids safe at the same time. She paced the room with the book in hand and began to take stock of her situation. She let her finger slide over the smoothness of the beautiful desk and stared at the globe.

She was missing something, but what was it? The Cirescos had lots of enemies, so somebody would have been in touch with them. Arms dealing might be getting harder, but she was sure they would find a way. If they were like Tio, they would try and keep the children safe.

Europe was a better base than the Americas. There were more countries from which they could deal weapons. Lizzy figured she could always begin in Italy — she knew the language well enough to get about and from there it would be easy to go anywhere.

Lizzy saw Sandro hug his father through the window and knew the conversation had gone well. Their bond was now stronger than ever. She couldn't wait until she could hold her children in her arms again. She just hoped it didn't take too long.

Seeing the smiles on Sandro's and Tio's faces at dinner, she knew all had been forgiven. After all, Tio did raise Sandro as his son, Sandro just never knew the truth. It warmed her heart to think one day soon it could be she and her children sitting around the table. But Tio was right, she had to be patient or who knew what could happen.

"Elizabeth, I would like to help you in your search for your children, I have finances that can aid...."

"Tio, I thank you. Really, I do. The amount of love and support you've shown me is more than I deserved. But, I have to do this on my own. I *need* to do this on my own."

"I had a feeling you'd say that, bella, so I am offering you a trade. Would you be up for that?"

"A trade, I don't understand? I sold my soul to the devil once, so you can understand my apprehension."

"Yes, I do. But, what I am going to offer you is a way to support your children by yourself."

"Go on," Lizzy said apprehensively. She was not quite sure where this was going.

"You see, you've been trained well with my army. Hell, you would have defeated Sandro if I let the match go on longer. My point is, you have talent and there are those out there that may be in need of your assistance."

"My assistance?"

"Your one of the best trained assassins Sandro has taught. And, I know your drive and determination. It may take you years to track down where the Cirescos went. But, there are those out there who can help you."

"Tio, so you'd want me to work for you?"

"No, I want you to work for yourself. But, we would be in communication with one another. I will help get you the jobs for the first little bit. Then, the jobs will find you."

She stared at Tio, total disbelief at what he was saying. True, it was a way of finding her kids, but as a killer? How could she do this? Lizzy wasn't sure if she could take someone's life.

"Tio, I don't know if I can. Ciresco is one thing, but others. He wanted me dead, he tried to kill me and took my kids. He made them think I was dead. For that, *he'll* pay. But, others?"

"The people you'd be after are no different than Ciresco. They have committed crimes and hurt families. Families that can't take their own retribution. But, you can help them and, in the process, earn money to help support your kids once you have them. It may be years until you see each other, but with these jobs you will never have to worry about money when that time comes. As soon as you're with them, you retire and vanish. No one will look for you because everyone who you would have helped will help keep your secret."

"So, you're offering me a way out. How would these people find me? How would they know of me? How do I do it without being caught?"

"My dear, you won't get caught. You do your research diligently, and wait for your best opportunity. The patience you will learn in this vocation will help you once you find Ciresco."

The more she thought about it, she knew it was the best option. Tio saw her come to a resolution and slid a manila envelope towards Lizzy.

"In there is your first target… *if* you decide to take it. You will find all the info you need to begin, as well as a passport and half the payment. The other half will be deposited into a safe account only you have access to. All funds will be transferred in this way."

Lizzy opened the envelope, knowing once she crossed this line there would be no going back. She also knew the amount of money in that envelope would help with her life. Immediately recognizing the target from a meeting with Ciresco, she read the bio and knew what to do.

"I'll do it."

"Wonderful. There will be a series of cell phones with each job. After every job is complete, destroy the phones and the information. I will know where you are and will arrange for the next job.

Just remember to ask each of the targets if they have seen Ciresco. They will help you if they believe it might save their lives. Know also this is your home. Come here whenever you need to, or even just to visit. Our family is small and you will be missed terribly."

"I will Tio. Often." She walked around the table to where he was seated, leaned down to place a kiss on his cheek, and gave him a hug. He would never be forgotten and would always be loved. If it wasn't for him and Sandro, Lizzy would have been lost. They had given her the strength to continue.

NINE

NICK

"NICK, IT'S BEEN months and nothing. She wasn't coming back."

"You're wrong, Ty. She's coming back and I don't care how long it takes to find her."

"She's gone... vanished. Even a psychic couldn't find her at this point. If she wanted someone to know where she was, we would have found some trace of her."

"She's out there, I know it."

"Then she's a ghost, and you know how hard they are to find."

"Did I tell you to go F yourself today?"

"Yep, just now."

Part of him knew Ty was right. Lizzy had vanished and the guy who helped her was doing a good job at keeping her hidden. She had connections; that was for sure. But whomever was hiding her had to know the truth. They had to be friends, but the hug from the picture looked like more. Nick knew should leave it alone, but couldn't. She was so close and then he lost her. It wasn't going to happen again. If she moved on with this guy, so be it. He still needed to know she was safe. Especially with what happened up north. Once he knew she was safe, he could move on.

None of this would have happened if I had kept my dumb ass out of jail in the first place, he thought. *Why did you run Lizzy? What's going on? I'm missing something, I know it.* It was only six months. What happened that you couldn't wait six months? He couldn't go back to her parents; they had moved and expressed how much they didn't want her in their lives. He had to find someone she would trust. There had to be someone.

Nick knew who it was. He just hated putting Dani in that position. Ty wasn't going to like it either.

*　　*　　*

LIZZY

She made her way from Tio's compound and traveled through South America into Central America, all the time doing research. The internet was a great help. People could be so stupid about putting way too much information on the Web. Everything could be found online if you looked hard enough. And with all the business training Ciresco paid for, Lizzy knew where to look.

She never stayed in one city long enough to get noticed and worked her way across the Panama Canal. As Lizzy traveled through Mexico and all its little villages, it was easy to see how someone could get lost. It wouldn't take much to vanish around these parts.

She used the money Tio had given wisely, hitching rides here and there with local village folk, taking the odd bus ride (and they were cheap down there not like home; just pennies), and staying the night at hostels along the way. It was just Lizzy, her backpack, and some toys of choice. The lighter she travelled, the faster she could go.

By the time she reached Puerto Vallarta and decided to rent a room, Lizzy still had almost every penny with which she started. It was going to be a while before she made contact and, considering what supplies were still needed, a hostel wasn't going to cut it. She needed to up her artillery — the lighter the better, but you never knew what you were going to need, and she wanted every angle covered.

She also knew Tio was concerned for Lizzy on her first job. He kept trying to send Sandro, but she wouldn't let him. Still, about three days into the trip she spotted Sandro not too far behind.

She guessed they both felt better that way. In a way, it made her feel better, too. But, Tio was right. Lizzy *had been* holding back that night on the terrace. She couldn't let Sandro get beat up by a girl. Today would be a different story, though. He didn't know she had seen him and that was to Lizzy's advantage.

She found a nice apartment overlooking the ocean. The price was right and she couldn't complain about it being fully furnished, as well. All that was left was to get a boat and store it away from the main area.

The next thing she needed was to explore and find out everything about the town. Lizzy wanted to know how the locals lived so she could blend in.

The airport was close to the main hotel area and marina, making access very easy. From her research, Lizzy knew the target liked to stay around touristy areas, it almost seemed so he could flaunt what he had. Before long, that wasn't going to be anything.

Lizzy made her way to the marina and saw some beautiful boats and yachts were docked there. Needing a quick escape was going to be easier than she thought. By the looks of the place, most people just came in and out for the day. There were some beautiful restaurants and walkways. When she saw the Lighthouse restaurant overlooking the bay, she knew it would be the perfect place to watch the world go by.

The beauty wasn't lost on Lizzy as she climbed the spiral staircase to the top. *Tonight*, she thought, *I would enjoy myself by watching the sun set over the ocean and thinking of Tio's*. She watched the birds as they flew by and glided on pockets of air with such freedom and abandon… at peace with the world. Soon, that would be her.

When she spotted Sandro below, Lizzy knew full well he had lost the trail. It wasn't hard, really, when she made myriad twists and turns through the whole town.

She fished an ice cube from her rye and ginger. What better way for a rude awakening than an ice cube down the shirt, she thought. No one ever said she had to give up her devilish side. Lizzy waited for the perfect opportunity and, oops, there it went. She watched the cube's graceful fall from its perch. And then… the moment of recognition as Sandro was caught and knew it. Doing her best impression of the royal wave felt wonderful.

"Well, are you going to stand there all day, or are you going to join me for a martini?"

Sandro shook his head and made his way up the stairs to meet Lizzy on the balcony. "How long have you known?"

"Since I crossed the Panama Canal. You didn't really do a very good job at hiding from me you know."

"Did you ever think maybe I wanted you to find me? Really, Lizzy, hostels? You could find a resort somewhere."

"Sorry!!! I didn't know your ass required a five star setting. The cheap way works so much better; less chance of being noticed."

"Yea, and a greater chance of getting bed bugs."

"Ha, ha, ha. Very funny."

"Who's laughing? So, darling. Now that you've found me, where shall *we* be lodging for the evening?"

"Well, I'll be at my apartment. What about yourself?"

"Where ever you are, I am. Plus, if you look like your married, people won't think much about it."

Damn! She knew he was right and loving every minute of it. As the waiter came around with her martini — always dirty with three olives — Lizzy looked Sandro squarely in the eyes. He was getting to her. She took the toothpick and slid an olive into her mouth (which was totally lost on him), but the man at the bar she was staring at, was squirming in his chair.

What better way to make a man fidget then the thought of something sexual. Sandro didn't know it, he had just helped make contact with her target. Men are so easily swayed. Sandro would find her apartment soon enough, Lizzy's current objective was to get the man at the bar. Not tonight, though. She would make him beg for it first.

As she quickly downed the martini, Lizzy let the stick with the two remaining olives slide past her lips. She let it linger, then slowly pulled the stick from her mouth. She stood up, sent a quick wink over to the bar, and was off. Men like the unattainable, she thought, and that's just what he was going to get.

Sandro knew not to follow as she left the bar. It was a signal they devised at his uncle's when we didn't want people to know where their relationship stood. If he was to follow Lizzy would forfeit her olives, but she wanted him to stay she would enjoy every one of them. The men thought she was always teasing him, they just never knew the truth.

Sandro had his usual, you think so, face on when she left the Lighthouse. On the way out, Lizzy gently rubbed past her mark at the bar. She could sense the sentiment wasn't lost. Tomorrow night he would sing and it was going to be an opera.

She knew full well Sandro couldn't leave right away, so Lizzy took some time to scope out her spot for tomorrow night: A nice little Italian restaurant just down from the Lighthouse. Her mark would be back tomorrow, but this time it would be where she wanted.

He was in his forties and was always after younger women. A nice dress and heels was lethal from the outside, but it was what was on underneath he needed to worry about. Tomorrow she would have to do some shopping, but her best friend was with her to help create the look.

It was about 20 minutes before Sandro finally made his way out. He was smiling, which meant the mark fell for it. The man would want to see why she rejected Sandro and left him there. Men were so predictable. Lizzy knew she had her work cut out for her, but this first job… he was making it too easy. Either that or she was being cocky. *Cockiness never paid. Ever.*

"I take it that's your mark. He was quite taken by you, he was going to come over before I came. You knew, didn't you? You had it all planned."

"Actually, no, I didn't. When I went up to the Lighthouse to lose you for a bit, he just happened to be sitting there. So I ordered myself a rye and ginger and waited to see what was going on. When I saw you, it all just clicked."

"Clicked, huh? Only you would see a link between the two."

"What better way to try to gain a man than to seem unattainable. You showed up just as I ordered my martini, which as you remember from Tio's house, proved to be a very sexy drink. By using our code, I knew he would feel like I left you for him; but I wouldn't be in his reach just yet. He'll have to return tomorrow to see if I'll be back."

"Oh, he will be back. He said so after you left. I went to the bar and sat a few chairs away to overhear him talking to the staff. He wanted to know who the cute brunette was at the table.

"Since no one seemed to know," Sandro said sheepishly, "I mentioned you moved into my building a few weeks ago. He thought you were too good for me. He *also* said he frequents there often and I said I'd make sure to let you know."

"What's this little bit of help going to cost me."

"Your house until this is done."

"You know," she laughed, "I'm only doing this because I love you right."

"I know. That's what friends do."

"Thanks for your help, Sandro. Come on let's get a shower, because you need one, and a good night's sleep."

"Sounds wonderful to me."

Tomorrow night would be the night. She wasn't going to stay in Mexico for long. Sandro would be in the background where ever she went, just in case. Whatever information her mark could give would bring Lizzy one step closer to her kids. It was all she could think about.

TEN

In the morning, she and Sandro were off to the market to make sure the look was right. Thankfully, the first store they went into had everything needed: A beautiful red dress cut down to the navel, hemline hovering just above the knees. Everything important covered, just barely... leaving you wanting more. The shoes were a deep, black patent leather with three-and-a-half-inch chrome heels. Beautiful and deadly in a wonderful combination. A black clutch and she was good to go.

The first thing Lizzy did when they got home was throw the shoes in the freezer. When they thawed they would mold perfectly to her feet. Next, she decided to take a quick nap and then get ready for the night ahead. Mr. X would not know what hit him.

As she tried to sleep, Sandro was talking to someone on the phone. By the sound of the conversation, it was his boyfriend. She had never met the gentleman, but if Sandro liked him, Lizzy knew she would, as well.

After tossing and turning for the better part of the afternoon, Lizzy decided to jump into the shower and get ready. Her children's images stayed with her every moment of every day. She wondered how much they must have changed in the 11 months since they were taken. They were seven already and probably getting ready to enjoy summer vacation.

She had to wonder what exactly the Cirescos had told them. Did they tell them she died? Did the Cirescos even let them mourn her death? How would they react when they saw their "Mimma" again?

Would she just be some distant memory or would they remember who Lizzy was and what she looked like? Every day that went by, the hurt grew, and the anger and need for vengeance just got worse.

"Until you're in my arms again my babies," she thought, "Mommy will always love you."

Sandro knew she had been thinking about the kids as soon as he saw her. They had an unspoken bond between them and knew when something was bothering the other. Like a brother, Sandro never pushed nor pried to get answers out of his friend. He just walked over and put his arms around Lizzy knowing the hurt she was feeling. He would be the first person she called when she got her kids back.

Tio and he would share their love with her children; her family would be complete again. Parts of Lizzy wished Nick was still with her, but he wasn't and life had to go on. She just hoped he found happiness in life and straightened himself out.

As she got ready for the night, even Sandro was shocked. Lizzy's dark, walnut brown hair, which she had dyed a few months ago, hung down her back in soft, sexy, bouncy curls. She put on some smoky eye make-up and pouty lips. The dress clung to every curve, and the shoes… well, they were just killer. She had everything ready to leave a man wanting more.

Under the dress, though, the story got even more interesting. Strapped close to her thigh, so as to stay invisible, was her dirk —just to be careful. In her purse was a small gun and some fishing wire, which always came in handy because you never knew...

It was a beautiful night when Lizzy left the apartment and made her way to the restaurant, so a nice walk along the marina was in store. It was on the way and the views were breathtaking. When she felt a presence behind her, Lizzy knew she was being followed… and not by Sandro. A quick glance as she passed a shop window revealed it was Mr. X.

As he was unwilling to approach, she put a little sway into her step and carried on, letting him admire the view for a bit. Lizzy could tell he was holding back as she neared the restaurant. Once inside, she picked a seat on the patio overlooking the marina.

A few minutes later he "arrived" and introduced himself. She was quick to block out his name as Mr. X suited her just fine. If they didn't have names, it would make things all the easier. She introduced herself as Lucia and they sat down.

"So Lucia, your neighbor told me you just moved here. Can I ask why?"

"Yes. For my uncle. My aunt just had a baby and because I was between jobs he asked if I wouldn't mind helping out for a few months. How could I refuse. This place is beautiful."

"And yourself," she asked. "Why are you here in beautiful Mexico?"

"Just a much needed vacation. The stress of my job sometimes gets overwhelming and I need a break."

"What kind of work do you do?"

"Shipping and receiving."

What a short, sharp answer. You could tell he didn't want to divulge any more on the subject. They enjoyed a nice dinner, watched tourists snap pictures here and there, and then made their way along the boardwalk.

As they walked past the marina, He explained the differences between the boats. If it made him feel good and smart, she didn't feel the need to interrupt. He went on to point out a boat close to her apartment and said it was his.

This was just getting too easy, she could just use his. But, that would just be too obvious. Luckily this was Mexico and anything could happen down here. No one would complain if there was one less drug lord.

He offered to take Lizzy on a boat ride the following day, but she made an excuse. With the dossier Tio had supplied, she knew what this man was capable of, so being in the middle of the ocean on his boat wasn't a real option unless Sandro was there. Instead, she thanked him for the evening and said they would meet again the following night at the Lighthouse — this time with Sandro in tow. He was here, so she might as well use him to her advantage. Maybe if the boat ride came up again tomorrow, she wouldn't mind.

When she returned home, Lizzy filled Sandro in on her plans and he thought them fitting. A man doesn't offer you a trip on his boat once and take no for an answer. It was a good thing she had bought three dresses that morning. They were *all* going to come in handy.

Over coffee the following morning, she filled Sandro in on revised plans. Hey, she is a woman and could change her mind; besides it was for the better. Instead of meeting at the restaurant, Sandro would wait on the boat.

The plan was for him to swim up along the side and sneak on board. Once there, he would send a text to let Lizzy know we were good to go.

As she got ready for the evening, Lizzy opted to change her look a little. Although she kept the gloves theme (because they didn't need to leave evidence), they were white tonight not black. The dress was a strapless yellow chiffon with an empire waist. The shoes were four-inch, white slip-on heels with silver detailing on the top. Her hair was positioned in a side sweeping bang, and she tied a soft bun off to the left side of her neck. She had found exposing the neck and collar bones was alluring to almost all males.

When Lizzy reached the top of the stairs to the Lighthouse, Mr. X was already waiting. She knew he had seen her coming because as soon as she reached the table, her signature martini was waiting. She leaned in to give him a kiss hello on the cheek and sat down.

She slid the stick with the olives out of her glass ever so slowly and took a sip of the martini. He was smiling. When she slid an olive off of the stick with her tongue and tossed it around gently in her mouth for a few seconds, Lizzy had him squirming in his seat. He had pre-ordered dinner and tapas were on the menu for the night — *nice, quick and easy,* she thought. When he finally asked her on his boat again, she planned to accept, but with her own plans.

As they watched the sun set from their table, Lizzy couldn't help but imagine simpler times. How just 10 years ago she had imagined such a different life. She had expected to graduate university with a degree in journalism, gotten married and started a family and life by now.

Instead, she was a hired assassin, her children had been stolen, she was alone, and would soon make the FBI's most wanted list if not careful. This wasn't the hand Lizzy had dreamed of, but they were the cards she was dealt. Poor Mr. X had no idea what was in store for him, but he would get what was coming to him. After her performance at dinner, she knew tonight would be the night. She didn't feel like dragging this on. No time like the present.

"Lucia," he breathed into her ear, "would you like to join me for a nightcap on my boat this evening? The dinner has been so wonderful and I would not like the evening to end so soon."

"That would be wonderful, thank you. But only for a quick drink. I do have to work in the morning and, with the baby, it will be an early day." She thanked the heavens Sandro sent the text he was in place.

As he took care of the bill, Lizzy excused herself to the ladies room to message Sandro they were on the way. One step at a time. This job was just the beginning of a new career and with Sandro there to confirm her accomplishment, she was sure Tio would send more jobs quickly.

As they left the bar and made their way down the boardwalk towards the boat, Lizzy could feel the excitement building inside. This man may have information that could lead her closer to her children. She would get out of him exactly what she wanted.

When they reached the boat, he motioned for her to board ahead of him. The boat was bigger than she first thought. Mr. X assured they were alone, but she knew better… although she did wonder where her dear friend was hiding. He knew this was her kill, he was just there for support and for that she was glad.

After Mr. X boarded the boat, he made his way to the galley to fetch some drinks.

Lizzy felt along the outside of her thigh to make sure the dirk was snuggly in place. All she had to do now was ensure he sat on her left because it was strapped to her right thigh. The garrotte was secure in her purse — all was good.

As he emerged from the galley, Mr. X made his way to join her at the stern. He sat beside her as she accepted the drink from him. Lizzy placed it on nonchalantly on the table beside her because if there was one thing she knew for sure: it was not to take a drink from him as it would likely be laced with drugs. It was how he took advantage of his women. But, not this one.

Lizzy knew she had to make her move. She leaned forward and placed a hand on his thigh. As she slowly slid it up his leg, she saw the excitement growing in his eyes. Her hand lingered upon his upper thigh for a few moments before she snatched it away.

"Sorry, I...I didn't mean to...

"No, no its fine."

He slowly slid his thumb up the side of her arm and then along her jaw line. Lizzy knew what he was thinking; she just had to get him below into the cabin.

"Are you sure?" she asked. "Do you mind if we go somewhere a little less visible... like down below. I'm sure it would be much more comfortable." She could see the anticipation for what he believed was going to come next.

"Yes, please, follow me."

He would soon find out they had completely different objectives. He followed Lizzy below while she made herself comfortable on his couch. He joined her and they resumed where they left off upstairs.

"Do you trust me?" she breathed into his ear.

As he shook his head in an emphatic, YES, Lizzy said, "Remove your jacket. Then the belt on your pants." He so thought he was going to get lucky. He was so wrong. If he was lucky, he'd co-operate and she would make it quick.

He was doing exactly as she asked and the excitement built in his eyes. He even kicked off his shoes in an attempt to save time. The poor bastard didn't know what was in store for him. As he sat back down on the couch, she needed to gain his trust. If it meant doing a little more than she wanted, so be it.

As he sat comfortably on the couch with his legs spread slightly open, Lizzy sauntered closer, leaned forward and braced against the back of the couch, her breasts ever so close to his face.

Slowly lifting her left leg so the dress rode up her thigh, Lizzy placed her foot beside his right knee. Then her right foot followed a similar pattern along his left side. As his excitement grew, she slowly lowered to straddle him — not her first choice of positions for the evening, but with the clutch resting on the window ledge behind him, it was the best place to be.

She felt him growing hard through his pants and rubbing up against her thigh. Men were so easy. Her hands slid around the back of his neck and up through his hair making him groan with want. As her body ground against him, his hand was busy fondling her breast. Her right thigh was tucked close beside the armrest of the couch so he couldn't feel the blade. She just hoped Sandro could see the show where ever he was hiding.

Reaching for the clutch with her free hand, Lizzy was able to grab the fishing wire. Not normal wire, mind you, this wire was good for hunting swordfish or shark — something that could tolerate a lot of tension without splitting. Wire in hand, she brought her hands together behind Mr. X's head and ground deeper into him. As a man who only imagined his own pleasure, and thinking he was getting exactly that, he eased his hand up behind his head.

"Oh, yea, that's it, just the way I like it..........what the...." It was right on cue. Lizzy quickly wrapped his wrists before he knew what happened to him.

"Like what?" she asked cynically. "The roughness...? the dominance...? I don't think so."

With a quick tug of the wire, and a sneer of pain from him, Lizzy knew it was properly in place. When she had scoped out the cabin on arrival, she noticed a convenient hook in the middle of the room. A little pressure at the right point on his neck and, bam, she bought five minutes alone. With Mr. X out cold, it was relatively simple to string him up in the center of the room.

"Nice work if I do say so myself."

"Thanks, Sandro. Where were you?"

"In the closet — no jokes."

"Hey, you lined that one up yourself. I'll let you wallow in it for a while. Now hide yourself before he comes to." As Sandro slipped back out of sight, Lizzy made herself comfortable on the couch, legs crossed and arms spread out across the back. She wanted to enjoy the show in comfort.

"What the fuck, let me go. Who the hell are you?"

"Someone you shouldn't have tried to screw."

"When I get down from this...."

"You're not going to, so shut up. Tell me what I want to know and then we'll see about undoing the string."

"I'm not going to tell you anything, you bitch."

"Sticks and stones. Really? Name calling is the best you can do. Now answer my questions, and I'll take it easy on you."

"Fuck you."

"So, it's going to be that way, then?" Lizzy rose from the couch and let her right hand slide down her side. Next, she slowly lifted her dress and knew the second he saw the steel of the blade.

"Who the hell are you?"

"Where are the Cirescos?"

"Cirescos? What the hell do you want with them?"

"That's really none of your business. Answer the question."

When she walked towards him was when he finally realized his legs were bound, as well. Lizzy slid the blade from its sheath and twirled it on her index finger. The look in his eyes said he knew she meant business. She traced the outline of his face with the edge of the knife as he tried to formulate an answer. He couldn't think fast enough as she made the first nick.

"Now, I'll ask you again, where are the Cirescos?"

"Europe."

With the blade still against his face making a slightly deeper nick, she pushed, "Europe? Well, now, that's an awfully big continent. Can you be a little more specific?"

"You bitch!" he sneered. "All I know is that he's in Europe doing business with some people I'd rather not be associated with."

"What people? The ones whose daughters you took advantage of. The ones you drugged and repeatedly tormented."

"You can't prove anything."

"Really? So why am I here then?" Lizzy gave him another quick nip to his throat, right beside the jugular. Not enough for him to notice right away, but in a few minutes he would. No one would miss this man when he was gone, not even his employees. She had to wonder how many of them he hurt.

"I told you what you wanted to know," he complained. "Now free me."

"You gave me the name of a continent," she countered. "How the hell do I even know you're telling me the truth?"

As the realization of his situation clicked in, so did his drowsiness. "What did you..." he stammered, "What did you do to me?"

"Well, if you really want to know? I placed a small nick at the side of your jugular. Now, your blood is slowly leaving your body. Just slow enough for me to keep questioning you."

She could see the gravity of his situation register in his eyes... he wasn't going to get out. Most men would beg at this point, not him. He was determined to be a hard ass right until the end. But it didn't matter what he said or did, there was no way he was leaving this boat alive.

"You know they will find you right," he warned.

"Who?" I asked. "Who will find me? No one even knows I'm here. No one knows my name. And I was hired through a third party. People want you gone and no one is going to seek revenge for you. Your own people can't stand the man you've become."

"*They* will."

"The *they* you refer to are the ones financing this." With that last pronouncement, Lizzy gave a quick thrust of the steel and her first mission was complete. She thought she might feel remorse of some sort for her first kill, but there was none.

Sandro came out from around the corner. From his smile, she knew he approved. "Never send a man to do a woman's job," he declared.

"Thanks. I just hope his info sets me on the right path."

"I messaged Tio confirmation. He's already wired the money into your account."

"Shall we, then?" And with that, they left the boat by slipping over the side into the darkness of night. No one would know they were there and it would be hours before anyone found the body. This was one case that would never make the news anyway. Lizzy guessed his employees would take the boat out to sea, dump the body and then sink the boat. Mr. X was a hated man worldwide, there would be no love lost for him. After all, his own family had paid for his demise.

As Lizzy and Sandro made their way down the street to the apartment, no one even noticed they were soaked. How he convinced her to go into the water, she didn't know, but she knew the risk of leaving the dock any other way. Luckily, she was an amazing swimmer. At that moment, though, the only thing Lizzy wanted was to get out of that wet dress and take a shower. The faster the smell of dirty water was off her, the happier she'd be.

She decided to call it a night after her shower so after giving Sandro a quick kiss and hug goodnight, it was off to bed. He thought she needed time, but really she just needed some sleep to begin planning her tomorrow. It didn't take long to fall asleep and when Lizzy woke up it felt like she had just closed her eyes, like she hadn't slept at all. She was also surprised to find Sandro gone. In his place was a note on the coffee table:

My dearest Lizzy,

If you are reading this, it's because I have already left. You were sleeping so peacefully that I didn't want to wake you. I talked to Tio and told him what an amazing job you did last night. He wired the rest of the money to your account and passes on the completion to your employers. In the envelope is your next job and 2 new phones. The blue one is for the job. The black for the next. You know the rules, destroy after each one. Don't use the black until the job is done and only keep the blue one long enough to complete it. Good luck and I love you. Remember I'm only a phone call away.

All my love
Sandro

A note. That was all she got. It was a simple reinforcement this was going to be her life for the next several years. In order to achieve the end result, though, Lizzy was ready for it and anything else the world wanted to throw her way. *Bring it on!* she thought. *You've already kicked me, beaten me and tried to kill me. I've survived and coming back for more.*

All that was left now was to clean away any evidence of her being here. She took out the cleaners and went to work. The apartment was paid in full until the end of the month, so no one would notice if she left early. A few hours later, Lizzy was on her way.

The envelope said open in France. So it was off to France. One down, who knew how many more to go.

*   *   *

NICK

"How was your holiday?" Nick asked his partner.

"Wonderful," Ty replied. "The beaches were great, the food was amazing and the weather was perfect. You should have come Nick. *You need a holiday.*"

"Yea, well, someone had to work when you were gone."

"Check out some pictures of this bar and restaurant. The food was glorious there."

Nick flipped through the pictures to make Ty happy. He did not really want to, but never would have heard the end of it otherwise. Then something in the last picture caught his eye.

"Ty, where was this picture taken again?" He held up the picture for Ty and hoped it was taken at the end of the trip not the beginning. It was too good to be true.

"That was four days ago, at a restaurant by the marina I was just telling you about. Why?"

"Now, Ty, look at the picture. Do you see anything that, say, should look familiar?" He was trying extremely hard not to lose his cool, but couldn't hold out much longer.

"Um, it's a restaurant. What are you getting at Nick?"

"Lizzy... Lizzy is in the picture. She's seated at the restaurant in your picture. How could you not see her? We've been looking for how long and she was right under your nose." He clenched his fists to keep calm, but it wasn't working and Nick took a swing at his friend. Luckily he *was* his friend and swung back.

"Calm the fuck down," he said. "That's not possible, I....we...."

"Spit it out!" he said.

"We ended up sitting beside them on the patio after the picture was taken. She left with the guy in the picture; they looked pretty comfortable. I didn't get her name, though."

"You're telling me you were right beside her and didn't notice."

"No, sorry. And, hey, if you would've come with, you would have been there to see her yourself... so don't blame me."

"Ty, we were so frickin close."

"I'll fax the picture to the restaurant to see if they've been back. Give me five minutes."

"It had better be the answer that I want."

So close, Nick thought. *He was right there. I should have taken the trip with him. I was so afraid of missing a piece of information, if I would've gone she would've been right in front of me. How could I have been so stupid and blind. I would have had my answers. This lead better pan out.*

"Nick, I talked to the owner, he said the man had been a regular for a while. And she had seen the girl only once before that. But not again since that night. Sorry man, were right back where we started."

"It's not your fault, and you're right. If I would have taken the trip, I would have had my answers."

He was right back where he started. Well, at least there was nothing lost. She would be long gone by now. From their luck to date, he knew that for sure. *But,* Nick wondered, *what were you doing in Mexico, Lizzy? What are you planning?*

ELEVEN

EXITING THE PLANE in Paris, Lizzy found it hard to believe she was actually here in one of the most beautiful cities in the world. She found a quiet corner at Charles de Gaulle Airport and took a seat. It was finally time to open the envelope Sandro had left.

Sure enough, there were two phones in it. She tucked the black one away in her purse and turned on the second. Next, she pulled out and began to review the info. No point in renting a room, especially if she didn't know where she was going to be. The dossier instructed Lizzy to go to Marseille with more information to follow upon her arrival. Well, here's hoping there was a quick way of getting there.

She made her way through the airport and found a ticket counter. Luckily there was a flight leaving in an hour.

"One ticket to Marseille please."

"Oui, c'est bon." But, the attendant had a funny look on her face.

"Do you speak English?"

"Yes," she said simply. "How can I help you? And, do you mind me asking why you would like to go to Marseille?"

"Business."

"Well, mademoiselle, be very careful. It is not a safe place for women who are alone."

"Thank you, I'll keep that in mind, but I'm sure that I will be fine."

"Stay away from the marinas and alleyways, they are not safe."

"Thank you again," Lizzy smiled as the attendant passed over the ticket and she made her way to the boarding area. That little bit of info was she needed. 'Not safe' was just up her alley and the marina was exactly where she was headed. After all, the worry should be for the poor fellow she was after.

The flight was quick, not like crossing the Atlantic. That was too much water for way too many hours for her liking. She swore Sandro was enjoying every minute of this even if he was not there. After customs she waved down a taxi — who better to take her around? Lizzy told the driver where to go and he just shook his head and said going there was just looking for trouble. He didn't know how right he was.

Finding a nice room to rent overlooking the ocean gave her a great chance to take in the surroundings. The landlord didn't even ask for ID when the room was paid for in cash. Just as she was getting bearings, her phone began to vibrate. Texting was a great way to disseminate information and this one pointed Lizzy toward a café where an envelope would be waiting. Quite conveniently, it was just down the street from her current residence.

She left the apartment with her blade in its secret place and headed over to the cafe. Lizzy ordered a latte and along with the order was a nicely folded envelope. She took the latte to go and made a stop at the pharmacy beside the hotel (it was time for a new hair color) and she was back on her way.

After kicking open the door to the room and scoping things out to see everything was good, she unloaded the latte and envelope onto the coffee table, threw down her keys and was ready for the next job. It was one Lizzy didn't expect — this time she was after a woman. The woman was supplying local teens with cocaine, but her employer wasn't happy when she sold to his son — a son who died of an overdose. He didn't want his hands dirty, but wanted her taken care of nonetheless.

Lizzy had a big problem with selling drugs to kids. Getting rid of rapists, murderers, wife beaters and drug dealers; as far as she was concerned, she was making the world a safer place. Still, it seemed the people doing the hiring were only out for their own family's retribution. There were no innocents.

Half the money had already been wired into her account, so she was able to begin. With paychecks like this, it wouldn't be long before she earned enough money to support her family for life. This amount was bigger than the last.

The woman's dossier included information about her local hangouts so she wouldn't be too hard to find. But first, a new hair style. It was time to get rid of the black, opting for a bright red and going a little shorter. Constant change would work well. Hair was the easiest thing to modify. A few inches here and there, different colors. It was time to have some fun.

After looking at the end result in the mirror, even Lizzy was shocked at the transformation. Red was a color she could definitely pull off, even though it wasn't one of her favorites. At least with her tan it wasn't as bright as it could have been.

She quickly changed clothes and armed herself. This job was going to be easy. In a seedy town like this, people weren't going to ask too many questions and, thanks to her intel, finding the prey was not going to be hard. She was always standing around the local hangout, waiting for the trouble makers to make their way down from school. This woman had no morals and not a clue about how to use stealth.

Once Lizzy saw her, she thought her mark looked familiar. She knew the woman, but couldn't place from where. Now this was going to bug her. If she could just hear her voice, Lizzy thought it would be easier to place how she knew the lady so she decided to hang back in the shadows for a bit and watch the situation on the chance her prey would say something. Sure enough, there was a group of teenagers heading her way.

"Hey," she called out to them. "Could you help me with something for a second?"

"Whatever lady, go find someone else to bug."

"But, I can pay you in return."

Kids were so easy, money was always a lure.

"What do you want lady? We're busy."

"Just help me move this product and bring me half the return. But if you don't......"

That was it! That voice, she had worked at the Ciresco's cottage for the summer. But, what was she doing here? How did she get here and start selling drugs? What a stupid idiot she was, selling to kids. Didn't she know someone would find out?

Lizzy made her way over and eased up behind the teenagers, appearing to be there for the sell, as well. But, she would wait until the boys were gone. She hated that they would have the drugs, but they were not her concern, her mark was.

"Hi, uh, I could really use some money myself, do you mind... if I... you know."

"What, you want to sell, too?"

"I really need some money and am flat broke. Give me a chance, I can do this. I have lots of friends." As if that was the magic word, she motioned for Lizzy to go with her.

"I'm not going to start you off with the hard stuff. Them I've used before, but you, let's see how you do."

As the woman opened the door to her warren, Lizzy could see she didn't go far from her stash. The entranceway was deceiving, but behind the wall she was hooked up. There was tons of product just waiting to be moved. Whomever wanted her dead had good reason. As she reached down to grab a brick of product, Lizzy seized her chance.

She threw her off balance with a quick shove, but wasn't ready for her swing back. Wow, she had a punch. It wasn't long before they were both grappling on the floor, but the woman was wasting her time. She had put her purse down when they walked in and it was way too far out of reach, now. After rolling around for several minutes, Lizzy finally had her pinned.

"Lila," she said harshly, "what the hell are you doing?" Her head spun around in recognition, but she wasn't ready for the blow she was about to receive. With her out, Lizzy grabbed the twine from her backpack and hog-tied Lila in a matter of seconds. Next, she went to all the windows and doors to check if they were locked because it was time for business.

As she heard her coming to Lizzy crouched down nearby and waited for Lila's eyes to open.

"Well, hello Lila, what brings you to these parts? Not enough people to sell drugs to back home?"

"Who the hell are you?" she sneered.

"I'm hurt, you don't remember me? You used to make my bed?"

"Excuse me?"

"Does the name Ciresco ring a bell?"

You could see the realization sink in. She knew who had caught her and she didn't look too happy to have heard the name of her former employer, either. Lizzy had to wonder, though, if the woman thought she was dead or not.

"You're… you're dead."

"Nope, pretty sure I'm not. See I'm still alive. Wanna feel?" I gave her a quick punch to the face. "Now, you are going to tell me where the Ciyrescos are. Do you understand?"

"Why should I tell you?"

"Well, I can make this quick or slow. Lately, I have been preferring the slower of the two methods, but that's entirely up to you. Which will it be? And remember, we're in a town where no one will give a shit if your dead or alive."

"The last I heard, they went to Spain, now let me fucking go."

"I didn't say that was an option now, did I? What's in Spain?"

"Hell if I know. They packed up after you died and went to Spain for business. They left me here in Marseille on the docks and I did what I had to to survive."

"Well, your means of survival didn't work out so well. You see, you sold some cocaine to the wrong person and, for that, you must pay."

Lizzy didn't wait for any kind of response; a quick twist of the neck and Lila was dead. She had no patience for hearing that woman's voice anymore. It would have just been whining.

Lizzy untied her victim and left. Whoever her supplier was would find her when she didn't show up. This town wasn't for her. She took a quick photo for confirmation and that was it — she was out of there.

As she stopped to get another latte on the way to her flat, Lizzy messaged the only address on the phone to say job complete. Once she received the other half of her money the phone would be destroyed — just like the last one — and on to the next job.

When she got back to my room, a quick linkup to the computer let Lizzy know the funds were there and the phone was gone.

It was time to turn on the next one.

And that became her life: a ring of the phone and a message telling her where to go next. And so on, and so on. The years seemed to fly by. Each one taking her to different places around Europe, but none leading any closer to catching the Cirescos. It was the odd few days in between jobs when she could follow any of her leads. And every time it was like she had gotten there just weeks after they left. But Lizzy was getting closer. She could feel it.

*   *   *

The more jobs she did, the more her account grew. She had more than enough to support her children for the rest of their lives. Lizzy was good at what she did and people knew they could count on her.

There was a very nice British family that paid for her services with a house: A beautiful villa in Tuscany. It had been for their son, but after he was murdered they wanted retribution. Once they received that, they decided the house would make a nice home for Lizzy's family. And his info about the Cirescos was bringing her closer to finding them. She now had the name of a school in Italy where his daughter went... with the Cirescos children.

It was summer now, so she'd have to wait until the fall. It had been 11 years since Lizzy had seen Tori, Anna and Tiano. Eleven years of hunting the Cirescos down. She had discovered so much over the years, how she ever trusted them was beyond reason. The more she learned, the more determined she became to free her kids. How could one man be so evil? How could she not have seen it?

Was I blinded by what the Cirescos had to offer? Lizzy thought. It had to be the only reason.

All the jobs she had taken, all the people she had killed. She had done it to track down her kids but, in the process, Lizzy saved countless others from the drug dealers, rapists and sycophants; not that she was much better in the life she chose. Hell, she was a hired killer. She would tell herself at least she got retribution for those who couldn't do it themselves. At least her employers could sleep knowing the people they paid her to hunt down would never hurt anyone else.

Those criminals were ones the law wouldn't get anyway. Their own families knew it. That's why they hired Lizzy. She was their means to the end. The wealthy had their own set of rules. Of course, some were criminals themselves, but they sought justice and didn't tolerate certain behavior. Even better, each and every family helped on her quest. They all did whatever they could for information so she could find her kids.

Some jobs were kept anonymous, which Lizzy preferred. The others were families she had previously met and who Ciresco double crossed. Their revenge on him was to help her and she didn't see a problem with that.

Now, as the end seemed at hand, all her old questions resurfaced. Would the children remember her? What would they say? How would they react? She had to be careful; after coming this far, she did not want to blow it.

It would be months before she would be able to find them — even if the Cirescos hadn't moved. They could have gone anywhere since her last bit of information, and it was the only lead Lizzy had. She would find them, though. She had to. It was the only part of her soul still holding on.

As she looked back on the last few years, she had never pictured this route for her life. This was the hand she was dealt. If she had only waited for Nick to get out of jail. If he only knew about the children. If only, if only… would have, could have, should have… the list goes on and on. So much could have been different. Did she really want different?

Her life had been an unending circle of occurrences. The fates had it mapped out long before she was born. Lizzy just wished they had consulted with her first. Everything in life happens for a reason. While she was not quite sure of the reasoning behind this event, it had better have a great end result.

Leaving for Tuscany was going to be an adventure in itself. There had to be answers to her questions. It wasn't a far trek from where she was, but with her luck anything could happen.

She wondered if the triplets were happy. If they were content in their lives. Did they ever get over the so-called loss of their older sister? And how were they going to react when then found out she was alive. At least she could thank Mrs. Ciresco for that. If she hadn't told her husband Lizzy was dead, she was pretty sure she would have been by now. Leaving loose ends was not something he did.

It had been a few years since she had heard from Sandro and Lizzy hoped all was well with him. He had so many of his own secrets and ghosts in the closet with which to deal. One step at a time for them both.

She also wondered if Nick had ever moved on. He must have by now, it had been 17 years. Years in which so much had changed. He may not have known about the children, but one day maybe she could bring herself to tell him the truth and let them meet each other. The first step, though, was getting them back. Whatever happened after that would happen. Right now that seemed like another lifetime.

We watch movies and read books about different realms. You have to wonder on some level if they exist. If you are like this there, or are you completely different. One never truly knows. Life is funny that way. Full of the unexpected as well as lots of surprises, good and bad. The curve balls, the anguish, the comfort... all of them tied together on some level. Our conscious being is defined in so many ways.

Lizzy really wanted to let her mind wander; there was so much to consider. This time in Tuscany would allow her to replenish, recharge and renew for the next and hopefully last step of her journey.

Her kids would be with her soon. She felt it in her bones. Now was when she needed to focus; where she would need all the resources she had developed. The Cirescos had better watch their backs for what was coming next as it was nothing they had ever seen the likes of before.

Deep down, Lizzy wished Sandro were with her. It would be nice to have a friend around. No matter how tough-assed she could be, she could use the emotional support. She just needed to make one stop on the way to her new home. She wanted to ensure she would be free and clear when all was done, that no one would ever take her from her children again.

Lizzy slid the card out of her pocket and looked at the address. This one stop was going to be worth it in the end.

* * *

NICK

"How can we still have nothing?" Nick asked. "It's been years since Mexico. How could she not turn up anywhere?"

"Maybe she just doesn't want to be found. Maybe she knows you're looking for her and doesn't want *you* to find her. She was under our noses for years, Nick, and we never knew."

"That's not the answer I'm looking for and you know it."

"It's never the answer you're looking for, but I'm going to keep saying it. You may be my best friend, but you are also the most stubborn, hard-headed person I have ever met and you know it."

Nick knew there was only so much Ty would put up with, but there was something missing. He was sure of it, but damned if he knew what it was. It had been years of sitting by waiting for her face to appear on another email; in another assignment. But there had been nothing.

Maybe he should have just given up and moved on with his life. It's what everyone had been telling him to do since the day he graduated college. College; Lizzy would have a field day with that. She knew how much Nick hated school. Because of her, though, he made something of his life even if she had no idea. Hell, Lizzy's own cousin told him to forget about her.

He had decided to wait until the end of the year; just six more months. If there was nothing by then he would finally give up. What else was there to do? He was almost 40 and had already spent half his life looking for Lizzy. The rest of his life would be spent living. If that's what everyone wanted, they'd get their wish. Six months, though. Six months...

* * *

LIZZY

She sat at her laptop wanting nothing more than to have some family: someone close she could confide with. After so many years alone, Lizzy had sent the odd email to her cousin, Dani, back home, but she had never left a reply address. She even made sure to delete the email account after a few days, only keeping it just enough to ensure Dani got the note.

Her cousin was the only one from the past she had kept in touch with and she kept her secret safe. All she knew, though, was that Lizzy left. Maybe if she told Dani the truth she could have the support she needed.

She kept staring at the screen not knowing where to start. This would be a big step. She needed family right now. Something was guiding, almost pushing her to send the email. If the last few years had taught anything, it was to follow her instincts.

Like the guardian angel on her back, Lizzy tattoos told a story. The daisy on her arm had the kids' names. When they were three, they asked why she wrote them on herself and Lizzy told them it was so they would be with her forever, where ever she was. The next thing she knew they had taken markers and drawn all over their arms when no one was looking. At least it was washable.

Lizzy's and their birth signs were on her lower back with a cross over top. The cross always reminded her to have faith, that everything happens for a reason. The guardian angel above the cross, with his wings wrapped around a woman: someone always there to watch over her. Whenever she needed peace, she just closed her eyes and concentrated on the one she needed most at that moment. Right now, she needed all of them.

She finally built up the courage and entered the email address. Her cousin and she were best friends growing up. Dani wouldn't judge and would probably have a shitload of questions for Lizzy to answer, but that was ok... *Here goes nothing...* she thought.

Dear Dani,

I know it has been a while. I know you get my messages and can't reply. There has been so much going on and I haven't told you any of it. You know I left and I can only imagine the reason that my parents gave you. But, right now... right now in my life, I need you more than ever. No matter how much of a hard shell I have on the outside, my insides need help. They're mush. There is so much I haven't told you, but if you are patient with me, I will eventually share it all. I am asking that you keep this to yourself and not mention it to anyone. Attached is my email address and I hope you will take the time to reply. But, I completely understand if you do not.

All my love

Lizzy xoxo hugs

She re-read the email a few times and hesitantly pushed the send button still unsure if it was the right thing. But it was too late to go back on it now. Only time would tell and hopefully Dani would be there. Lizzy couldn't blame her if she wasn't. She hadn't been much of a friend or cousin. It had been only one sided for so long.

She logged off the computer because spending the next few hours in front of a 15-in. screen would be terrible. Besides, the train ride was almost over and her house in Tuscany was waiting. Getting it ready for the kids would take up most of the summer. Mind you, it could only take that long because there was no way Lizzy could spend a season pacing around waiting for the leaves to change color. She also took the time to scope out the school were the kids went and checked out the rest of the local area.

Strategic planning came into play. Every avenue had to be covered. If it took a few extra months so be it. She hadn't come this far to screw it all up now. They finally were all in the same country. The toughest part now was going to be to play it safe and not let any emotions get the best of her.

Lizzy had only been to the house once when she was passing through Italy and had wanted to see what she actually owned. It was quite impressive: a beautiful villa with a cobblestone driveway and rolling hills.

There was a small staff which she agreed to keep on as she didn't want anyone to lose their jobs. The previous owner told her the butler and maid were his most trustworthy employees. As the pair were getting close to retirement and loved the property, everything worked out great. She just hoped they were ready for teenagers.

She gave a quick call to the villa to let them know she was on the way. There were some toys stashed in the garage that needed a little TLC and Lizzy wanted to be sure they would be ready for her arrival.

Gianni and Mina knew about everything. When she took over the house, she wanted them to know what they were getting into. Both of them were more than ready.

"A little adventure is always welcome, Miss Lizzy. Don't let my age fool you...." Gianni had said. She gathered there was more to him, but only time would tell.

TWELVE

THE TRAIN RIDE was nice; it gave her lots of time to think. Too much, maybe. The things your mind can come up with are unbelievable. Trying to plan for every possibility when there were so many different outcomes. Instead of living in her head, Lizzy decided turning the laptop on was probably a better idea. There had to be something on there to keep her entertained.

As soon as she logged on the little email prompt was flashing. It had been so long since she had seen it; it took a few minutes for the prompt to register. Sure enough, it was from Dani. She could only imagine what her cousin had to say.

> *Lizzy when I figure out where you are, I'm going to kill you. All these half msgs and CRAP! What the hell is going on? You know you're completely insane, right.*

> *How the hell could you take off like that and run away. You left your mother in such a state. Nick was up my ass looking for you when he got out. And all I get is a shit load of msgs from you, where I can't f'n reply. You send this cryptic msg now asking for my help, but not to tell anyone. WTF! Seriously! WTF! Love you, but cuz, come on? What the hell did you get yourself into? Where the F have you been? Why now after all these years? Answers, sweetheart! I WANT ANSWERS!!! Did you ever think to ask about my life? Maybe I needed you.......breathe.......breathe........ BREATHE.......*

*I'll read what you have to say, not going to say if I agree or
even like whatever it is you've been up to. (deep breath) But
Lizzy, come on. What happened? Tell me what happened.*

*Your extremely PISSED OFF cousin
xoxo (bullshit)*

Lizzy stared at the screen for a long time. She had known her cousin
wouldn't be happy, but she didn't think Dani would be like this. OK,
she was pissed and she couldn't really blame her.

Run away. That's what her parents told everyone? Sure, so they
didn't look like asses. Whatever helps them through the day? Wait until
Dani finds out the truth. Let's see what she thinks, then.

Lizzy guessed she should have asked what happened in her life — it
had been almost 20 years. Of course she would be married with kids
and a family by now. As long as she was happy. Lizzy had to consider
what to write back, though. Should she tell her slowly or all at once?

As the train came to stop, she realized it was time to pack up her
crap and get off. She would have to get back to Dani later as Gianni
would be waiting. At least she was going home to somewhat of a family.

Whenever she called the house, Gianni and Mina would tell her
how smoothly everything was running. Truly, both of them had lived
there for so long it was like their own home. Lizzy even told them to
live in the main quarters, not the servants' one, as she was never there
anyway. Someone might as well enjoy the place. She only hoped they
were ready for the surprise of having more people permanently.

The ride to the villa was beautiful. The only other time she had
been there, Lizzy never took the time to enjoy the scenery. Although
she recalled the beauty, she had not truly appreciated it.

When she got out of the car Lizzy just stood there and enjoyed
the view; the lush trees and gardens, the serenity of it all. It was like
something out of a book. This was where her family would live; where
they would heal from the wounds of the past, and where, hopefully,
everyone would come to understand why everything had to happen
the way it did.

Lizzy went straight to the arching, solid wood entrance door. It was so simple and elegant. Gianni was there and opened it as if on cue. The smell of lemons and oranges greeted her. It had been such a long time, since her time at Tio's, when she had smelled anything that good. Since then, it had been nothing but run-down motels and hostels — wherever was cheap, quick and unlikely to ask questions. She finally had an actual a home.

Inside the door old iron fixture hung from the high ceiling to just over your head. Off the foyer to one side was a staircase curving ever so slightly as it climbed to the second floor. On the other side of the entrance was a small sitting room which led to her office. The cathedral window in the office overlooked the terrace and the grounds. The view from her desk would always take everything in.

The office connected to the kitchen. With its granite counters and stainless steel appliances, this was where she planned to cook as well as where they would eat as a family.

When Lizzy entered the kitchen that first time, the smell of fresh baking met her and almost immediately put her on the hunt for chocolate chip cookies. Discovering them cooling on the counter, she grabbed one and let her teeth sink in slowly, savoring the taste for as long as possible. And... it was just a cookie. Still, she grabbed a few more for her exploration of the house.

Two sets of french doors exited the kitchen onto the terrace. She opened the first set to find a beautiful chaise and decided to take a minute and enjoy the surroundings. There was a patio table and chairs beside a railing overlooking the crystal clear pool. Gianni and Mina had put up hanging baskets around the patio. There were grape vines growing up the side of the trellis, as well as cherry and fig trees on the property. It was so picturesque. If the rest of the house looked as good as everything she had already seen, life was going to be easy.

After a short bit, she had to tear herself away from the view because Dani would be waiting for a reply and she had to face the inevitable and get it done. Gianni had already put her laptop in the office so there was no time like the present.

She would just have to tell Dani everything with no beating around the bush; let the cards fall where they may.

Dani,

OK I get it, you're pissed, you have every right to be. What I'm going to tell you though… You have to promise me you won't tell anyone. Yes, I should have asked how you have been, and about your life. Maybe after I tell you my story, you will understand better.

Here it goes. I DIDN'T RUN AWAY. They kicked me out. Yes, kicked me out. I told them I was pregnant and Dad threw a bird. He told me to get out and never come back. The ass even held the door open for me. Ok, close your mouth. Yes, I said pregnant. I took a job over the summer as a gardener. When the lady found out I was pregnant and alone, she offered to help. They took me in. They wanted to adopt my children. I said that if they wanted that I was part of the deal. I had already lost my parents, Nick was in jail, and I was scared and alone. And yes, I said children, so stop re-reading to check.

I found out it was triplets. They accepted me and the package deal. They sent me back to school, gave me a job in the family company. It was great. Up until they tried to have me killed! Yes killed. Stop pausing, keep reading.

The lady told her husband I died… to protect me I guess, but they took off with my kids. I went to one of his ex-business partners and asked for help. Which he gladly offered! The family wasn't as nice as I thought. Tio (the ex-business partner) helped me and trained me. And I have spent the last 11 years searching the world for my kids.

They were told I died. They were taken from me and I am close to getting them back. Hopefully soon! I know I haven't been the best friend or cousin. And, for that, I am sorry. But, I could really use someone to talk to. Even though we can only email each other. I hope you will be there for me. Nick never knew I was pregnant, so please if you ever see him don't tell him. I will if I ever have the chance. I can't tell you where I am, only know that I am safe and healthy, and in the one place I have always dreamed of going. I can't tell you what I do, or where I am, but please keep my secret.

I hope you understand
Lizzy

Her hand was on the track pad with the arrow hovering over the send button. It had to be done. Lizzy hoped for the best and clicked. Knowing Dani, the email would be printed and re-read a few hundred times before she wrote back. It sounded completely absurd. Hell, it was her life. She lived it and thought it was crazy.

With the message sent off, she needed to have a chat with Gianni and Mina. They needed to know what they were in for. She just hoped they didn't judge her as it was the last thing she needed. As if on cue they entered the office. Having been alone so much over the last decade it was something Lizzy was going to have to get used to.

"Gianni, Mina, can you please have a seat. There is something I must tell you."

"No need Miss Lizzy..." Gianni began.

"Just Lizzy, please. That whole MISS thing... Ya... No."

"Lizzy, Mina and I have already been told everything by the owners. That's why we are still here. They gave us a choice. With our backgrounds, we thought it would be the perfect place for us to be useful again. Don't get me wrong. We like our jobs, but we miss the adventure."

Adventure? Useful? What are they talking about? And why should the old owners tell them? It's none of their business. OK, deep breath.

"How? More so, *why* is it that you know?"

"When the previous owners hired us, it wasn't to be butler and maid; it was for our military training. I was a weapons specialist and Mina a nurse. But as we aged we wanted to stay on as butler and maid. Disguised as we were, no one ever thought otherwise. We had come in handy over the years. If we can help in any way, please ask."

"OK. So, if you know everything and what I do, you must realize I will be bringing my children back here to live."

"Yes and we have prepared for that. The house is fully secure and reinforced. We'll hold up to pretty much everything. I've kept your vehicles in good repair. As they aged they were traded in, and I have added a few just in case they might be needed over the years. They are in the garage. There is also a fully loaded armory behind the staircase."

Lizzy was blown away. They were ready to help. Everything had been kept in peak condition for her return and there was no need to worry about stock because everything was already here. First stop, the garage. She had to see what was in there.

"Thank you Gianni… Mina! I don't know what to say. Let's make this a home for my children. Let's bring them home. And, Gianni… show me were the garage is please."

Gianni's eyes lit up. She guessed he got the reaction for which he had hoped. With them here, Lizzy knew her house would be safe.

Gianni led her to the garage and when the door opened, shocked wasn't the word. The collection of cars was amazing and they were all hers. Trucks, SUV's, sports cars, motorcycles, dirt bikes; he had thought of everything. By far the best were the Ducati and the Acura NSX.

She was in heaven. All of vehicles were polished, fueled and ready to go. Even better, they were in varying years. Some old, some new, but nothing that would draw too much attention.

Her need for speed was met. Lizzy reached over and gave Gianni a hug and thanked him. He didn't have to do any of this, but the fact he did was amazing.

When they headed back to the house, Mina had already made a wonderful dinner and she insisted they join her. There would be no maid and butler when it was just them. They would eat as a family and discuss everything so everyone was always on the same page. She didn't want any surprises anymore.

After the meal Lizzy relaxed in the chaise on the terrace to see one of the most enjoyable sunsets in years. Amazing tones of reds, oranges and golds shimmered in the evening sky. Brazil would have been the last time she let herself enjoy it. Not anymore. Going forward, she would enjoy each and every one.

After the sun slipped below the horizon, Lizzy believed Dani would have checked her email by then. Everyone has everything on their hand-held so she would have seen it within minutes. She went to the office and grabbed her laptop before taking a shower to ease away the tension. When she slipped into bed and logged in, sure enough, there was a message.

Lizzy,

HOLY CRAP!!!! Ok, so........um......yes, stalling, I know. But wow, how? What? Yea. Can't believe it! I'm just blown away. I don't understand. Putting everything aside, I'll be here for you anyway that I can. I won't tell anyone......it's just so much to take in......I erased the email so my husband won't see it. I just can't believe it. I hope you get your kids back soon....I'm at a loss; I don't know what to say. Msg me whenever you need me. I'm here. Don't worry.

Dani.

She did not even know at what point she began crying, she just felt the dampness on her cheeks. It was amazing to know she still had family, someone to talk to. She had put herself out there and wasn't rejected. Dani had come through when she needed her the most.

It was time to tell Sandro where she was. Not that he would come any time soon. But she needed to let him know she was ready!

* * *

Dani sat with her cell phone. She re-read the email she had just sent and quickly hit the red X in the corner of the screen. She had promised Lizzy she wouldn't tell anyone. This was going to be a hard secret to keep. But she had to for her cousin's sake. Dani could hear her husband calling her from the kitchen. She tucked her cell into her jeans pocket and went to see what he wanted. This was going to be harder than she had thought.

Dani had already been keeping the secret of all the emails over the years. Lizzy didn't know what she was asking, but Dani would do it. She had to keep her cousin safe.

"Hey, Hun, what were you doing?"

"Nothing. Just fooling around on my cell."

"I'm just heading out. It's gonna be a late night. I have that case closing I was telling you about. Then it will be a few weeks off for both of us. We could use the break."

"Oh....Good....Glad to hear. Be safe. I'll see you when you get home. Love ya, Tyler."

"You too."

Dani let out a sigh of relief as she watched her husband leave. If he was going to be home for two weeks, her phone was going to have to be on silent. She didn't need Tyler seeing any of Lizzy's messages. That wouldn't be good at all... Just as she completed the thought, her phone decided to go off. She pulled it out of her pocket to read another message from Lizzy.

Thank you, Dani. Thank you so much. I appreciate everything you're doing for me. I know it's a lot to ask. Just know that I'll be happy very soon. And on the plus side, I get to see things I've only ever dreamed about since I was a girl.

Love,
Lizzy

Dani snatched up her keys from the counter and went out to grab a coffee. She left through the garage and didn't hear Tyler come back in the front door.

"Dani? I just forgot my bag. I'll see you later." As Tyler reached for his bag, he noticed Dani's cell on the counter. As he picked it up to take it to her the screen clicked on. When he saw the name on the screen, he stood there. It was from Lizzy. After all these years... Why now? Tyler made a quick call to say an emergency came up and wouldn't be in.

He had to get to the bottom of this.

Tyler was already feeling anxious. It had only been 15 minutes since Dani left, but he wondered where she went. He looked up again just as her car was pulling into the driveway. He waited for her, not sure what to say. He just held the phone against his head.

"Tyler, I thought you went............" Dani cut herself off when she saw him sitting on the couch. She reached down to her pockets and realized he had her phone. By the look on Ty's face, there were going to be lots of questions. "Ty, I can expla........"

"Explain what. I've been busting my ass trying to help Nick find her and all the while you've been emailing her. What the fuck? You know Nick keeps looking for leads and here you have one."

"It's not like that; I just got the first message I could reply to late last night. I had to find out what was going on first. She's my cousin, I had to know."

"Wait! That you could *reply* to? How long Dani? How long was she emailing you?"

Dani knew it was time to tell Ty. She would just have to leave out a major detail. She owed her cousin that much.

"Every now and then she would send me an email, but when I tried to reply the account was always closed. No address, no number, just a 'Hi, it's me hanging in there. Miss you!' and that was it. If I told you, you'd have gone straight to Nick and you'd still be running in circles. Last night she sent me an email saying she needed me. If not for anything else, just to talk to."

"Every now and then? For how long?"

"Um....since she left......but wait....I know......last night I was finally able to reply and then she wrote back. She didn't say where she was; just that she wanted some family. That was all." The look on Ty's face told her he needed to process. Lizzy wouldn't send messages anymore if she knew that Nick was still friends with her. She just hoped Ty would see her point.

"All right. We have to tell Nick. You know that, right? No more secrets. Let me see the emails."

"I can't, I deleted them. It was hard enough keeping it from you, but I also had to respect her wishes.

"And she didn't run away, Ty. Her parents threw her out. She just made some really bad choices."

"There's an understatement. I'm going to the office; Nick should turn up there eventually. Since I bailed on him, he'll have to go back. I might as well start the paperwork for the case he's on."

Ty gave Dani a kiss on the cheek. Even though he was mad, he knew she kept the secrets for a reason. Still, he was dreading his best friend's reaction. He just hoped Nick would be in an understanding mood.

THIRTEEN

Nick could have killed Ty for leaving him stranded. He better have a good reason. Seeing Ty's car in the lot when he pulled up was not going to give him any brownie points, either. He threw the door open and stomped into the office to make sure he got Ty's attention, but by the look on his friend's face, Nick wasn't sure if he wanted to know what the emergency was.

"What the fuck? You left me stranded. I could've used the help tonight you asshole."

"Nick, sit down. There is something I have to tell you."

"Just spit it out. Come on, man."

"Dani got a message today..."

"Yea, so?"

"It was from Lizzy."

"From who..."

"You heard me right. Dani had left her phone on the counter and I saw the email from Lizzy when I picked it up. Apparently, she's been getting them for years, but this was the first one Dani was ever able to reply to. I just found out, man. Sorry. That's why I canceled for tonight."

"What do you mean *years*?" Nick said as he threw the chair at the wall. "All these years we've been looking for her and Dani has been getting emails. *And* not telling us."

"Where are you going Nick?..."

"To see your fuckin' wife......I have a few words for her!"

"You're not driving. Get in my car, I'll take you."

"You better get there fast, too. Because the longer it takes, the madder I'm going to get." Nick knew Ty was right; driving wasn't such a good idea in his current state. When he saw Dani, though, she had better be ready for all the questions. He was not going to stop.

All these years spent looking for leads and there was one right under his nose the whole time. Dani better have a good reason for keeping it a secret all these years. The real question was: why now? Why did Lizzy all of a sudden want contact with her family? It didn't make sense.

He could feel himself beginning to breathe again as Ty pulled into his driveway. Nick had been holding his breath the entire ride. In just a few more minutes, some of his lingering questions would be answered. He hoped they would be answered was more like it. For all he knew, Dani did not know any more than him.

"Nick, let me ask the questions? She's my wife and I left kind of pissed off earlier."

"Yea, fuck that!" he spat back at Ty. He of all people should know better. He knew Nick wasn't joking either.

When they entered the house, Dani was sitting on the couch. Her hands were balled up into tight fists, tissues clenched in them. He could tell by the look in her eyes, she was sorry. But he didn't need or want sorry. Nick needed answers.

"Dani....."

"I know, Nick. I know. I'm so sorry... I... she..."

"It's all right. Just tell me everything, please, and don't leave anything out. You know everyone already thinks I'm nuts for still looking for her all these years. I just want to bring her home, Dani. I need to bring her home."

Dani told him everything. How Lizzy emailed her the day she left. How she could never reply. She would just open accounts to send the email. Whenever Dani tried to reply, the address would come up as unknown. Lizzy had asked her not to say anything and Dani didn't want to get Nick's hopes up. She didn't think Lizzy had ever moved on though, either. She had never mentioned if there was a man in her life... ever. Just 'Hi, I'm good' and that was it.

Then there was last night's email, the one she deleted. At least this time there was a return address. A place to start. It would take some time to find its origin, but it wasn't impossible.

"What was different about yesterday's email, Dani? Why does she want someone to talk to now?"

"I don't know. Maybe she is missing family. All those years by herself, who knows? None of us really knows her anymore." Dani knew. She just couldn't tell Nick; that was Lizzy's job. "Nothing out of the ordinary. She didn't say where she was? What she was doing? Anything Dani? Think."

"Nick, I wish I had more to tell you. Really I do. She just said she wanted someone to talk to. I wrote back and gave her shit for doing this to me all these years."

"Does she know our connection? Does she know that we still talk?"

"No, I never mentioned it. She just wrote that she was happy and seeing things she had always dreamed about. That's it."

"Thanks, Dani. Just let me know if she messages you back, please. Give me her email address, as well. I'm not going to message her. It's just so I can start tracking her down to bring home.

"Ty," he added, "can you give me a ride back to the office?"

"No, I'll take you home and pick you up in the morning so you can't do anything stupid."

Nick gave him a sideways glare, but knew he wasn't going to win unless he walked home and that was just too damn far away. So much for a few peaceful weeks. Now that he had this, there would be no stopping him.

After Ty dropped Nick off, he went straight to bed and turned on the TV. His mind wouldn't relax, though; the night's learnings opened so many new possibilities, so many new avenues to search. He just had to find the right one.

*   *   *

Lizzy

When she checked email the next morning, there was nothing from Dani. With the time difference, though, it didn't surprise her. There was, however, an email from Sandro. He was more grounded than she thought.

> *Lizzy,*
>
> *I'm so happy to hear from you. It has been so long. Hope all is good with you? You are getting closer to finding your kids. I'm in Europe and not too far from you. I'm coming to help. Are you ready for me.....lol.....I'm ready for you. I'll be there on Sunday.......try not to get into too much trouble before I get there. That way, we can have some fun together.*
>
> *Sandro*

So, she thought, *he was already in Europe.* Lizzy wondered what could bring Sandro over here because he hated the continent with a passion; he believed everyone was too high up on themselves.

She decided a shower was in order before letting Mina know they would have a guest staying for a while. She hoped they liked Sandro. He was bound to be his exuberant self here more than anywhere else. Maybe that was it: he finally came out of the closet. Every girl needed a gay best friend to tell her when she was being stupid. Sandro fit that bill to a tee.

She took her coffee and went to sit by the pool. It was a wonderful way to spend the day and it had been so long since she had been able to take some time to just relax. A day of nothing was just what the doctor ordered. Well, at least a few hours. She would begin the next stage of her search after lunch. Even though the Cirescos didn't know she was looking for them, they would always be hiding. And, Italy was big with lots of places to hide.

When her cell chirped, Lizzy knew the day would be cut short. Someone wanted something. She looked at the screen to see it was a job. She should have just sent a text back saying 'on vacay, it will be a few weeks.' But when she saw the name, everything changed. Tio wanted someone found. He never made a request like this before and after all the help he had given, it was the least she could do. The request actually took her to a place Lizzy wanted to go anyway — the town her parents were from.

A quick reply and all was confirmed. He would send the information tomorrow. Now, what to take to Bari? There were so many choices in the garage; which one should it be?

Lizzy slipped back into the chair and held the cup to her lips, letting the warmth sooth her. Tio had brought her this far, helping him was not going to be a problem at all.

* * *

Nick

When he looked at the clock it was 4am. *Hell*, Nick thought, *I don't care. I know where she is.*

"Ty, wake up."

"What the hell? This better be good."

"I know where she is. We leave in a few hours. Don't tell Dani, I don't want Lizzy to know."

"Fine, whatever. I'm going back to sleep."

"Be here in an hour, I just booked our tickets. And, grab your passport."

"What the hell am I supposed to tell Dani?"

"We're going on a job and will be back in two weeks. Hell, I'll give you tickets to take her to Hawaii when we get back. Just be here!"

He knew where she was. The only problem left was finding her. Why the hell had he not thought of this before?

Ty was good, he showed up at Nick's place grunting and saying he owed him. Hawaii was not going to be cheap; but it would keep Dani happy.

The most trying part of this trip, though, was being stuck on a plane for eight hours. All he wanted was to be there and begin the search. Nick realized Italy should have been the first place he looked years ago. Lizzy always wanted to go there; it figured she would end up there. But, he still could not figure out why she contacted Dani now.

What was happening in her life that she was reaching out for family now? Was she in some sort of trouble? Did she run out of money? Something was not adding up. It didn't matter how many times he went over it in his head, Nick would have to find her to truly know.

As the announcement came that the plane was getting ready for landing, Nick and Ty just looked at each other. Time would tell if the lead paid off. There were a lot of questions, but he knew where to begin.

*   *   *

Lizzy

Sure enough, Tio's message came first thing the next morning. It wasn't a death warrant this time, only a warning. The man she had to find needed a message delivered. One he wouldn't forget any time soon.

Lizzy had four days to prepare and Bari was only five-and-a-half hours away, but she could make it in three if she took the right ride. It wasn't like Tio to make these requests of her as he had Sandro. Maybe Sandro was just here on holidays and needed to relax.

The request was simple enough. Besides, it would not take long at all, especially if everything was already set up. She just had to show up, do her job to get the message across and leave. It was going to be nice and easy.

Gianni would help Lizzy prepare and it would give her a chance to know him better. They already had some great conversations over the last few days, and he and Mina were amazing. She was glad they decided to stay. The added support would come in handy.

It didn't hurt that Gianni's age was misleading; he was in better shape than most 30 year olds and was ready for some of the action he had been missing.

Mina obviously missed taking care of someone. Years of not doing it after the military left her with only Gianni to baby. Part of her longed for the excitement again. Depending on how things went, she was likely to see some soon.

Lizzy wondered if she would be the same when everything was said and done. Would she miss the thrill of it all? Could she just go back to a normal life? She would eventually find out.

Gianni and she spent the next few days training. He was completely up for it. He missed the fight as much as she did and it was nice to have someone with whom to spar. She had been looking forward to Sandro's coming just for that.

The rewards of physical activity were always best when the other person was a willing participant. She would be better able to fine tune techniques and just battle for fun. It had been years since they sparred. Luckily Sandro was always up for the challenge and, after having developed a few new moves over the years, Lizzy was sure she could surprise him.

She was up early the next day to grab a quick swim and get her heart going as the anticipation built. Her mark would not be there until 2:00 pm, so she had plenty of time as it wouldn't take long to get there on her bike. It also helped the speed limit was more of a guideline than anything else. Besides, they would have to catch her first and Gianni assured Lizzy there would not be any problems with the modification he made to the bike.

She grabbed a towel and made her way back to her room, all the while imagining what it would be like to have family roaming the halls. It wouldn't be quiet and subdued. It would be noisy and hectic. *I couldn't wait,* she thought. After throwing on a pair of black leather pants and a white, open back shirt she was ready to go. She grabbed her jacket and helmet from the chair and made a beeline for the garage.

There, gleaming in front was the red Ducati 1098R with 80 hp and 8000 rpm of torque. She was in heaven. It may not have been the most expensive bike in the garage, but it was by far Lizzy's favorite. She knew her baby would get her there no questions asked. Quick and sleek... what more could a girl ask for. She flipped down the visor and zipped up her leathers. This was one ride she would enjoy. The speed alone gave me her an adrenaline rush. Nothing ever felt as good as when she closed her eyes, started the bike and let the power flow through.

In no time at all, she reached an old building surrounded by trees and green space. After parking the bike, she made her way on foot to the wall of the building. That would be where she found her mark. Who knew why he thought he was there? It didn't matter. He wouldn't be expecting her and this place was out of the way so no one would see their exchange. After his lesson, a quick run through the trees to her waiting bike and she would be gone before anyone knew the difference.

Once she had visual confirmation, Lizzy waited until the target came closer. He seemed to be enjoying the scenery, so she just blended in like another tourist. It didn't look like it would be difficult to get her point across.

*   *   *

NICK

"Nick, we've been all over the country. She's not here?"

"She is. We just have to find her."

"You're a stubborn asshole, you know that. How long do you think we can keep this going for?"

"Until I find her, Ty. Until I find her."

"You could be chasing air as far as you know. You're playing a hunch based on a conversation 20 years ago. People change. This Lizzy you're looking for is nothing like the Lizzy you knew. They are two completely different people."

"I know. But that doesn't mean I'm going to give up."

"Yea, I'm going to get ice cream. I'll see if they have dumbass flavor for you while I'm at it. I have no idea how I let you talk me into this shit."

"You let me talk you into this shit because your life would be boring without it."

"Boring would be nice, Nick. There is nothing wrong with boring."

Ty brought the cone back to his friend; wanting to throw it at him. Nick wouldn't know boring if it bit him in the ass. As they leaned against the cars, they could hear a commotion in the distance. Ty glanced over and knew the look in his eyes. Nick needed to blow off some serious steam.

"Don't even think about it. I'm not calling Dani to bail us out of jail in another country."

"Just shut up and eat your ice cream."

As the noise got closer, they could see two figures fighting. The skill level they could see in them, one or both of the combatants would end up seriously hurt by the time the fight was done. They were grappling on the ground and throwing each other against the trees. Either this happened often or Nick and Ty were the only ones who noticed. Everyone else in the area just seemed to go about their business.

One of the fighters was much smaller than the other, but he was holding his own. The guy was quick and lethal with his jabs and kicks. Sometimes people just need to learn when to stay down in a fight. Not this guy, he just kept going, almost like he was fighting for his life. He wasn't going to let up.

With a final kick, the bigger of the two was thrown to the ground. The smaller one in black booked it to a bike parked on the curb. He started it up without taking a second to look back and didn't notice the other guy get up.

Everything had happened so fast. The bike had only moved a couple of meters when the shot went off. The next thing we knew, the bike was on top of the fighter in black.

Nick and Ty ran through the traffic. They had to move the guy on the bike before he was run over by oncoming cars. By the time they got to the bike, though, the shooter was gone.

"Ty lift the bike, I got him."

"I got it. Just get him off the street."

As Nick dragged the body out of the street, he realized it wasn't a guy at all. Even with the helmet on he could tell it was a girl. Definitely not what he was expecting. She had fought so viciously and was now lying there. He rested her head in his lap and gave her a moment. She

RYENN GINGER

was bleeding and it took her a few minutes to get her bearings. As he moved to take her helmet off, her hand shot up and she shook her head no.

*   *   *

LIZZY

She didn't know how she ended up with her head in Nick's lap, but she recognized him as soon as her eyes opened. No, before. At first, she thought the sound of his voice was a dream; that maybe the bullet wound had been mortal and her mind was playing tricks. But now, seeing him looking down at her… this couldn't be happening! She did NOT need this complication. What was he doing here? Why now?

As she tried to get up, Lizzy knew the hit had been pretty hard, but she had to get out of there. She needed to get away from Nick. As she could feel her body sway, Nick reached out instinctively to support her and she quickly pushed him away. *Not now!* She thought. *I can't do this now.*

Lizzy walked over to her bike and rested her hands on the seat. She just needed to clear her head. *How had any of this happened? Why was fate being so cruel?*

*   *   *

Nick and Ty had given the biker the space she obviously wanted, but they could see she was losing blood. The wound was not going to kill her, but it was bad enough to make her weak. As she tried to mount the bike, Nick stopped her.

"What the hell do you think you're doing?"

"Leaving. Why? Do you have a problem with that?" Lizzy *so* did not have time for this.

"Yea. You just got shot, lady. And you're obviously not steady on your feet. If you get on that bike you'll kill either yourself or someone else and I'm not living with that on me."

"Well I have to go, so it's not your problem. Where are my keys?"

Nick looked over to see Ty had the keys in his hand and wasn't about to give them up.

"Listen, we'll drive you and your bike where ever you have to go. And I'm guessing that the hospital isn't the place you were headed either."

"I can drive myself." She just needed to get her keys and get out of there before the cops showed up.

"Not happening. It's our option or nothing."

They didn't really leave her with much of a choice. The only problem was she didn't want Nick to recognize her. This day had gone from good to crappy to downright shitty in a heartbeat. Nick was here and all she wanted to do was go to him. But *that* Lizzy had died years ago and *this* Lizzy wasn't ready to deal with this yet.

"Fine, but I ride with him," she said to Nick. "You take the bike and follow. I hope you guys have enough gas to drop me off, though, it's a long drive."

She took off her helmet and handed it to Nick. With her skull cap and glasses on he wouldn't be able to tell it was her. She made her way over to their car and climbed into the passenger seat. This was *not* how the day was supposed to end.

FOURTEEN

"I'M TY, AND I'll be your driver for the day. Please buckle up and enjoy the ride."

"Was that supposed to be funny?"

"Hey, I would have been more than happy to drive the bike, but you let him do it. So now I get to babysit you. If it were up to me, I would have left you there to fend for yourself. My guy over there is a little messed up right now, though, so I tend to let him lead."

"Great! Just get on the highway and I'll give you directions as we go."

"And where is there, darling?"

"First, don't call me darling. Second, the where *there* is you'll find out as we go."

"So, the ride is going to be like this is it?"

"What? You wouldn't give me the keys. It's your own fault we're in this mess."

"Fine. Just stop bleeding all over the rental."

She had forgotten she was bleeding.

And what the hell did Nick have to be messed up about? she thought.

As she unzipped her leathers, Lizzy couldn't tell if Ty was shocked she was packing or if he had expected it. She really didn't care either way. Getting out of the jacket sleeve was the only way to get at the wound, but that would have to wait for a bit. She couldn't do anything until home, anyway.

She just had to figure out a way to get rid of them before Nick discovered who she was. By the way Ty was acting, Lizzy knew it was not going to be easy. She also had to figure out where she went wrong with the mark. Nothing like that had ever happened before. Her targets never got away, let alone got a shot off at her. It did not make any sense, and she was also sure the guy would not get the message to stay away. She was going to have to tell Tio.

And then there was going to be the next day. She might not be hurting at the moment, but Lizzy definitely was not looking forward to the morning. Even more than the physical pain, she dreaded seeing Nick again. Old wounds were already opened from the day's experiences and she was unprepared for their full force.

She kept her skull cap and glasses on for the entire drive. It was hot, but she had to be safe. Every time she looked in the side view mirror to watch Nick, she could swear he was enjoying the ride. What the hell was he doing here with this guy?

When she reached for her cell to message Gianni she realized it must still be on the bike. It would have to wait, but she needed him to work his magic as soon as she got home. Things were about to get interesting.

When they stopped for gas she could tell Ty wasn't impressed with the situation. It was obvious he did not want to be carting her ass around and would rather have been enjoying his holiday. After four hours on the road, though, at least it was not much longer. The ride had been quiet and gave her time to plan.

As she felt the jacket sleeve begin to get stiff, Lizzy knew it would have to come off. Better to pull it off while the wound was still a little wet instead of after it dried and the movement pulled it open again.

She eased the sleeve down her arm while undoing the zipper. It hurt much more than she thought it would — probably because her arm had become stiff from lack of movement. Mina would have to pull the bullet out when she got home. Luckily, there didn't seem to be any major damage. All she had to do was keep her arm still so the bullet did not damage anything else.

"There's a towel in the bag on the back seat if you'd like to use it," Ty shrugged.

"Thanks. Are you trying to be nice?"

"No, just saying. The car is a rental and we don't need to explain the blood."

Twisting her body without hurting her left arm was harder than she thought. Once she settled back in the front seat, Lizzy just let her arm hang to take all the pressure off.

"What's that?"

"What, you've never seen a tattoo before."

"Yes, but there's so much blood on it I can't see it."

"It's a daisy."

"A daisy? Why a daisy?" Ty couldn't believe it.

"Not that it's any of your business, but it's my favorite flower. Don't they have daisies where you're from?"

"Yes, my wife has them planted in the garden out front. They were her cousin's favorite flower… Lizzy."

"Excuse me?" This couldn't be happening. How did he know who she was?

"Lizzy. You're Dani's cousin."

"I'm sorry, you're……."

"Cut the bull shit. I am not in the mood after the day I've had."

"Does he know?"

"I didn't know until I saw the tattoo. He's been looking for you."

"You have to get him out of here. He can't know it's me. And how did you find me?"

"It was a fluke. We were eating ice cream when you came running out of the trees. By the way, who the hell taught you to fight like that? You could've been killed."

"It's not your concern."

"You're bleeding in my car and apparently we're family. It's my concern."

"Wait. You married Dani….. She told you……"

"No. I found your last email by accident. She kept your secrets so don't worry. But, why did you leave? That's what we don't understand."

At least they didn't know the truth. For that she was glad. Dani had kept her secret.

Now all she had to do was convince Ty to get Nick out of here in the 15 minutes before they were home.

"Ty, I need your help. You have to get him out of here. And I'm not going to answer any questions so don't even ask. After I get out of the car, you take him, leave, and don't ever look back. Please, promise me."

"He's not going to buy it. Give me a reason."

"No reason. You can make up whatever you want. Just take him and go. You can't be here." Lizzy choked on the words as she said them. Nick couldn't get involved. There were too many things that could go wrong and she couldn't hurt anymore.

This guy Ty had to take Nick and leave. She had already hurt him enough; he didn't need to learn the truth now.

"You know Nick better than that. He's not going to just want to up and leave, so either you come up with a plan, Lizzy, or we're going to be staying for a while. When he finds out it's you… the shit is going to start flying."

"Well, if you do your job right he won't find out, will he? Just get him out of here and stop asking so many questions. Turn right up ahead we're here."

Ty was shocked by the view when he made that right. His face made it obvious he thought Lizzy had done well for herself. The house was massive and the garage was any man's dream.

"Get him to leave the bike out front and I'll see you later."

As soon as the car came to a stop Lizzy jumped out and ran to the front door to warn Gianni. She was definitely going to need his help now.

God bless him, Gianni opened the door as she approached.

"Gianni, whatever you do, don't let them in. Stall as long as you can."

"Who is it? What's going on?"

As they were coming up the driveway, there was still time to quickly brief Gianni.

"It's Nick, but he doesn't know it is me and I'm trying to keep it that way. Just keep him outside as long as you can. Where's Mina? I'm going to need her nursing skills. I'll be in the office."

"Lady Lizzy, you are truly one of a kind."

"And that's why you love me Gianni, I'm the excitement in your life. Now cover for me please. By the way, his friend knows, but I don't know how long that he can stall Nick."

"Your wish is my command......" Gianni rolled his eyes as he thought to himself *that girl knew how to get into more trouble than anyone he knew.*

*   *   *

NICK

As he pulled up the driveway, Nick caught a glimpse of the girl running into her house. Of all the ungrateful things to do after they helped her and brought her home... And what a home it was. She was definitely into something, *maybe she could be of some use,* he thought.

He pulled the bike up beside Ty and turned the motor off. Despite the long ride, Nick had actually enjoyed it. He couldn't remember the last time he that had felt free.

Ty was leaning against the car waiting for him. By the look on his friend's face, Nick knew something was up, but Ty's sunglasses kept him from reading his expression.

"So, she just ran inside and left you out here?" he said more harshly than he meant. "What? You couldn't charm her, Ty?"

"Charm? That girl is definitely not one you'd charm. You were lucky, you got to ride by yourself. I had to deal with her. Let's go, now. I'm not in the mood anymore."

Ty hoped his friend bought his line. He needed to get Nick out of there even though a part of him wanted Nick to finally know the truth. This Lizzy was not who his friend had been searching for all these years; this Lizzy did not want to be found.

"Yea? Not buying it. We just drove her all the way here without even a thank you."

"It was your idea to bring her home, not hers remember."

"Yea, well, something doesn't add up. Besides, if she's connected she can help us find Lizzy. She will know this area better than us."

That's for sure, Ty thought, *but he wasn't going to like what he found.*
Ty could not let this happen. Not now. This girl would break Nick's
heart even more than it already was. The Lizzy he wanted was long
gone. Nick would not even recognize this person.

"I say we get the hell out of Dodge, go home and say fuck it to the
rest of the search. She's not here and you know it."

"I don't give a shit," Nick said stubbornly. "We're here and I'll at
least get a thank you." He turned and started for the door. Nick would
use whatever leverage he could if this person could help in their search.

*   *   *

LIZZY

"Lizzy, really?" Mina scolded. "Another gunshot wound? And always
the same arm, too. We're going to have to do something about this."

Mina smirked at her friend — because that is what she and Lizzy
had become. The age difference didn't matter. They understood each
other.

"Just pull it out so I can get this jacket off. I don't want to ruin
another shirt."

"At least you chose one with no sleeves this time. It makes it easier."

"Yea, it's white so unless you want to get the blood off it I suggest
we leave the jacket on until it's done."

She cringed as Mina removed the bullet and cleaned the wound. It
would need a few stitches but Mina was good, so no worries there. Her
worries were still sitting on the front driveway. She should have installed
sound on the cameras out there; at least she would know what they were
talking about. Ty had obviously still not convinced Nick to leave. She
remembered how stubborn he could be when Nick got something in
his head. She just hoped Gianni could get rid of them.

When she glanced at the monitor again, Nick was no longer standing
by the car. *He was making his way to the front door!* she screamed
internally. His friend obviously did not succeed in getting them to leave.
Now for the problem she was not ready to face at all. When the knock
at the front door finally came, she had no idea what to do next.

"Mina, you're going to have to stall them until, he's fed up and leaves. I can't deal with him right now and he can't learn the truth."

"Honey, you can only run from your problems for so long until they catch up with you. You know that better than anyone."

"Well, this problem can wait a few more years," Lizzy said. By the pounding on the front door, though, she knew it probably would not be that way for long.

As Mina left the room, Lizzy shrugged off her jacket. She would just have to wait them out. They couldn't stay that long. It may take a quick drink, but when they realized she would not be coming, they would leave — they would have to.

*   *   *

NICK

"Nick, you're going to break the door," Ty pleaded. "Come on, they obviously don't want us here. Let's just get in the car and go."

"Not going to happen. I want answers and I'm not leaving until I get them."

"It's your funeral, not mine." Ty mumbled to himself.

"What was that?"

"Nothing. Let's just go."

If there was one thing Nick did not do well, it was give up. He could stand there and bang on the door all day. Ty thought they would have to open the door at some point out of pure frustration. And, as if on cue, he could hear the locks shifting on the other side of the door.

"Sorry, Sir," Gianni consoled them. "The miss required some assistance and thanks you for your service. There's no need to see her."

"Yea, there is," Nick said as he pushed through the door to stand in the entrance. "Until I hear it from her, I'm not going anywhere. Now, you can either show me to her, or I'll find her myself."

Maybe this was what Lizzy needed; to confront her demons and get closure. She would yell later, but Gianni was doing what he thought was right. "Right this way gentleman, I'll show you up to the terrace."

As he led them down the hallway and through the kitchen, Gianni hoped the office door was closed. As he turned the corner, though, he realized it was open and gave Lizzy a smirk. The two men couldn't see it, but it would give her time to get organized.

* * *

LIZZY

Seeing Gianni smirk as he walked by, she knew what he was up to. He was like the father she had always wanted. *Pretending to know what was best for me.*

She could have killed him for bringing them through the kitchen. What if they had seen her? Ty already knew, but she was not ready for Nick to know. Gianni would have to get rid of them… one way or another.

Mina offered them beer as they sat out on her terrace. *They were making them comfortable,* Lizzy thought. *That wasn't part of the plan.*

At least now she could get close enough to hear their conversation and maybe see why they were here.

Nick leaned in his chair overlooking the balcony and just enjoyed his beer. He *had* earned it after all. Four hours of driving and then the woman whose life they helped save did not even have the courtesy to say thanks.

"You have that look in your eye, Nick. What are you planning?"

"Nothing… just enjoying the beer."

"That's bull shit and you know it. Whatever it is, just forget it and finish your beer."

"Yea, okay… whatever you say," he said knowing he would do whatever it took to find the woman. He wasn't going to leave until he did.

Ty knew his friend was up to something. The two of them needed to sort their shit out and he wasn't going to stop them. The sooner it was done, the faster he would be able to go home. Luckily as he saw Nick polish off his beer rather quickly he knew it would not be much longer.

Nick pushed his chair back and left the table. Lizzy had a feeling she would find out soon enough where he was going. She just had to make it to the hallway and back before he saw the pictures on the table or he would know.

She went through the main office door, slipped around the corner and quickly flipped the frame over. *Crap*, she thought, *there were a few others further down the hall.* As she quickly went around hiding pictures, Lizzy could not help pausing to look at one with the kids. All her decisions came flooding back.

Lost in that contemplation she did not hear Nick walk in. By the time she realized the mistake, it was too late. She put the frame down and made an attempt at the office, but she had been seen. She just hoped he wouldn't follow.

* * *

As he entered the hall and saw her, Nick knew he couldn't let it go. He saw her put the picture frames down and was going to say something, but thought better of it. He wasn't going to let her get far, though. They had some unfinished business.

Nick picked up the pace to follow her and she in turn sped up until they were both at a run. Although she made it to the room ahead of him, Nick was close enough to stop the door from closing with his foot. He had her now and wasn't going to stop until he got his answers.

When she realized the door wasn't shutting, Lizzy panicked. She couldn't meet him like this. Not now. She wasn't ready. Hell, there would never be a right time. In truth, she just didn't want any of this at all.

She put all her weight against the door knowing she would be no match for him. All that was left now was to keep her face hidden, but that would be a problem.

Nick pushed open the door knowing he had her trapped. She was going to answer his questions one way or another and he wasn't leaving until she did. Even though he knew his efforts were not appreciated, it no longer mattered.

Just... a... little... more... force...and... he stumbled into the room as the door suddenly flew open.

Momentarily stunned, Lizzy jumped out of his way. Anticipating her move he reached her more quickly than she had expected and pinned to her the wall, his body pressed up against hers. She couldn't think straight. They had not been this close in years and she hated how her body responded to his.

He was in her house... her office... standing against her. He was wearing a pair of jeans, running shoes and a fitted t-shirt. It seemed like it was just yesterday they were so close. His hair was still curly, but a little shorter. It was all she could do to keep from running her fingers through it. She knew this line of thinking wasn't good and had to get out of this position.

Ready for her move, he shifted closer. He had seen her fight and was well aware of this woman's capability. On some level, though, he knew they wouldn't hurt one another. It just felt so right... and it had been a long since he let himself get this close to a woman. He had to get a grip on his hormones or they would be his downfall.

She just looked vulnerable. Her hair was dark and flipped over in a sexy way. Her skintight leathers hugged every curve provocatively, and while her blouse went around her neck, he could feel there was no back. Without realizing it, his hand had made its way to the arch of her lower back, the other resting on her neck. His forehead lay on top of her head and neither of them moved, afraid of what could happen. It just felt so good... so right.

FIFTEEN

So MANY THOUGHTS were going through her mind, she didn't know if she wanted to get caught or run away. On some level she just wanted to lose herself in the moment; to be lost in Nick's arms, but she wanted, no needed to get away. Life always had a way of playing cruel jokes on people, Lizzy just hoped it wasn't her turn to be played.

Her breath became ragged as the contact lingered. She knew this could go either way and Lizzy needed to get out of the position she was in. She didn't need her memories getting the better of her. She didn't want to hurt him and felt the need to move, but even this small contact was keeping her from thinking straight. Lizzy could think of only one way to make move quickly and knew what she had to do…

"Hey, Nick," she said. "Do you mind getting off me please? I really don't want to have to hurt you."

"How do you………." Nick was stunned by the voice he just heard. It couldn't be. Not after all the years of looking. Here? Now? This wasn't happening. It couldn't be happening.

He slowly backed away from her, but without giving her enough room to escape. He had to see for himself; to make sure his mind wasn't playing tricks on him. After so many years of searching, for her to just fall into his lap this easily. It couldn't be real.

With one hand on her back so she couldn't move, he used the other to brush her hair off her face. When he saw her eyes he knew it was true. The amber color brought back so many memories.

He didn't remember the Lizzy of his past being as strong as this person — the viciousness when she fought. She had changed. Something in her life had changed her, but it was still her. He could still see the old Lizzy.

With Nick staring into her eyes, she remembered all the reasons she had fallen in love with him so many years ago. As the emotions came flooding back, she couldn't let herself get lost… she needed to focus. He wouldn't be able to forgive her once he found out everything she had done in the years since they had known each other. All Lizzy could think now was she needed to get rid of him before he did find out.

"Nick, come on. Move already, would you? Yes, it's me. Now get off." She pushed him away to get some space.

Nick eased himself back and ran his hands through his hair. He just couldn't believe it. They were actually in the same room.

He didn't know if he wanted to hug her or hit her. But, having seen how she fought, he opted to keep his hands to himself.

"What the hell, Lizzy?!" Nick blurted out. "What are you doing here? What's with the house? Where did you get it from? Why were you…?"

"Okay already," she cut him off. "I'm not going to answer any of your questions. You just need to leave and I'm asking you nicely. Go now, please." It killed her to ask, but she was not ready to deal with this yet.

"Leave? Yea, I don't think so. You have some explaining to do."

"Explain what? You were in jail and I made a new life. I didn't ask you to like it, I asked you to leave."

"That's not happening," he said. "I spent almost two decades looking for you. Now that you're here, you're going to answer my questions."

"I'm not going to answer anything. You don't own me! I'm not the same person I was all those years ago."

"From the display in the park, I can see that. What happened to you Lizzy? What changed you?"

"Life changed me. Now I've answered a question and I've asked you to leave. So leave. And take your friend with you." Lizzy needed him to go, and soon. It didn't matter how many years her emotions had been shut off, she didn't want them to come flooding back now, not when she was so close.

Nick grabbed her by the wrist. He knew as long as he kept physical contact with her, he had a chance at breaking down her walls. He pushed her against the wall, trying to get her to focus.

When he touched her, Lizzy knew she would be done if she didn't break it quickly. He left her no choice — she didn't want to hurt him, but her need to move was greater.

She shoved him in the chest to send him staggering back a few inches — it wasn't much, but it was just enough for her to be able to move.

Ready for her, Nick kicked her in the ankle causing her to fall to her knees. But when he reached down to hold her again she kicked back and sent him flying. The two of them began rolling around the floor.

Lizzy knew she could hurt him, where to hit and inflict as little or much trauma as possible, but it was Nick and she just couldn't.

With all the commotion going on in the office, it was only a matter of time before Gianni, Mina or Ty made their way over to see what was happening. They either chose to ignore it or had their own problems. Lizzy knew Gianni wouldn't leave her, though. He was like a father and would always make sure she was all right — even though he knew she would be.

After several more minutes of them rolling around, the office door finally opened.

"Are you going to stop them?" Ty said as he looked over to Gianni. "Because I'm not, this has been in the making for years. They need to settle this shit one way or another." He just turned around and left. Ty wanted it done so his friend could move on with his life.

"Mina," Gianni agreed, "let's go. She can hold her own."

Before leaving Mina looked at Lizzy and said, "Honey, you can't run from your demons forever. No time is better than the present to face them." With that, she turned and left with Gianni.

Lizzy realized she wasn't going to get the help she wanted. She didn't need it, but neither did she want to be alone. She had been by herself for longer than she cared to think about.

She chose to stop fighting and once she was on her back, just laid there.

"I'm not going to fight you anymore, Nick. I just need you to go. Please, just go."

As she felt her tears welling in her eyes, she fought to regain control of her emotions. Her friends were right, but she didn't want to do this now.

"You know me better than that," Nick came back. "I'm not giving up until you tell me what the hell is going on. You can do it today, tomorrow, hell next week for all I care, but I'm not going anywhere until I get answers. They said you had demons to fight and I'm not leaving until you talk!"

Resting back on his knees Nick looked at her and could see she was fighting herself, he just didn't know why.

"Some things are just better left in the past, Nick. Leave them there and get off me."

He raised himself up and extended a hand to help her rise. The stubbornness in her wouldn't accept his help and she pushed his hand away.

He moved out of Lizzy's way, but never took his eyes off her. She was hiding something and he was going to find out what it was. As she stood and leaned against the desk, he felt for her. He knew Lizzy and something bad had to have happened for her to be like this. She always fought for what she believed was right; he just had to figure out what that was.

"You're not going to get any answers here, Nick. So just pack up and go home."

"What and leave you here to get shot again? By the way, why the hell were you fighting with that guy anyway? He was three times your size. How's your arm?"

"My arm is fine. It's not the first time and won't be the last."

"What, you get shot at often?"

"No....the guy got a lucky shot. It won't happen next time."

"What are you talking about? Next time?"

"Like I said, none of your business. Stay out of it."

"I watched you get shot and you want me to stay out of it. What's going on?"

"Well, right now I'm going to take a shower and relax. I'm hoping by the time I'm done you won't be here."

Lizzy looked over her shoulder as she left the room. She knew he wouldn't listen, but needed time to evaluate everything that had happened.

"I'll be here when you're done. I'll just ask your butler what rooms Ty and I can use for the night."

Watching her leave killed him, but he wasn't going anywhere and she had better get used to the idea. At least with her out of the room he could do some snooping on his own. The computer in front of him was going to be the place to start.

Nick waited to hear her go up the staircase. After making sure no one else was around, he made his way back to the desk hoping he would come across something. The last thing he needed right now, though, was having someone walk in while he was rummaging through her stuff.

He began lifting papers gently, making sure not to move any of them. He had a feeling Lizzy knew where she placed everything. Next, he gave the mouse a shove to see if the laptop was on. To his relief it was. To his dismay it was locked. Whatever files she had on it, she didn't want anyone to see. He'd have to find a way in, but had already spent too much time in the office. He didn't want her butler to walk in on him so he left through the kitchen entrance and made his way back to the terrace to find his friend.

He found him sitting with a smirk on his face, Gianni and Mina beside him and not at all surprised when he came out. They had known he would come; the only question had been how long it would take.

"So," Ty opened, "did she hand you your ass?"

"No, but she's hiding something. That much I know."

"Nick, you do realize Lizzy won't tell you anything don't you? Just ask these two."

"We'll just see about that." He gave Ty a glare he knew his best friend would figure out.

"Sir, may I show you out," Gianni broke in. "I'm sure my Lady has asked that you leave."

"Yes, she did. But we're not going anywhere, so you can show us our rooms for the night. *And* I've already told her we're staying."

"She must not have been happy about that. When she wants something, she always gets her way."

Gianni knew they wouldn't be leaving. He just hoped they were ready for the truth… whenever Lizzy was ready to reveal it.

"Yea, well, that's her problem not mine. I haven't spent almost 20 years looking for her to just leave now that I've found her. If you don't want to show us to our rooms, we'll just find them ourselves."

"Mina, show the men to their rooms." He looked to Nick as he said, "Put that one in the blue room."

Mina saw Gianni smirk as he said it, but confirmed, "The blue room? You're sure, Gianni?"

Smirking and knowing it was for the best, he sighed, "Yes, I'm sure."

As she walked the men to their rooms, Mina knew Lizzy wasn't going to like it. Gianni was Right, though. Lizzy was a daughter to them and she needed to deal with this one way or another.

Maybe once she realized telling him was for the best, she could put the past to rest. Deep down, Mina knew Lizzy still loved Nick. There had never been another man in her life. If she could find a bit of happiness with him, it would be for the best. Putting Nick beside Lizzy's room wasn't going to go over well with her, but it would give him a chance to gain her trust.

"Nick, your room is over here. Ty you are across the hall. I warn both of you, she has a temper and I'm sure it's brewing as we speak. You chose to stay, just be prepared for when she sees both of you again. She kept her restraint before; I make no promises for next time. You're on your own with her. Also, we are on her side, not yours."

"Thanks Mina, I'll make sure Nick gets the message." Ty looked over to his friend to make sure the point was clear.

"I'm not here to upset her," Nick said. "I just want the truth. Can you understand that?"

"Better than you know," Mina confided. "Dinner will be served in an hour. Go shower and rest, and put on some clean clothes."

They had almost forgotten everything that had transpired earlier in the day. The two looked down at themselves and agreed showers were in order. And clean clothes never hurt anyone, either. Nick figured he should at least make a good impression after all these years.

Lizzy paced her room wondering how this day happened. She never lost a target before. Her reputation alone always brought compliance. How did this mark get the better of her? Why now? If things had gone as usual, the mark would have gotten the message and she would have gotten out cleanly. She would never have run into Nick and he wouldn't have ended up at her house.

What was she going to do know? He obviously wasn't going to leave until he got the answers he wanted. And she was not about to willingly give them. Lizzy needed to come up with a new plan.

It was already July and only a few months left until everything fell into place. With Nick here now, everything she had worked so hard for could be ruined. She wasn't going to let that happen. All she needed to do was get rid of him and quick.

Lizzy caught a glimpse of herself in the mirror. After rolling around in the dirt and then the struggle with Nick in her office, she looked a mess. Her arm was still killing her and all she really wanted at that point was a shower and some clean clothes. She would deal with the Nick problem later, she thought to herself.

As she eased into the shower the water washed over her; she hoped it would wash away her problems, as well. At least the heat eased her every muscle and fiber of her aching body. The grime and dirt rinsed off her body and out of her hair.

Lizzy found she was exhausted after all the surprises that day. Not surprisingly, she also found no appetite for dinner. She decided to just dry off, put on a pair of shorts and a tank top, and then slip into her welcoming bed. *Just a nap*, she thought. *Just to recharge,* she told herself. As her head hit the pillow, she fell instantly asleep. Her body finally told her she had enough for one day.

Nick and Ty had washed up for dinner and made their way back downstairs. Neither of them was surprised Lizzy didn't come down for dinner. They had thrown her for a turn today and, even if she had changed, she still needed to deal with the situation.

In hopes of keeping things simple, they decided not to snoop tonight. It might put too much attention on them and would be the quickest way of getting thrown out. The men figured they would just let the couple lead the discussion.

Ty received a call on his cell phone and stepped onto the terrace leaving Nick alone at the table with Gianni and Mina.

"So," he opened, "how long has Lizzy lived here?"

"She just moved in permanently this year," Gianni answered. "She only visited infrequently in the past few years."

"Does she travel a lot for work?" Nick pushed.

"You could say that. If you're trying to get answers, though, you best ask Lizzy yourself. Whatever needs to be said is between the two of you. Not us." Gianni gave Nick a stern glare to make sure he understood.

"You are right about that. She can't hide in her room forever."

Nick looked through the window to see Ty was done with his call. Something was troubling his friend. That usually meant Dani had called. He guessed Ty would tell her where he was now since they would be here for a while.

It hit him like a ton of bricks. He needed Dani to get closer to Lizzy. Who better to help than family?

Nick grabbed his phone, ordered the tickets and sent Dani a quick email. It would be a surprise for them all. *He just hoped it wouldn't backfire in his face.*

"Is everything Okay?"

"Yea, she's pissed I won't tell her anything. You have no idea what it's like to have a pissed off wife."

"Dani will get over it. I'm sure."

"You've met my wife, right?"

"Yes, I have. And when she gets here, she will be more than happy to blame me for everything, not you."

"Gets here? Nick, you didn't? You know she's going to kill you, right?"

Nick smirked at his friend from across the table. Of course, he was right. But it would be another person on their side and it never hurt to have someone else in your corner.

"Yea, well.....I'm going to bed, it's been a crazy day and I need sleep."

"Do you remember your way?" Mina asked.

"It's the third door on the right, right?"

"No, second."

"Thanks," Nick said and left the table and made his way up stairs. A good night's sleep was in order to think clearly.

"Um....Mina," Ty said, "it's the third door."

"Yes, it is the third door. But her door is the second."

"This is going to be ugly."

"Not our worry. They need to straighten this out and she can't avoid him forever."

"If they start fighting again, I'm not stopping it. They can have at each other for all I care."

SIXTEEN

As HE MADE his way up the stairs to his room, Nick hadn't realized how tired he actually was, both physically and emotionally. After spending years looking for someone, he hadn't realized the stress it had put on his body. It was like being stuck underwater with the pressure pushing at him from all sides; one could only last for so long. Now that he'd found Lizzy, the constant stress had disappeared and he could breathe again, but he felt mentally and physically drained.

For once he was looking forward to sleep — to dreaming. The nightmare was over. Lizzy was safe and sound in her room and he didn't have to worry where she was living or if something bad had happened to her. She was there and they were under the same roof. Even though she wasn't the same girl who left all those years ago, he could sense the old Lizzy was still inside somewhere. She might not have wanted to be found but he needed to remind her of who she used to be.

As Nick reached for the door handle to his room he just wanted to see her. Even though he didn't know which room she might be in and she would probably throw him out, he wanted to know she was safe. He knew, though, she would have to adjust to having him there.

Nick entered the dark room just wanting to rest. He spotted the bed as he closed the door and made his way to it. Once there, Nick realized he was in the wrong room. Maybe he had someone helping him on the inside, after all. Mina had directed him to Lizzy's room. He just stared for a moment at her lying there, sleeping so peacefully.

She must have been exhausted, she was flopped on the bed in a pair of shorts and a tank top, she looked like the old Lizzy: without a care

153

in the world. He just wanted to take care of her and make up for all the lost years. He wanted to protect her, even though he'd seen she didn't have a problem protecting herself.

Nick knew his next thought would lead to his undoing, but he didn't care. It had been so long and he just couldn't help himself. He eased off his shoes and lay down on the bed next to Lizzy, doing his best not to wake her. As soon as his head hit the pillow, he let himself fall into a deep, restful sleep. He would deal with the consequences when she woke up and found him there... not a moment before.

His dreams were filled with memories and how different things could have been for the both of them. If he had never gone to jail and been there for her when she needed him most... He dreamt of a future where they were married with children.

Sadly, reality seeped back into his thoughts and he was stuck behind bars for being a stupid idiot. Married with children was not what the universe had in store for them.

Lizzy felt the warmth of someone next to her and let herself enjoy the dream of a normal life. So many years were spent searching; and being alone. All she really wanted was a family and a home to call her own. The family she was going to get back, the home she now had. Seeing Nick that day had reminded her of how different things could have been. She shouldn't have run away; she could have waited for Nick and told him the truth. In her dream, she lived the life she wanted even if it was just for a moment.

To have someone there, someone to comfort her when she needed it. She was strong and could give herself credit for that, but every now and then the wondering got the better of her. In her dream, Lizzy was comforted by the image of Nick beside her. She wished on some level it was real, but because it was only in her head, she knew she was safe. He brought out a side of Lizzy she had put to rest years earlier. He was still the only one for her and would always be, but he couldn't know that, it would change everything.

Lizzy's warmth beside him felt right. Nick woke when she curled her body into his. He savored the moment, knowing when she woke up it wouldn't be pretty. But having her next to him was something that he had longed for. All he wanted was to prolong the moment and he wasn't going to ruin it.

Lizzy snuggled closer to Nick in her dreams. There, she could take the image wherever she wanted. She slowly slid her arm up along his chest to the back of his neck and let her fingers slip into his hair. It felt so real... a little *too* real. She had dreamed of being with him for so long, she could hear the beating of his heart in her ear as her head rested on his chest.

Reality sank in; Nick was in her room — lying in her bed. She instantly pushed away and shoved him off the bed.

"What the hell are you doing here?"

"I...the wrong...don't throw that!" Nick backed away before she launched the lamp at him.

"You're in my friggin room!!" Lizzy screamed as the lamp flew towards the wall beside his head. She wanted to make her point.

"Lizzy, come on just relax. I just fell asleep."

"Yea, in my bed. What are you doing in my room? In my house?! I asked you to leave!"

"I'm not going anywhere. I told you that last night, Lizzy. The faster you understand that, the easier this will all be."

"Leave! Now!"

"No."

"Nick, don't make me force you out of my house. You won't like it."

Nick walked over to her, knowing it probably wasn't the smartest idea, but he needed her to realize he was not going anywhere. In a few quick steps he was resting his hands on her shoulders letting her know he wasn't leaving.

"Nick I want you to leave. Now don't make me do something I may regret one day."

He reached around to the small of her back and said, "You won't hurt me Lizzy. You don't have it in you. I know you."

"No, Nick. You *knew* me. I'm not the young, naive girl you knew all those years ago. A lot has changed."

"Yea, so? I'm not the same Nick either, sweetheart. What's your point?"

"You need to leave," she pleaded, "now." Being this close wasn't helping her. It was all she could do to hold on to her instincts.

"Not going to happen. You have some explaining to do, so come on honey explain."

"You know you're not leaving me any choice right."

The reality of who she had become set in. Nick felt something cold against his collar bone. He had a feeling what it was, but he didn't even see her grab it. Still, he didn't want to give up. *His* Lizzy was in there. He just knew it.

"Move the blade, Lizzy. Be nice now."

"I stopped being nice years ago so get used to it. You're in my house and I want you to leave."

"You won't do it, I know that."

"You don't know anything." She pushed the blade a little harder, not enough to break skin, but enough to ensure he got the point.

"I know something changed you and I think that I was part of that. You're not *this* person, though. Maybe you are now, but that's not *who* you are. I'm sure the real Lizzy is in there."

"The real Lizzy died years ago. This is who I am and I really don't care if you like her or not. It's not your choice to make. Now, I've asked you nicely to leave. The next time, I won't be so nice."

Lizzy felt him removing his hands from her arms, no matter how much she really wanted them there. She didn't want to do it; didn't want to hold it to him like that, but he left her no choice. She eased her blade back. As he lowered his arms and turned to walk away from her, she could feel her heart breaking all over again. She wouldn't drag him into her mess; he didn't need to know anything.

He knew she needed her space and that he should have left while she was still asleep. He was still in shock over the fact she had pulled a blade on him — and where did she get it from so fast anyway? Lizzy had been right about one thing, she had changed. Leaving was the only thing he could do.

No matter what she did, though, he wasn't going to stop until he found out why. She would have to get used to that. As he closed the door behind him, he needed to see if his surprise had arrived yet. Why not add insult to injury? Something had to give at some point.

Nick spotted a picture on the table as he walked down the hallway. He was about to stop when he heard the front door opening. The picture would be there later. He just hoped the person at the door was the one he expected.

After he shut the door, Lizzy sank to the floor. She thought she had been dreaming when slipping next to the body in her bed. No one had ever gotten close to her in her sleep without her knowing before. He made her careless and she couldn't afford that at the moment — even if lying beside him felt right. When he was near she couldn't think straight. Hell, she had pulled a knife on him, the one man she vowed not to hurt any more than she already had. The worst part was he didn't even know it. She just wanted him to leave no matter what her heart was saying.

Lizzy got back up and went to the closet to throw on some yoga pants and a t-shirt. As she put her hair up in a ponytail she thought to herself, *Today is going to be a busy day. I needed to focus and train.* No one and nothing was going to keep her from reaching her goal.

The training room wasn't far off. Even if they passed each other in the halls she figured she could make it quick not give him the time. Lizzy knew hoping Nick would leave was one thing, but his actually going was something entirely different.

She left her room and headed towards the stairs glad not to have run into anyone thus far. The faster she made it to her destination, the happier she would be. As she descended the staircase quickly and scouted the hallway ahead, Lizzy didn't even try to hide her smirk. She liked dodging the enemy; it was what made her so good at her job in the first place.

Luck in her favor, she decided to make a quick stop in the kitchen to grab a bite. Unprepared for who was sitting at the table, Lizzy stopped dead in her tracks to make sure she was seeing correctly. It couldn't be... There, right beside Nick, was her cousin, Dani. *He   had   called   her cousin.*

"Dani......"

Dani rushed out of the chair to her cousin. She still didn't want to believe what Nick had told her was true.

Lizzy couldn't believe Nick had brought Dani here. She didn't know if she wanted to kill him or thank him. Lizzy needed family now and that's exactly what Dani was. As she hugged her cousin, Lizzy finally knew she had someone she could talk to; someone who would understand, and someone who knew the truth.

"Lizzy! Oh my God, Lizzy! It's really you."

"Dani?!! When?... How?... Nick!"

"Nick called me last night and asked me to be on the first flight out. When he said he'd found you, and since my husband was here, as well, I couldn't resist."

"Glad to see I came in second there."

"Shut up Ty, you know she's here for you. And I did promise you two a trip."

"Nick, this doesn't count as the trip. This is still business."

Lizzy didn't care about Nick or Ty at the moment. She had her cousin with her. Dani was the one person she needed most at the moment. From Nick's reaction, he knew he had succeeded in making her happy. She hated that look in his eyes.

"Ty, she's my cousin and I'm taking her for a while, so see you. Dani I know you just got off a long flight, but we need to talk."

"Talk is one thing we have to do."

"Dani come with me please. Boys, I hope not to see *one* of you later." As she glared at Nick, she hoped he got the point.

Lizzy escorted Dani down the hall to the garage — she needed to get away from the house so they could speak privately and without prying eyes. They entered the garage Lizzy went straight to the dirt bike. While she knew her cousin would think she was nuts, she needed to talk and didn't care at the moment.

"Dani, do you still remember how to ride?"

"Yea, why?"

"Does Ty know about your past?"

"No. I never told him."

"Then he's in for a shock isn't he." Lizzy laughed and threw her cousin a helmet. The two of them used to live on dirt bikes when they were younger.

Dani started the bike and followed Lizzy down the path in the yard. She heard the 'What the fuck!' come out of her husband's mouth fading behind her. Oh well, they all had their secrets. She had forgotten how much she loved to ride; the thrill of the wind whipping through her hair and the adrenaline rush as the RPMs on the bike went higher.

This was going to be a good day. She had her cousin back and they were going to straighten the mess out. First, though, Lizzy was going to have to tell her how she was able to get a house like this, as well as get used to the she was going to be spending a lot of time visiting.

Lizzy left the path and parked the bike once she knew they were far enough away to have some privacy. Gianni knew where to find her if needed since they were in her regular place.

"Lizzy, it's been so long. Tell me what's happened, have you found the kids yet?"

"No, but I know where they will be. It just won't be for a few more months."

She filled her cousin in on all the details of her life. She was happy Dani didn't ask too many questions. She mostly just sat there and listened. The questions would come, that was for sure. But it felt nice to confide in someone for a change; someone, who actually knew everything and wouldn't judge.

Lizzy saw that her cousin needed a minute to absorb everything, so she took a moment to sit there and run her hands over the grass as she used to do when she was a little girl. The action was so carefree and long forgotten; Lizzy was surprised at how good it felt.

"You know you have to tell him, don't you, Lizzy?"

"Dani, I can't. He wouldn't understand... Think of the life I led then and the life I lead now. I'm a completely different person."

"So is he. Don't you think he has changed over the years, as well?"

"Yes but...."

"Lizzy, he's been looking for you since he got out. You owe it to him."

"What do I say? 'Oh, by the way, Nick, you're a dad. Oh yea, and I took off with your kids who are now in the hands of arms dealers and I've spent the last 11 years ridding the world of scum bags for money while tracking them down.'"

"Well, maybe not exactly like that. But you have the general idea."

"Dani, I can't tell him. First I need to get my kids back and these people are dangerous enough, without having to worry about someone else getting hurt."

"He has a right to know and you've kept it from him for long enough."

"Dani..."

"Lizzy..."

"Dani... No."

"Lizzy... Yes. And you know I can do this all day right."

"Fine, but I'll tell him when I'm ready."

"You have until tonight and then I spill the beans."

"At least I know one thing about you, Dani."

"Yea, what's that?"

"You haven't changed." Lizzy looked at her cousin and they both began to laugh. Thankfully, some things didn't change.

Lizzy knew she was right, but how was she going to tell Nick. How do you tell someone you have taken away a part of their life they can never get back? It wasn't something she could go back and change. She took off with his kids, denied him a chance of ever knowing them, and now they were teenagers. At least she had gotten their first six years before they were taken from her. Nick didn't even get that.

* * *

With the girls gone, Nick had the opportunity to look around. He knew Mina wouldn't stop him; he just hoped she would keep Gianni away. Lizzy looked determined to talk to Dani, so he hoped that they would be gone for a while. Together, he and Ty would be able to cover more ground. He wasn't sure what he was looking for, but there had to be something that would lead him in the right direction.

Having already checked the office the previous night, Nick thought he might have better luck in her room. He already sent Ty to check the garage and saw Mina talking to Gianni on the terrace, so there was no time like the present. As he made his way up the stairs he remembered the picture in the hallway and went to get it, but it was gone. Someone didn't want him to see whoever was in the picture.

As he opened the door to Lizzy's room, he realized how big it was. It was dark when he entered last night and this morning... well... there were other problems. He knew Mina had already been in to tidy up because the bed was made and everything was neat. Nick went to the night-table and opened the drawers but found nothing. It was the same with the closet and dresser. As he got more frustrated, Nick continued his search knowing there had to be something, anything about what she did for a living.

As he walked over to the dresser again, Nick noticed there was another picture. He had been so concerned about the drawers and boxes he didn't think to look at the photographs at first.

He lifted the frame and saw it was of three small children. Could she be married? Was that why she freaked out that morning? Was she worried her husband would find her in bed with another man? Then he remembered there were no male clothes in the room.

Nick carefully placed the picture back where he had found it and decided to check the other rooms. The first few were where he and Ty were sleeping, so he made his way down the hall and noticed one room was set up for kids, but all the other rooms were empty except for a bed and dresser. There were no pictures or clothes or anything personal.

Nick went back to the children's' room and looked a little deeper. He noticed there were no clothes in the closet or dressers, only a few stuffed animals and some pictures of Lizzy and the children. The pictures ranged from infants to what looked like six or seven years old. Maybe, he thought, she was married and lost her husband and kids in an accident. That could explain the change in her.

Losing your children and husband could do anything to a person. As he sat on the bed holding the penguin in his hand, he never heard Lizzy enter the room.

"What are you doing in here? Get out."

SEVENTEEN

"Lizzy, what happened?"

"I said get out! No one is to be in this room, NO ONE!!"

"I'm sorry, just talk to me."

"You don't know anything, please just go." Her eyes were filling with tears. It wasn't supposed to happen this way. She hadn't wanted him to see the room. She wanted to tell him first, but not like this.

As he walked over, Nick could see the pain in her eyes. It didn't matter he hadn't seen her in years. He knew Lizzy and could tell when she was hurting. She took a step back, but Nick knew it was only her own defenses she was worried about. No matter how much of a hard-ass she tried to be, he always knew the truth.

"Why couldn't you just leave? Why are you still here? I want you to go now!"

"Lizzy, I'm not going anywhere. Someone hurt you. I can see that just looking at you, so stop with the bull shit and tell me what's up."

"Just leave please," Lizzy said as she turned her back to him. She didn't want him too close because she didn't know if she could handle it.

"No. I'm not going anywhere, Lizzy." As his frustration grew, Nick walked over to the window to give her some space; always keeping her in his full view. He rested against the window ledge to wait her out. There was nothing else he could do until she was ready.

Lizzy turned around knowing he wasn't going to leave. She knew this conversation needed to happen. Dani told her if Lizzy didn't tell him she'd do it herself. This was something that needed to come from Lizzy. It was her mess and she had be the one to clean it up. Deep down, she knew it would be a relief to finally let him know what she had done to him without his knowledge.

Forgiveness would be too much to ask. But what was done was done and there was no going back. Lizzy decided to move forward and took a deep breath, walked over to the night stand to pick up the photograph he had been holding when she walked in and she wondered what Nick had been thinking when he looked at it.

She sat in the middle of the bed and held the frame in her hands remembering the day the picture was taken. It was right after the children were born. She was their mother in every sense of the word. They were hers; she should have just left then, went to find Nick and told him everything. But she hadn't and that was her biggest regret.

The sun was glowing from behind him, making his expression hard to interpret in the shadows. Part of her was glad he hadn't left, but she was still mad he had stayed.

"Are you going to tell me what happened?" Nick knew she couldn't see him properly by the way she was squinting. He also knew he should move closer, but wanted to give her the space she needed. He would know when the time was right.

"Happened to whom?"

"Your family? Your husband and kids? That's who the people in the pictures are, isn't it? Were they killed in an accident or something? Is that what made you so cold?"

"No, they were taken from me and I have been doing everything and anything to get them back."

"So where's their father, then? What did he do with them?"

"It wasn't their father who took them?"

"Tell me what's going on Lizzy? Why did you leave? Why were you living under another name? And, why the Cirescos?" Nick knew he had gotten her attention with the last question. He sat down in the chair across from her. He could tell if she was lying by the look in her eyes and she knew it.

Lizzy leaned her head forward and stared at the picture. "How do you know about *them*?" she asked.

"Funny story. Let me enlighten you…

"After jail and your vanishing," he explained, "I went back to school and became a private investigator. I thought it would help in tracking you down after you up and vanished. Imagine my surprise when, years later, a doctor hired us to find out what happened to one of his patients. See, she left the hospital completely alive. But her obituary said she had died days before. Out of concern he hired us to find out what happened. Can you guess whose picture came through with a different name on it?" He could see her attention increasing, but he did not want to push too hard. At the same time, Nick needing Lizzy to realize what he had been through.

"Mine."

"Yes, yours. We tracked down where the Cirescos lived and went looking for you. It looked like you left fast, though. Oh, and nice hiding place by the way… under your bed. Some things never change. Now do you mind telling me why you were living with arms dealers? Inquiring minds want to know."

"What else do you know?"

"We tracked you down to Mexico, where you left the airport with a man. I guessed he was your husband. You guys seemed awfully close."

"Husband? No, I never had a husband."

"So he's just the father of your children, then?" Nick knew he was being snarky, but couldn't help himself.

"No, he isn't the father of my children, either. He is just a good friend who helped me out when I needed it."

"So, then, who took your children? And what's going on?"

"Okay, after I left Mexico with my friend, Sandro, he and his uncle helped me get back on my feet. They trained me. You see, I was going to do anything I had to in order to find my kids."

"Then who took your kids?"

"It's a long story....."

"It's a good thing I have time, then. I'm not leaving, Lizzy, so at least let me help you."

She saw Dani walk by the room and hesitate in front of the door and knew she had to tell him. Dani gave her a nod and the confidence to continue. Then she closed the door so they wouldn't be disturbed and Lizzy was ready to continue.

"When I went to work for the Cirescos I was pregnant and didn't tell them. It only took a few months for Mrs. Ciresco to figure it out, though. I was sick and tired all the time. She had always treated me like her daughter since they never had any children of their own. When she took me to the doctor I told her what was going on.

"Being a single mom was going to be hard enough, but when I found out I was going to have triplets it was a whole new problem. She and her husband offered to adopt the children, but I didn't want to be away from them so I made a deal: I pretended to be their daughter and let them raise my kids as their own. They were wealthy, I was naive and scared. But it allowed me to be a part of my children's life and make sure they would want for nothing.

"Things were great for the first six years. The Cirescos put me through school and gave me a job. Then they tried to kill me and took off with my children.

"I know Mrs. Ciresco lied and told him I died or I probably would really be dead by now. I may spare her for that, but when I find him I won't have any pity."

"Why not involve the police and let them help?"

"I was supposed to be dead. How would that look? I only had the original birth certificates and nothing else, so I called Sandro. He met me in Mexico and took me to his house in Brazil. After I told him and his uncle the truth they helped and trained me.

"After that, I started taking jobs to remove people whose families wanted retribution. Every job brought me closer to finding the Cirescos. See they had made a lot of enemies over the years; enemies who were more than willing to help bring them down.'

"They trained you? To do what?"

"I was a paid killer. I took out people the law couldn't. Rapists, killers, drug dealers — the scum of the earth. With the money I earned doing that, I'm more than capable of raising my kids and not working once I have them."

"So where's their father, then? Why are you doing this by yourself?"

"He wasn't around?"

"What, he just left you alone with triplets on the way? What kind of creep did you hook up with?"

"He wasn't a creep. He never knew about the triplets because I didn't tell him. I couldn't find him?"

"So he took off on you? Lizzy why didn't you do better for yourself? Why get messed up with a guy like that?"

Smirking, she knew once he found out the truth he would be dumb struck. He didn't think her smart enough to meet a decent guy, not realizing he was the one who wasn't around when she needed him. He had gotten himself thrown in jail for being stupid. If *he* had been smarter, they would never have been in this mess in the first place.

"He wasn't around because he had gotten himself thrown in jail for being an idiot."

"Nice, you're a paid killer and you hang out with criminals. What happened to the Lizzy I knew?"

He couldn't believe she had let her life get to such a point.

"I was young and scared, Nick. The one person I needed wasn't there for me. Shit, I didn't even know I was pregnant until he was serving his sentence. When I went to his father to find out where he was the old man was drunk and couldn't give a rat's ass about what I was saying. I did what I had to do and you have no right to judge me for that."

Lizzy got up from the bed and walked over to the window, the picture still clutched to her chest. She knew she was in the wrong all these years, but his judging her wasn't helping the situation. He still hadn't gotten it — he simply thought she had sunk very low. As she heard him take in a deep breath across the room, she knew he was choosing his words before he spoke again.

"Okay, so he left you alone. Why didn't you wait for him?"

"My parents kicked me out with nowhere to go and no money to my name. I had to do what I felt was right at the time."

"Lizzy, how old are your kids?" The realization was beginning to sink in. Nick had been the one to leave her alone by getting his ass thrown in jail. It was his fault. He was the father.

"They're going to be 17 this year." Lizzy watched him sink down into his chair stunned by this new information. All he could seem to do was sit there and stare at her while he processed everything he had just been told.

Lizzy had taken off because she was scared. He was the one who had left her alone. He was a father and never knew. What had been going through her mind when she found out she was pregnant? How scared must she have been? All alone and pregnant, her parents throwing her out... After all these years, all the searching, to finally find her and realize he was the cause of her leaving. He wanted to be mad at her; to be furious for not telling him. *But* she had tried. She went to his father. It was no surprise his dad wouldn't help her, he never helped him or anyone else, the bottle was always more important.

When he finally lifted his head from his hands, he could see Lizzy standing rock still, as if afraid to move. This Lizzy, who didn't fear anything — hell she had been shot the day before. But, now, she was afraid and he knew he was the cause of it. It was like she was waiting for a bomb to go off. Nick had every right to start yelling and screaming, but he knew it wouldn't get them anywhere.

"Why didn't you wait for me Lizzy? Why did you take off?"

"I wanted to wait, Nick. Really I did. That was my original intention. Get a job, get through the summer and find you when you were released. I didn't want anyone to know I was pregnant because I didn't want their pity. If my own parents wouldn't help me, I didn't want anyone else to either."

"You could have waited…"

Nick got up from the chair and walked over to her by the window. He could tell she was nervous by her reaction.

The closer he came to her, the more she just wanted to turn and run. It was an alien feeling; *she* didn't run from anything anymore. People ran from her. As he got closer she knew it was time to face everything that had happened. She had to account for her actions, but she had to keep her walls up. Lizzy couldn't afford for them to crumble now, not when she had come so far.

"Once I found out I was pregnant with not one baby, but triplets, everything changed. Hell, we wouldn't even have been able to support ourselves, much less give them the life they deserved. The Cirescos made me an offer and, trust me, it wasn't an easy one to deny. I could give up you and the meager life we could have, or give the children lives you and I could only dream about."

"You didn't even give us a chance."

"I was scared, alone and pregnant. They offered to give my kids everything and the opportunity to stay in their lives at the same time. How could I not consider it? It was the hardest decision I ever made to leave you behind, but it had to be done."

Lizzy wiped her cheeks with the back of her hand, not even sure when she had begun to cry. It was too late... the walls she fought to keep so firmly in place were beginning to crumble and there wasn't a dam thing she could do about it.

Seeing her standing there, fighting against her own emotions, Nick knew she was trying to will herself to stop crying; to regain control. She was strong, but he wasn't going to let her do this herself.

He had already missed out on even knowing his children. Now, he would do whatever it took to get them back. He took the last step closer to her and drew his Lizzy into his embrace. He needed her just as much as she needed him. Having just found her, he wasn't going to let her get away.

"We'll get them back Lizzy. I promise you we will get them back."

"I can't let you help me Nick," she said as she pushed herself back from his arms. "You could get hurt. You don't know these people the way I do. Let me finish what I started." She began this and wanted to be the one to finish it.

"Well, you know it won't happen that way. You just told me I have three kids who are 17 years old. These people tried to kill you once already; you're not going against them alone. I'm helping you and *then* you can tell them."

"I made it this far on my own. I think I can handle the rest."

"Put your stupid pride behind you, Lizzy. With mine and Ty's help, we *will* get them back."

"Wait, your and Ty's help. They don't know you. Hell I don't even know if they remember me."

"There is only one way to find out. You just need to either accept we are doing this together or put up with me following right behind you."

She could tell he wouldn't give up. Hell, how could she even think Nick would give up now after he had spent all these years looking for her? She also knew it would be a lot easier with his help. The Cirescos didn't know him so he might be able to get closer than she could. After all, she knew where they were going to be. Lizzy had to be smart, though. She couldn't let her feelings for him put them at risk.

"Fine," she said, "we do this together. But you need to know what you're up against. Who these people really are."

"I did my research on them when I was looking for you. I know exactly what I'm getting into."

"Then I hope you're ready. This is going to be a fight to the end." She turned from him to look out the window with the knowledge she could count on Nick. Her heart broke for her past decisions, but once they found their kids maybe, just maybe, she could have the semblance of a normal life.

He reached from behind to wrap his arms around her waist. As Lizzy leaned back into his chest, he knew she still cared. They were going to get their family back. Hell, it began to sink in: he had a family. *They* would be a family when this was all done.

He rested his chin in the crook of her neck; it felt right. This was how it should have been all these years. Maybe Lizzy was right, if they had tried to raise the kids when they were younger, he might have resented her. He wasn't in the right frame of mind all those years ago. Even though she had taken them and herself away from him, he was the man he was now because of her. For that he was grateful.

"We need to go tell Dani and Ty what's going on."

"Dani already knows, I'm sure she told Ty while we were in here talking. You guys need to be prepared for what's next. You'll need......."

"We'll be fine Lizzy. Just have faith, OK. Now can you tell me about my kids, what their names are? What they were like?"

"Sure, and by the way, your kids are just like you. Devilish, in every way."

"So you didn't really get that far from me at all then, did you?"

"Nope. Not at all." As she leaned into his chest, she felt like she was home. They were going to do this together. She continued to tell him about the kids, what they were like up until the Cirescos took them. Their zest for life, their giggles, and their temper tantrums. She could feel herself smiling at the memories, ones she was glad to share with him. He had missed out on something she couldn't replace, but they would have their whole lives to try.

"You do realize, Nick, you need to be prepared. I'm different from who I was then. I have done a lot of things wrong. But I am trying to make them right now."

"I can only guess at what's gone on, but I'm positive there was nothing you weren't forced to do in some way or another. Just tell me what you know and we'll go from there."

They heard a commotion downstairs and Lizzy knew they had to go check it out. Only one person knew where she was and, by the sounds of it, he had just arrived. As they made their way down the flight of stairs the person going at it with Ty in the entrance wasn't who she expected. Sandro was doing his best to pull the guys apart, but Ty didn't want to stop. Nick jumped over the railing to intervene and she couldn't figure out why until she caught a glimpse of the man's face. Then *she* went in for the kill. She didn't care how this guy got into her house, there was only one way he was leaving.

Lizzy pushed past Ty and Nick without care, the man was hers. It was owed to her. She got hold of him and shrugged off Nick as he tried to grab her. It didn't take long for Nick to realize he needed to stay out of her way. Ty holding him back help, as well.

Nick didn't see her pull the knife. Hell, he didn't even know where she had hidden it. In one second she shoved him, and in the next she held an eight inch serrated blade in her hand. She had definitely changed. As he felt the need to get back into the fight and help her, he realized that she was holding her own. As well, Gianni was standing there and didn't seem to want to intrude.

"Let him go, Ty. She can handle herself."

"If I let him go he'll end up on the other end of that blade," Ty pointed out as he felt Nick struggling to get free. Still, he knew this was a score Lizzy had to finish. Gianni had told him everything about her the other night. Nick just needed to stay out of her way or he would be the one to get hurt.

Nick was surprised as he watched Lizzy and the man rolling around on the floor. He knew she could fight, but this display wasn't what he had expected. She not only held her own, hell the other guy couldn't get a shot in otherwise. Lizzy kept the upper hand. Whoever had trained her knew what they were doing. As she pinned the guy to the floor, her knees on his shoulder and knife pressed to his throat, he didn't know if he should have been proud or help the poor guy.

"How the fuck did you find this place?" Lizzy asked the intruder. "You got off lucky the last time you son of a bitch, but not this time."

"You crazy bitch, what the fuck are you doing here? I thought I shot you. I should have aimed higher."

"Buddy, you got luck, but it's about to run out."

"LIZZY STOP!!!!!"

The blade against the man's throat, Lizzy knew the voice behind her. But why he was asking her to stop, she'd love to know.

"Sandro! What the hell? Since when do I ever stop?"

"Get off him, Lizzy."

"Fuck you. This asshole shot me. Finishing him will be a pleasure."

As Sandro looked back and forth between Lizzy and the man she was straddling, things became clearer. *She* was the one he had fought in the park the other day. The only question was why?"

"Lizzy, get off him. For me, please."

"Sandro, if you want me off him, tell me who the hell he is."

"He's my boyfriend. Now will you get off him?"

"Well your boyfriend was on my hit list, so I'll need a better reason."

"Wait, you're Sandro's Lizzy?" said the man underneath her. "Why would I be...? Wait, I promise not to do anything. Just move your blade." He had heard about Lizzy and knew if she did move there would be a good reason behind it. She never stopped until she got her mark, but why was she *his* mark?

"Like I can trust you?" she hissed back. "You fricken' shot me. And I never lose."

"Well, someone paid me to get rid of you and I'm guessing the same thing on your end. For Sandro's sake, let's figure this out." He held her gaze knowing it might be the only way for her to see the truth in his words.

If someone wanted her dead, she was going to find out whom. Lizzy eased the blade off his throat and pulled herself cautiously away from him. She wanted answers and wasn't going to rest until she had them.

Sandro rushed over to help his friend and Lizzy guessed he didn't know anything about what was going on.

Why had someone wanted her dead? And, who had sent this guy after her? There was more to this; Lizzy just had to find out what. It took everything she knew to control herself with her mark standing in front of her. She saw Ty had finally let Nick go. Now, she just hoped he stayed where he was. The testosterone in the room was going to be unbearable if things went south.

In order to stay ready for anything, Lizzy kept her blade casually in her hand.

Sandro breathed a sigh of relief. "Thank you, Lizzy. Now do you want to tell me what's going on?"

"All I know Sandro is when a job comes up, I make sure it gets finished. The only reason his blood is still in him and not all over my foyer is for your sake, not his."

"But, who would hire you to kill him?" Sandro was getting more confused by the minute. No one knew this was his boyfriend. It was something he kept to himself.

"Your father. He told me everything I needed to know about this guy and said he was the final clue in finding the Cirescos. I've come this far, Sandro. You know what they did to me. Did you really think I would just let it go?"

"Letting it go was never your strong point, Lizzy. But, why would he put a mark on him? Where's the file?"

She nodded over to Gianni to retrieve the file from the office as everyone looked just as confused as she was. Something wasn't right? It just didn't add up. One way or another she would get to the bottom of it. Right now she had more questions than answers going through her head.

Lizzy glanced across the room to where Nick was positioned and wondered what he must be thinking. This was a side of her he had never seen. As she twirled the tip of the knife on her index finger her frustration only mounted.

Gianni handed the file to Sandro and they looked at each other realizing this was just the beginning. Sandro flipped through the pages with concern on his face.

As he walked over to hand the folder back, Lizzy knew they needed to talk. After a quick nod, Sandro followed her. She looked over at Gianni knowing he would give them their space and keep everyone from following. Lizzy closed the door behind them leaving the other entrance open a crack. She could count on Gianni to be there just in case; Nick probably not far behind. All she had to do was make sure Sandro didn't notice the other door.

"Do you mind telling me why your father would want your boyfriend dead?"

"The file doesn't make sense," he said. "Why would he want you to kill him for doing the same things you do? And why did he say father hired him to kill you? Something isn't right Lizzy."

"No shit. Tio doesn't know I missed my mark, and I'm guessing your boy toy didn't tell him either. We just need to find out why. Anything coming to mind?"

"Nothing. Why would he help you all these years and then suddenly want you dead."

"Because there is something he doesn't want me to know. There's more going on here than either of us knows Sandro. The problem is to get the upper hand we need to figure out what."

"What are you suggesting, Lizzy? You have that look on your face." He knew her well enough to know when she was plotting something and the glint in her eyes told him so.

"Well, if we were both hired to get rid of one another, then only one of us should be alive."

"You're not going to kill him, Lizzy."

"Oh, relax and get your panties out of a bunch. I won't kill him yet if that makes you happy, but we will have to fake his death. Luckily, Tio only ever wants a photo confirmation. When I send it and your friend fails to report, he won't have a choice but to accept it. He knows neither of us would give up, so it's going to have to look real and not easy either."

"So you want to fake his death, make it look as real as possible and tell Tio you killed him? You don't think Tio will just send someone else after you?"

"I'll be counting on it. But your friend will have to keep out of sight. That way I'll have the upper hand, not Tio. I'm not stopping until I get my kids back, Sandro. So don't even think about getting in my way."

She didn't take her eyes off her friend to make sure he registered everything she said. If Tio wanted her dead, he was going to have one hell of a fight on his hand. He wouldn't be prepared for what was coming.

"Sandro, are you sure he doesn't know you guys are involved?"

"I told him I'm gay. Not that I had a boyfriend."

"All I'm saying is: what if he knew? What if Tio has known all along? By getting rid of your boyfriend there would be no scandal. By making either of us kill the other he made sure you would hate whoever succeeded if you should ever find out."

"Then he would have been planning this for a while. He knew when I was going to be in Italy and he knew I was coming to see you."

"Yea and he knew I would still have my information because I wouldn't be sending it until today with the time difference. I need to send the message within the hour so get your boyfriend and we will take the picture and explain everything after."

As her friend left the room, it didn't take long for Nick and Gianni to walk through the other door. She knew they had heard everything so she wouldn't need to explain. By the looks on their faces, they also knew finding her kids was getting harder by the minute.

EIGHTEEN

"So what are we going to do now? Whoever this Tio is, he wants you dead. If he hired this guy to kill you, he will send more."

"I'm counting on it."

"Do you have a death wish, Lizzy? I know you've changed, but..."

"If he thinks I killed Sandro's boyfriend he will use it to break our friendship. I want him to keep sending people after me. He's up to something, and I haven't done this all these years to just give up now. Whatever he doesn't want us to find is big and that makes me want to find it more.

"And," she continued, "you're right Nick, I have changed. I just hope you get used to the new Lizzy because she and the old ones are great friends. Now you're either going to go home and stay out of it, which I doubt, or you're going to stay and help. The choice is yours. To our advantage, Tio doesn't know you're here so you'll help in more ways than you realize."

"You have that look in your eyes."

"Gianni, we're going to need some papers drawn up. I think it's time Nick goes back to school."

"School?" he asked confused. "What are you up to?"

"Do you trust me, Nick?"

"Do I have a choice right now?"

"No."

"Then I trust you." Nick knew her mind was going a thousand miles a minute. This new Lizzy didn't leave anything to chance. Whatever plan she was formulating, he knew it would be pretty solid.

When the office door opened with Sandro and his friend coming back in, you could tell his boyfriend was not happy he was going to play dead. Once they filled him in on the plan, though, she knew he would see the light.

"All right," Lizzy began, "so we know Tio wants both of us dead. We also know if one of us killed the other, Sandro would hate whoever succeeded. So this is my suggestion, you pretend to die, Sandro calls Tio tomorrow to tell him what happened and says he is going to get back at me for killing you. That should buy us a few weeks. In the meantime, you two are going to help me train Nick and Ty so they can help with the Cirescos."

"The Cirescos," interrupted Sandro's friend, "that's who you're looking for?"

"Yea, Tio said you would have information about them. If you do, spill it."

"They bought a villa about 30 miles from here not too long ago. Their kids will start school nearby in a few weeks. My cousin was hired as their bodyguard."

"Interesting. Well at least Tio didn't lie about you being useful. Now the question is why did he want us to off each other? Your cousin can't know you're alive, by the way. For now, you can't talk to anyone."

"That's fine. I want answers as much as you do."

As Lizzy prepared to send the confirmation she encountered something new — people weren't usually so cooperating. This time, though, both needed answers so they had to make sure this worked.

Once the message was sent off and Lizzy confirmed Tio transferred the money into her account, it would be time to get started. First, the money would have to be moved into an account Tio didn't know about. Using some contacts she had developed Lizzy would make it look like she made some big purchases.

Next, she showed Sandro and Ty where the training room was, but kept the weapons room to herself. There are some thing's people don't need to know. She would show Nick, though, when she had a chance.

Once everyone left to do their own things, it was finally just her. So much had happened in the last few hours, she was glad for the moment alone. It had gone from just being her, Gianni and Mina to her, Gianni, Mina Nick, Ty, Dani, Sandro and his boyfriend. No matter the challenge, though, Lizzy would take the world on if it meant getting her kids back sooner.

Nick was about to start that part. Because the Cirescos did not know him, he could get close without drawing attention. If they knew she was this close, they would leave in a heartbeat. She hadn't worked so hard for 11 years to blow it all now. She was glad when Nick entered the room. They needed to talk about what was being planned, and Lizzy knew Gianni would have completed his tasks in mere hours.

"You know," he opened, "this new you is a little devious."

"Devious," Lizzy came back, "is that the best word you can come up with?"

"No," he smiled, "but it's the politest. You have a lot on your plate. What can I do?"

"How's your English?" she asked.

"My what?"

"Gianni is getting the papers ready. You're going to be the new English teacher at the kid's school. You can gain their trust and find out about them. We need to know everything we can. They don't know you, and I can't take the chance of them recognizing me."

"So I get to pretend I'm a teacher? Are you nuts?"

"Yes and no, I'm not. You're the private investigator, just think of the files you will have access to. This will be great."

"Only you would think me going back to school is great."

"Thanks! Come with me, I have something I need to show you?"

"Really!"

"Not that... and I see your mind still only works one way."

"What's wrong with that way."

"Don't get me started."

With everyone else outside, Lizzy led him down the hallway towards the garage. She wanted him to know where she kept everything... just in case.

"There's a room in the house only Gianni, Mina and I know about. But I need you to know where it is, as well."

"What kind of room? A little bit of fun......" He knew from the way she held her shoulders, Lizzy was smiling even if he couldn't see her face.

She led him into a room and shut the door behind them. Why she wanted to show him the utility closet, he had no idea; there was nothing to awe him in there. When he was about to say something, though, he saw her punch in a code into the wall and watched a door slide open. He couldn't even see the key pad she used. Next, she motioned for him to enter and then followed him in as the door closed automatically and the lights came on.

"This is my toy room, well one of my toy rooms. I wanted you to know about it in case anything happens and you need something." Lizzy watched as he took in the room; it obviously was not what he had expected.

"Your toy room? You have more guns and grenade launchers in here than a small army. And these are all yours?"

"Well, a few are Gianni and Mina's, but yes most are *all* mine. Pick the one you like and keep it with you. You never know when you're going to need it. Sandro and his friend can't know about this room, though, so don't mention it. There are two accesses; the first one was how we came in and the second I'll show you on the way out. The lights only go on after someone enters and the door is shut. They will go off as soon as you punch in the code to leave. The keypad is in the picture, you just run your hand along the trees, then touch the artist's name."

"Do I even want to know where these weapons all came from?"

"Probably not. Just know they are here when we need them. Now follow me." In the corner was a staircase he hadn't noticed earlier. Beside it was what looked like a fire pole. As Lizzy led him up the stairs she knew it was dangerous to give out so much information, but he needed to know where they were.

At the top of the stairs Nick found himself in what looked like a dressing room. As they walked through the door they were back in her bedroom — that explained the pole; she could get down to the armory in a hurry. He remembered seeing a door to the garage through the utility room, as well. She had thought of everything.

Lizzy was afraid to even ask what he thought. It wasn't every day you took someone through a weapons room and ended up in their bedroom. It was who she was now; she just hoped he understood. She watched as he looked around the room. The last time they were in there, she wasn't prepared for his being there, now she didn't want him to leave.

Sensing her thoughts, he took the gun out of the small of his back and placed it on the dresser. Nick moved across the room to Lizzy, grabbed her by the waist and drew her into him. His forehead on hers, Nick stared into Lizzy's eyes knowing this was the next step. Wherever they went from here they went together.

Just having found her alive was enough for him. After all the years of wonder he now had her and wasn't about to let her go... no matter what.

She tilted her head ready for their lips would meet. It had been so long and she never was able to say goodbye when she left the first time. They had never shared their final kiss and it was something she need at the moment.

Nick leaned in for their lips to meet. It felt like their last kiss had only been yesterday. Scooping her up into his arms, he crossed the room to Lizzy's bed. All he wanted was to hold her. They had already been too many years apart and all the old feelings resurfaced, if they had ever even left. He was content to hold her in his arms for the time being. When they found their children, he would make sure they were never apart again.

NINETEEN

THANKS TO ALL the training Sandro and his friend, Eddie, were helping with, Lizzy knew it wouldn't be long before this would all finally be done. Nick had started his job at the school and even though the kids weren't back from vacation yet, he was able to meet their teachers and get a feel for the layout of the building. One step at a time. She had waited so long, patience was what she needed now but her anxiety was building. She could do this, she *would* do this, and she was going to have her family back.

As the summer rolled along, Lizzy and Dani were happy they could catch up on all their missing years. Although Lizzy wasn't completely shocked to find her father had never asked about her, she had expected more from her mother. It was her loss choosing to miss out on everything in the end.

Nick used the rest of the summer to get to know the "new and improved Lizzy," as she called herself. The one who knew how to get what she wanted and was not afraid of anything except her emotions. He learned all about her since the time they separated. He admired her determination, seeing the commonality in his own determination to find her all these years.

The kids would be starting school the following week and he was glad he'd be the one to bring the news of them to her. That he would be able to tell her what they looked like and who they've become. They were so little when they were taken and had grown almost into adults in the 11 years since. He and Lizzy would help guide them. He only hoped they would be willing to accept the truth. He was afraid they might resent Lizzy for everything that happened. Only time would tell.

As he read through their files, Nick discovered they were good students with good grades, but they had authority issues.

Tiano had a knack for causing trouble, Anna loved to play people off of each other, and Tori liked to challenge authority. They were definitely their kids. There wasn't much information in the files about the Cirescos, however. Other students had comments about parents, but their file only noted their names.

Nick was grateful to be able to design the lesson layouts. His first objective was to get to know the children. He taught two English classes and they were divided into the two —apparently all three of them in a single class made it stressful for their teachers. He would have to test that theory to see how far they were willing to go. The information would go a long way in determining what he and Lizzy were dealing with.

Sandro and Eddie ran him and Ty through the paces when he returned from school. They wanted to make sure they were ready for anything. Lizzy wasn't joking when she had said Nick and his oldest friend needed to be trained.

Nick enjoyed watching her spar with Sandro. Even though he was afraid on some level she might get hurt, he knew that was the old Lizzy. This one dished out as much, if not more, than she received. She could hold her own.

After the match, Sandro walked over to where Nick was sitting. "You know, Nick, the two of them can't be in the same room with each other for more than five minutes," Sandro said of Lizzy and Eddie.

"Neither of them strikes me as the losing kind," Nick agreed. "We just need to keep them apart."

"I believe they should have it out, but in close quarters. This anger isn't good. It keeps them from focusing and will make this blow up in their faces."

"Sandro, I'm not going to tell Lizzy to take it easy if they spar. And you damn well know Eddie won't go easy either." Nick didn't like where the conversation was going.

"Lizzy needs to do this," he pushed. "You remember the old Lizzy, Nick, and have just met the new one. If she doesn't get rid of the anger by fighting Eddie, it will be her vice. She needs to let it go."

"They'll kill each other. No way."

"They won't. There will be rules."

"Do you really believe either of them is going to listen to rules?"

"If we're in there with them," Sandro pointed out, "they won't have a choice. They've stayed apart for weeks, and the tension is only getting worse. This needs to be done now. Go get Lizzy, I'll get Eddie and let them finish this and move past it."

"You're nuts, you know that Sandro? She'll kill him. She's been dying to."

"She knows her limits. There are still rules in our little world. They will listen. After all, I trained both of them."

"You let her decide." Nick knew the tension had to be eased, but didn't want it to be this way. He was there the last time they fought and knew how skilled they both were. This could only end one way.

Nick left Sandro on the terrace and made his way down to the pool where he knew Lizzy was relaxing. He didn't want to suggest the sparring match, but Sandro was right. He knew the new Lizzy better than Nick. She looked at peace sitting there at the edge of the pool, her feet dangling in the water. He knew she was just moving the water with her legs, making little circles. It was something she had always done.

Nick walked up to Lizzy, slipped off his shoes and took a seat on the ground beside her. Without saying a word, he tried to see what she was looking at in the distance. She was lost in thought and he was glad for the quiet. He placed his hand on hers and gave it a slight squeeze. It was a small gesture, but one he knew she appreciated.

"You'll have them back soon, you know. Our kids."

"Ya. It's just been so many years. I can't imagine what the Cirescos have told them about me or if they even remember me. It's been 11 years and they were so young."

"Lizzy, they loved you. They'll remember. Trust me." He knew how he would find out for sure, too.

"Thanks. You always know what to say."

182

"Yea, well you're not going to like the next thing. Sandro thinks you and Eddie need to relieve some frustrations before it overtakes both of you."

"Really, now? I'm in!"

"That's it. You're in? I remember the last time you two fought. Do you really want to do that again?"

"Yep." As she stood up, she looked down at him.

He knew by the look in her eyes she was excited. What he couldn't understand was why.

"Are you coming?" Lizzy asked.

"What? Now? You want to do this now?"

"Yep! There is no time better than the present. Plus, you got me all excited."

"That got you excited."

"You can either stay here or come and watch. Your choice. But this is going to end today."

"Yea, that's what I'm afraid of."

"Have faith. Besides Sandro takes it too easy on me."

"That's easy?"

"Yea, that's easy. You should see us when we both actually try."

If all their practicing had been easy, as she said, Sandro was probably right. Maybe this was just what she needed. Ty better be there to hold him back though. She was still just Lizzy to him and he didn't like the idea of her getting hurt. He didn't mind seeing Eddie get knocked around a bit, either, he just wanted to be the one to do it.

As Lizzy made her way to the terrace, she just wanted this to start now. Sandro would have a catch though, he usually did. For weeks he had kept them apart as much as possible, she had no idea why he had chosen this moment. When she saw the smug look on his face, she knew he was up to something.

"I see Nick told you."

"Now, Sandro. We do this now." She said looking between him and Eddie. She guessed from Eddie's expression he was already filled in.

"There are house rule to this. You're not allowed to kill each other… it kind of defeats the purpose. And no bone breaking, we don't have time for the pair of you to heal. Just a good old fashioned, dirty fight."

"That's it?" Eddie asked. "Those are the only rules? I'm game Lizzy if you are?"

"Let's go, I've waited too long for this. And," Lizzy added, "no interference from either of you two. Get it."

Lizzy looked between Sandro and Nick, knowing they would be the only ones to break them up.

"You two will do this in the training room," Sandro said. "A little extra padding doesn't hurt."

Sandro pushed his chair in and led the way through the house to her training room. Completely padded, it was designed especially for this. Outside they could find ways around his little rules with furniture and foliage. In here, it would just be them. Their anger was going to be shelved today.

Lizzy knew Nick wasn't happy about this, but she was just too excited. She wanted redemption. She was going to finish this, if for nothing other than her own peace of mind. The rules were set and they would both abide by them. Sandro had taught them both and they wouldn't let him down.

Breaking the rules was not negotiable. But saving yourself from the one breaking them was allowed. She wouldn't betray his trust. Lizzy just hoped his little boyfriend felt the same way.

As they entered the room, she saw Ty. She was glad he was there for Nick's sake. Her old boyfriend was bound to do something stupid and Ty would be able to stop him.

As soon as the door closed with just the five of them in the room, Eddie made the first lunge. He just didn't expect her to be that fast. He was big and quick. She was quick and feisty. Steady on their feet as they danced around, each combatant looked for the other's weaknesses.

Lizzy glanced over and made eye contact with Nick and, before she knew it, Eddie had her on the ground. In that split second he had taken her and he wasn't gentle about it, either. The full frontal blow took Lizzy down, but she was far from out. She planned to use Eddie's bulk against him.

Still, Sandro had just made his point. She realized Nick couldn't be with her when she went after the Cirescos. He would be her downfall.

As they grappled on the floor trying to get the advantage, Lizzy quickly got the upper hand. Men always underestimated her and that was an advantage. Although Eddie wouldn't take it easy on her, being quicker than he thought was always good.

Sandro was a good teacher; he knew both their weaknesses but didn't offer any hints. He wanted the fight to be fair and for both of them to get it out of their systems.

The two of them needed each other to bring down the Cirescos; they just didn't know it yet. Why his father had made the mistake of setting his friends against each other, he didn't know. With their help, though, Sandro would soon find out.

He watched as the pair of them positioned and repositioned. They were fighting like he had never seen before and it seemed they weren't going to stop. Just when he thought Eddie had Lizzy she would turn the tables, or vice versa. They had already been at it for 15 minutes and there was no clear winner. The two of them were evenly matched. He saw Ty holding his friend back, and thought Nick needed to learn she could do this herself.

"Nick, relax they're fine."

"End it, Sandro. They've been at it long enough."

"No, not yet. They need to finish."

"If you don't," Nick grimaced, "I will."

"If you do, you'll get hurt and then she'll kill *me*. Let them finish Nick; just sit back and watch the show."

The show? Nick thought Sandro was nuts. He was watching the woman he loved have her ass handed to her by a psychopath.

Heeding Sandro's advice, Nick took a few seconds to actually watch what Lizzy and Eddie while trying not to worry about her. When he allowed himself to actually see, he was surprised to realize it wasn't Lizzy whose ass was being beaten, it was Eddie's.

By letting him think he was winning, she was tiring him out, simply waiting to make her move. Lizzy always moved herself out of the way before he could get the big hit in. She used his aggression for her own benefit and made far more direct hits that Eddie.

Eddie had gone hard from the beginning and you could see he was tiring. The whole time she had led him to believe he maintained the upper hand.

Once Lizzy saw her chance, Eddie was down in one quick move. She applied a very little pressure and he was out. He would be asleep for a while. While Sandro say no killing, he never said no sleeping. He clearly wasn't impressed, but she had won. Even though Eddie was the first job she failed to complete, after this bout it was finished in her mind.

"Your boyfriend should be awake shortly. You can tell him thanks for the work out. It's so much better than with you, at least he tries."

"He's not going to be happy having been beaten by a girl, you know."

"At least he's alive. Tell him no hard feelings, Sandro. You two deserve each other. Now if you boys would excuse me, it's time for a shower."

As she left the men in the room behind her, she knew Nick would quickly be on her heels. The boys could talk amongst themselves while she took advantage of the moment to confront Nick. In the end, she couldn't afford the distraction. It had already almost cost her the fight. Luckily she didn't have to share that knowledge with anyone. Still, Lizzy wouldn't take the same chance again.

TWENTY

Nick could see the look in her eyes when she ended the fight. Something was bugging her. Once he got over his fear for her, he admired her skill. Even though he already knew this was what she had been up to all these years, it was still hard to believe. Using her opponent's strength against them was her secret weapon. Her marks mistakenly assumed she was not capable and Lizzy used it against them.

Nick knew Lizzy needed a few minutes before he joined her, so he hung back a few minutes with Ty and Sandro. Eddie was sleeping like a baby on the floor. If she had wanted to finish him, she'd have had no problem.

"Your girl is one hell of a fighter, Nick. I wouldn't want to be on her bad side."

"You trained her, Sandro. Lizzy told me the story, but pieces seem to be missing."

"When she called me and said she needed help after Ciresco tried to kill her, I knew something was up. With some of the training she had already received from Ciresco as he trained her to protect her own children, my uncle offered her help.

"She was lost, alone and outraged. What's more, she was a good friend to me and I promised to help her in any way I could. Her determination was something I had not seen in a long time.

"Throughout her training," Sandro continued, "Lizzy kept saying she 'would do anything it took to get back what's mine.' And she has. After coming this far and being this close, we all need to get her kids back. She needs them to go back to being the happy girl I met so many years ago. The anger has taken over, but with you being here, she's smiling again. That I like. We may both be killers, but we're not heartless. We do what we do for a reason. A means to an end. I promised I'd help her all the way and I stick to my word."

"You're a good friend, Sandro. Thanks for helping her."

"I love her like a little sister," Sandro confessed. "Don't hurt her."

"She's not getting out of my sight for very long ever again. Don't worry."

Nick left Ty and Sandro to talk and went after Lizzy. He hoped and expected she would be done with her shower by the time he got there, but secretly hoped she was not.

As he pushed the door to her room open, he heard the water turn off and his heart lightened a little with her nearby. He knew what he needed to do and she was not going to run this time.

As Lizzy dried herself, she caught a glimpse of her tattoos. It had been so long. They reminded her to be strong. She had worked so hard and come so far.

In a few short weeks, she would have everything for which she had worked so hard. The angel with wings wrapped around her cross reminded her to have faith and know someone was always looking out for her.

Lizzy was smiling to herself as she wrapped the towel around her and left the bathroom. She wasn't shocked to see Nick staring out the window. It had become his favorite pastime since he came to the house.

She crossed over to him and wrapped her arms around his waist. As she rested her head on his back Lizzy felt his hands on her arms. This was what she longed for.

She did not know how to tell him he couldn't be there in the end. It was killing her, but it was for both of theirs safety. She could not risk something after what happened in the sparring match.

"Hey," Lizzy opened.

"Hey.....how are you feeling?"

"A little sore, but fine. I think Eddie's idea to take a nap was a good one right about now."

"Somehow I don't think Eddie will think his nap was a good idea," Nick laughed.

"You're probably right. But it was better than the alternative."

"Probably."

"Nick," she said slowly. "You can't come with me when I go after the Cirescos."

Nick turned instantly to face his soul mate. "Excuse me? Are you nuts?" He thought she must be nuts if she thought he was going to stay away.

"No," she said simply. "Because of you, I could have lost today. I could see the worry in your face and that's when Eddie made his move. You're a distraction to me. One I like, but not in a fight. I can't have that happen again."

"You're not going without me."

"It's not your call."

"The hell it isn't. I saw you fight, when I actually took the time to watch I realized what an amazing fighter you are. I was worried when you saw me. I know what you can do......."

"I can't take the chance of you getting hurt."

"I'm going with you, Lizzy. You need me. Hell! You need all of us. We are doing this together. You need to get that it through your stubborn head. I'm not going anywhere."

Before she could reply, he leaned down and captured her lips with his. He figured if they were busy, she would not have time to argue.

Lizzy knew full well Nick was trying to distract her, but she didn't mind. It had been a long day, her muscles and joints were sore, and she just needed to relax and get some sleep. If Nick was curled up next to her while she slept there were no complaints. After waking up to find him in her bed that first night, she did not want him anywhere else.

The comfort she felt around him was wonderful. He made her feel whole. He filled that part of her heart she had lost so long before. Their kids would fill the rest. She had a home, a family that was going to fill it, and friends who would support them. It made everything worth while.

Nick sensed how tired she was and walked her over to the bed to tuck her in. As much as he wanted to join her, there was something he needed to do first. She fell almost completely asleep as soon as her head hit the pillow. He went to his old room to grab his bags and brought them back to the room they were already sharing.

After rummaging through his bags, Nick found what he was looking for then grabbed a quick shower and slid into bed with Lizzy.

He wrapped his arm around to hold her close. A position to which they had become accustomed; an unconscious need to know the other was nearby. He knew she still kept her blade close by, but was glad it was on the nightstand instead of under her pillow as before. Things were changing.

He placed a soft kiss in the crook of her neck and felt her snuggle closer. He was home. He was not going to stop until she was fully his and would never let her go again.

As Nick slipped her hand into his, she didn't notice the ring he slid onto her finger. He hoped she liked it when she woke up. Making her his wife was long overdue. He smiled inwardly as he drifted off to sleep with her tucked close. It just felt right.

TWENTY-ONE

THE SUMMER DREW on and the fall semester was now only days away. Nick had become accustomed to the campus and eagerly watched as the students returned. He still did not like being back in a school (even if he was the teacher this time). Even more, he hated not knowing which kids were his. All he could really do now was bide his time. He thought all the years of looking for Lizzy would have made him patient, but that did not happen.

Tiano and Anna were going to be in his first period class, while Tori would be in his third period. He was glad to have second period free. He would need the time after meeting the first pair to review.

It was all Nick could do to sit at his desk in the classroom and wait patiently for the next 48 hours to be done already. All teachers were required to be available for returning students' questions and he had to make it look real. He was not sure what Gianni had done to get him the job, but he was entirely sure he did not want to know.

He had no idea why Gianni had selected English for him to teach and not physical education. Gym teacher he could have pulled off easily. But this... this was going to be a long shot.

He flipped through the files on his desk, not exactly sure what he was seeking. Lizzy wanted this over with as fast as possible and he was not about to argue. The hardest part right now was going to be keeping his cool if he ran into the Cirescos as anything was possible this close to school starting.

As the students filtered past his door while roaming the halls, he longed to go back in time to see how things might have been different;

191

not that he would change much. His life choices made him who he was, but it would be a chance to tell his younger self to smarten up faster.

He felt a need to get out of the classroom for a bit and decided a walk through the grounds would be nice. It would be nicer if Lizzy was with him, he thought to himself, but he knew it was impossible. The remote camera she was watching everything on, at least, allowed him to pretend Lizzy was there for the ride, even if she was not there in person.

The camera was Lizzy's idea. She wanted to see everything as it happened so she had firsthand knowledge.

He made his way to the common area coffee in hand. Despite the benches, flower gardens and statues scattered throughout, there was no serenity to be found. Hundreds of students wandered about. Some sitting, some walking, and everyone catching up with friends they hadn't seen for a while.

Nick smiled to himself as he couldn't help but remember their simpler times. Without any worries or cares yet, he hoped they enjoyed it while they could. At that age, they couldn't wait to grow up; at his age, he would give anything to go back and enjoy one day of nothing.

A commotion behind him broke into his thoughts. As much as he didn't want to get involved, as a teacher he didn't have a choice.

Nick edged past the group of onlookers to get to the center of it all where two of the students were fighting. He hated breaking up girl fights. As he stepped in and received a blow to the side of the head, he assumed neither of them knew he was the new teacher.

The other students looking to see who the interloper was as he cast them a look which made his point clear.

"Enough! That's it! Both of you to my class room, the rest of you find somewhere else to be unless you're involved in this." He looked over to the girls and said, "Follow me and don't say anything."

Nick didn't really care if the two girls wanted to fight. His cheek was killing him, whoever's fist he got in the way of had one hell of a swing.

As they reached his class, Nick directed the pair to the opposite side of the room and instructed them to take a seat.

"I don't care who threw the first punch. Really, I don't. You two want to fight, do it somewhere else. I don't have time for your teenage bull shit."

"Sir, who are you? You have no right......"

"I'm the new English teacher here, so yes I have every right. If you don't like it, take it up with the Dean. Now tell me what's going on?"

"She started it....."

"Oh yea, like I'd want anything to do with........"

"Oh fuck off, you know you did........"

"You're a wench you know that........"

"Really, you're the one to talk......."

"Shut up the both of you. You're giving me a headache. Policy says I'm to report this to your parents and I really don't feel like doing that kind of paperwork today."

Lizzy had to be getting a kick out of watching this. He could almost see her smirking wherever she was.

"You can't call our parents; they won't be back for a few weeks still. That's why we're here early."

"Are you two related?"

The girls looked back and forth between each other. They usually avoided confrontations with their parents. If they could get this teacher on their side, this year might be better than last.

"Yes, we're sisters."

"Sisters?...You couldn't find an easier way of settling something than beating the shit out of each other."

"Umm, I don't think teachers are allowed to swear, sir."

"I'm the exception and I really don't care. I don't want to see it again. Just sit here and don't talk for a few minutes while I decide what to do with you."

Nick didn't want to be in this position, he hated it. He was the teacher though and knew he should report the fight. But he needed to get the students to like him if he was going to find his kids.

His phone buzzed in his Pocket and Nick pulled it out to see a message from Lizzy. After he ignored it and the phone went off again, he knew he needed to look.

'ARE YOU HAVING FUN YET? IT SEEMS LIKE IT OVER HERE.'

'HAHAHA, VERY FUNNY :P WHAT DO YOU WANT ME 2 DO, I'M THE TEACHER REMEMBER'

'LUCKY U, HAVE FUN :P TTYS :D'

As he ended the chat, he knew Lizzy was enjoying every moment of his torture. As a student walked past the door and gaped inside, Nick still needed to do something.

"Psst, psst," he heard the interloper hiss. "What did you two do this time?"

"Shut up before you get us into more trouble."

"Suckers!"

"Would you care to join us?" Nick asked the young man whose head was sticking in the doorway. Nick had not wanted more shit to deal with, but why the hell not.

"I hope you are enjoying this, Lizzy," he mumbled knowing she would hear him.

"What did I do?" the young man asked.

"Disrupted me. Now, sit down."

"Wow. The new teacher is a hard ass, where are you from again?"

"None of your concern," Nick gave back "And you're right, I'm the new teacher. As to being a hard ass, you have no idea."

"Hey, I just wanted to see what these two did this time? They're always getting into trouble."

The boy sat leaning on the back legs of his chair, a move Nick had been famous for in high-school, as well as detention.

"What these two did is none of your business. And the next time you walk past my class, unless you're in it, keep walking."

"YES, SIR! See ya, girls; I don't want to be near mom and dad when they find out. Later."

"Wait, what did you say?" Nick looked at the student as he rose out of the chair.

"I don't want to be in their shoes, they are always getting in trouble...."

"Oh, like your any better," one of the girls blurted out.

"Ya, look who's talking."

As the three students began arguing with each other, Nick just sat there. *It couldn't be*, he thought, *not this way*. Lizzy must have been thinking the same thing on her end because as soon as he reached for his cell to call her, it went off in his hand.

"Nick, you don't think...."

"It's possible....."

"They're so big....."

"Do they look......?"

"I don't know Nick, it's been so long. You have to find out." Lizzy wanted to rush over to him. She knew these were her children; she just needed the proof first.

"You three sit down and shut up," Nick began. "Now tell me who you are? And what the hell is going on?"

"Well, my sisters are known for getting into trouble, our parents pretty well washed their hand of them years ago. And me, well, I'm the....."

"You're what, Tiano? A pain in the ass, a trouble maker. Come on, we can't wait to hear this one."

"Shut it Anna, who asked you? And don't even bother, Tori. You're just a drama queen, anyway."

Nick watched as the siblings bickered with one another and knew they were his children. Lizzy was right; they were just like him, but they were just like her, too. He needed to keep his cool, he couldn't blow this. He had been prepared to meet them in class the first time, not fist fighting in the school yard. It should not have surprised him, though. It was where they would have found him at the same age. He took a deep breath to focus.

"All right, would the three of you please just sit and calm down for a moment. Now, tell me exactly what's going on. Tiano, don't talk yet. You two tell me everything.

"Not how the fight started, though," he continued. "You're siblings, I get it. Why did you say your parents washed their hands of you? Don't they send you here?"

"Yea, they send us here all right; and to friends' houses and everywhere else. The only time they really bother with us is when we get kicked out of school. If we get kicked out of this one, though, it will be military school."

"How long has this been going on for?" Nick asked trying to remain calm. He didn't know how long he could hold out. Ty and Sandro were probably fighting to hold Lizzy down at the same time.

"I don't know, since we became teenagers," Tori said. "We were all cute and they wanted us around when we were younger, but once the hormones kicked in dad had enough and sent us off to boarding schools. The less contact with us the better."

"And your mother?" Nick pushed.

"Yea, she's a prize. Too busy socializing. I guess she realized kids hindered that, so the less we were around the better."

"What about any other family member? Is it only the three of you?"

"Yes, but there was....."

"Shut up Tori, you know that doesn't matter."

"No," Nick fished, "Tori if you were going to say something, feel free to say it." The opportunity was there and he needed to take it.

"No," she said, "there's nothing."

"Oh Tori," Tiano said, "who cares? Tell him. What my sister is trying not to say is we had an older sister who died when we were kids. We never knew how Mimma died, but mom and dad never talked about her after it happened. It was like she didn't exist."

Nick knew that piece of information would get Lizzy's attention. They remembered her. Well, her name at least. It was the opening they were seeking.

"Do you guys ever talk amongst yourselves about your sister, Mimma?" Nick asked.

"Not really. Only that we miss her. It was about this time of the year when she died."

"I still say she ran away," Anna blurted. "She knew what they were like. Do you blame her?"

"Anna!" Nick said. "Why would you say that?"

"All I remember is mom and dad packed us up saying we were going for a holiday and Mimma had to work. A few weeks later they said she died. But they didn't look sad at all. Dad actually looked happy."

At that moment, Nick thought, *happy wasn't the word for it*. Nick hoped the children would understand everything and forgive Lizzy once they knew the truth.

"Do you guys spend your whole school year here, then?"

"We go to friends in the summer," Tori said with a tinge of sadness in her voice. "But besides that, yes, here mostly."

Nick thought talking about Mimma had brought up memories she did not want to deal with.

"If you're not going to punish us, can we just go?" she asked. "I'm done with this."

He did not want to punish his kids, but Nick needed to maintain the pretense of being their teacher so he bought himself some time.

"You can go for now, but come back here at three and I'll tell you what I've decided. Tiano, that includes you, as well."

Nick had an idea but he had to run it past the dean first. He just hoped it would work. He also needed to call Lizzy as he was sure Gianni and Ty were tired trying to keep her back by that point.

*　*　*

She couldn't believe it. They remembered her. Her kids remembered her. And those people had basically dumped them off at a boarding school when they were done with them. She was not surprised about him. But Mrs. Ciresco, she had wanted so much to be a mother. How could she just give it up; did she get bored? It did not make sense? Having wanted payback for everything they had done to her was one thing, now she wanted revenge for her children, as well.

It was not fair to be shipped around from place to place, dealing with them only when there was trouble. It was no wonder they were fighting at school.

Lizzy's children had grown and she couldn't wait to reunite with them. But she couldn't afford to mess up now. After all the years of searching, they were mere meters away and it took everything for the guys to contain her. She had to be smart, there was no other choice. When her cell rang she knew it was Nick.

"I take it you saw everything?"

"Yes, can you guess what I'm thinking?"

"It's not that hard, Lizzy. How badly did you hurt Ty and Gianni?"

"They're big boys. They'll be fine." She glanced over at her friends. By the looks on their faces they knew they did what had to be done.

"So where do we go from here Nick? I know what I want to do."

"Trust me. I have an idea and it's right up your alley. I'll fill you in when I get home. Oh, by the way, did I tell you I loved you today?"

"Yes, by the ring I woke up with on my finger after you left. We'll talk about that when you get home."

"See you soon, Lizzy."

Nick snapped his phone shut and went straight to the Dean's office. He knew his request might be denied, but it was a brilliant idea, if he did say so himself.

TWENTY-TWO

Ty and Gianni forced Lizzy to go home after she got off the phone with Nick. They both knew what she was capable of and were not going to let her blow it all now.

Still in shock over finding out her children remembered her, Lizzy paced all around the house in an attempt to control her urge to rush over to the school. She had come this far and couldn't let her emotions get the better of her. This was what she trained and searched for. This was the reason why she had become who she was.

Nick had a plan and she needed to put her trust in him. Having waited this long to find them, people would think patience was her strong point. Today it was not. She would be amazed if she lasted until Nick returned home.

It felt like hours had passed instead of only minutes and staring at the clock was not doing her any good. Lizzy had to find something else to focus her energy on.

Lizzy made a bee line for her room to change. She hoped a swim would let her burn off some energy and think at the same time. She wanted a clear head when Nick told her his plan.

She picked out a nice red '50s-style bikini, grabbed a towel and made her way down to the pool. As Lizzy dived in the warm water felt great against her skin, washing away her fears and bringing everything into perspective. She knew her cousin would find her soon, but for that moment she need the alone time.

Ty would make Dani give Lizzy some time to herself, but she would only stay away for so long. Deep down Lizzy didn't want her cousin to ever leave. It was nice having family around.

With every swim stroke, Lizzy felt her emotions getting sharper. Her mind was focused, for the first time and should could see clearly The controlled breathing calmed, the water soothed and the air cleansed. The fibers of her being reunited with one another after having been ripped apart all these years.

Lizzy dove deep to the bottom of the pool where she could feel the pressure build for just a few seconds. The serenity — no noise, no people, just her thoughts. As she pushed off the floor, Lizzy allowed all the tension to leave her body as the surface approached. All the built up anxiety and emotions., Everything that had ruled her for so many years was gone. Lizzy felt the warmth of the sun against her skin when she broke the surface and knew her soul was complete. Ready for the next leg in the journey, she let herself float at the surface and moved her hands side to side... at peace.

Lizzy had not realized how much tension had built up over the years. Her body felt newly calm and relaxed. As she placed her arms under her head and crossed her ankles, she allowed herself to enjoy the day; she was utterly free.

Sensing someone looking at her, Lizzy knew she was being watched and eased one eye open to find Dani smiling at her. Lizzy was happy for someone with whom she could talk.

"Enjoying your swim are you, cousin?"

"Absolutely! Just warn me if you're going to jump in. I'm quite comfortable at the moment."

"You always did love swimming, Lizzy — except when we went to the beach."

"Hey there's fish in that water. I prefer the nice, clean pool, thanks."

"Ty told me what happened today? How are you doing?"

"Great. They remember me Dani. That's more than I could have hoped for. I got to see what they look like. The picture was not very clear, but I could see how much they've grown up.

"They're almost adults," Lizzy said wistfully. "I missed out on their childhood." She made her way over to the side of the pool and lifted herself onto the ledge. She grabbed the towel that Dani was holding for her.

Dani handed her a towel and asked, "So what are you going to do now? And throwing me in is not an option."

"Ha, ha. I'm relaxing on a lounger and waiting for Nick to get back. He said he had a plan, so now I have to wait to find out what it is."

"Lizzy, waiting isn't your strong suit. Actually, I was surprised when Gianni told me you were at the pool. I thought you'd be training."

"I needed to clear my head, Dani; you know swimming always did that when we were kids. I think I deserve an afternoon off anyway."

"Frig! You need a few years off."

"As soon as I get my kids, I'll retire! Now sit down and relax in the sun with me, would you."

"You don't have to ask me twice. By the way....."

"No by the way's, it's time to do nothing. Whatever you want to ask, do it later. I'm actually relaxed for once and I don't want my brain to work right now."

Lizzy closed her eyes and basked in the sun as she let herself enjoy the rest of the day. When she woke up still beside the pool, she could not remember the last time she had actually had a restful nap. Sure, she had slept through the day before, but only ever out of need. She saw Dani was still sleeping and smiled. It reminded her of when their parents took them to the beach as kids. They would just lay there and tan all day long without a care in the world.

Lizzy should have let Dani wake up on her own, but she just could not pass up an opportunity. She grabbed a glass from the table and took a few steps towards the pool to fill the glass and throw some water on her cousin for a wakeup call.

Just as she was about to launch the water, Lizzy saw Nick approaching and let her cousin off the hook, sort of. She placed the glass on the chair by her feet so it would splash on her when she moved.

Everything in place, Lizzy grabbed her towel from the lounge chair and made her way towards Nick. By the smile on his face she knew he was happy with whatever he was planning, she just wanted to know what it was.

Before she could ask, though, Nick scooped her up in his arms and placed a trail of soft kisses along her neck. As she was enjoying his distraction, Lizzy figured a few extra minutes would not hurt.

"So," she finally asked, "do you want to know what I did today?"

"Nope, not right now... a little busy here."

"Yes, I can tell," Lizzy persisted, "but it was a good day."

"I take it you didn't hurt Gianni or Ty, then."

"Only a little, but they were holding me down."

"Lizzy I don't want to know." Nick set her back down on her feet, quite pleased with himself. He had worked out a great plan that would cause the least amount of damage and give them their children back by the end of the weekend. He just had to fill her in on the details.

"Are you going to tell me, or let me start guessing?"

"Did you tell me you love me this morning?"

"Nick, you know the answer to that. Please, I'm being good right now," she said a little more tensely than planned. "What's going on?"

"Let's go inside and I'll fill everyone in at once. It'll save having to repeat myself. This is going to happen fast though, I'm warning you. And probably without as much violence as you and Sandro are planning."

"Well, that doesn't sound like a whole lot of fun now, does it?" She gave him a smirk as her cousin's squeal made them both turn. To be woken up by a sudden splash of water is never fun.

"Okay, Dani, let's go do some planning."

"Lizzy, I'll get you back for that."

"Be glad Nick came when he did or you were going to get woken up in an entirely different way."

"I don't want to know, do I?"

"Probably not. But I'll save it for another time. No worry."

Dani following close behind, they made their way up to the main house to find everyone. She guessed it wouldn't take long as Gianni would have started to hunt everyone down soon as he saw Nick's car pull up in the driveway. The only question was what was he planning?

By the tone in his voice he thought it was going to be easy. Things never were easy where the Cirescos were concerned, though. If they were she would have had her children back years ago.

Until then every two steps ahead she took came with one step back. But this... finding them this easily? Alarm bells were going off, she just needed to figure out why.

Everyone, including Eddie and Sandro, was already waiting when they reached the office. Luckily she and Eddie had found a way to put their differences aside. Sandro did not know the details yet, but the two of them had an entirely different plan.

Lizzy knew how anxious everyone was after the news earlier and hoped Nick would get to the point quickly. Thankfully, he had never been one to take his time on anything.

He was prepared for the onslaught of questions that flooded him the instant they walked through the doors. As soon as everyone calmed down Nick figured he would begin; there was no point in trying to talk over the noise. It didn't take long; Ty knew the look on Nick's face and helped shut everyone up.

"As all of you know, upon breaking up a fight at school today I found the kids. And, it seems, they are just like *both* their parents."

"If you mean stubborn and itching to pick a fight then, yea, they are just like you." Ty said with a smirk on his face.

"Like I said, the three of them are quite sight. They are quick on their feet and apparently have a habit of getting kicked out of schools around the world. They told me if they were kicked out of this one, their next stop is military school. And, if they get put into one of those; well, getting them out is going to be a whole lot harder."

"So, we need to get to them before they pull another stunt," Lizzy interrupted. "Why does this all sound familiar?" Lizzy was looking right at Nick because he had the same track record growing up.

"So," Nick continued with a sigh, "I went to speak with the Dean of Students regarding them. We agreed the children had been through a lot and needed someone to guide them."

"And, of course, you said you'd do it, didn't you?" Ty knew how Nick's brain worked. He had to have something up his sleeve.

"Yep. You see, every school has washed their hands of all three of them. Apparently, their parents simply drop them off and that's it. They only come when they cause trouble.

"So," Nick went on, "I proposed that maybe community service should be their form of punishment.

Somewhere off campus… where they could see what life was like outside of school."

"What are you getting at Nick?"

"The Dean and I decided we would give the kids a chance to redeem themselves," he said smiling. "I mentioned I was staying at a rather large property of a friend just outside of the city; how it had lots of room and needed help fixing up. I suggested the kids spend their weekends helping out as their punishment and at the same time see how other people live."

"And he went for it?"

"Not at first. But when I told him I was just like them when I was younger and it took someone doing the same for me to smarten me up, well…"

"Left out the part about jail, did you?" Lizzy smirked. "I guess you didn't want to tarnish your image." By the sideways smile towards him, he knew she liked the plan.

"Today is Thursday, so they will be coming home with me after school on Friday for the weekend. It's our chance to get to them without interference. The Dean will call the Cirescos Friday night after we leave and tell them about the plan to deal with the triplets. So, if anything is going to happen it will be on our grounds, where we have the advantage."

Lizzy did not want to believe anything Nick was saying; it was all happening so fast and something didn't seem right. The one thing she had learned over all those years working was: when something seemed wrong, it usually was.

As much as she didn't want to admit it, the look Eddie had given her meant he had similar misgivings. The two of them needed to talk. She hoped together they would be able to figure it out, but first they needed to get away from everyone else and Gianni would help with that.

She glanced over to Gianni and saw he was on the same page. She was glad Gianni and she thought alike. Since the day they met, they had always been an unspoken communication. It was nice. A quick glance was all they needed to feel one another's thoughts. It had come in handy during certain situations.

As everyone left the office, Lizzy walked around and took a seat at her desk to wait for Eddie to come back in the side door. Gianni asked Sandro, Ty and Nick to join him so that took care of them for a while. Dani and Mina had gone to the terrace to enjoy the sunset, so this was their best chance to talk. She looked over to the Eddie as the door closed behind him and knew it would be a long night ahead.

TWENTY-THREE

ALARM BELLS WERE going off. Lizzy knew in her gut something was not right. She just could not put her finger on what vital piece of information was missing. It may have seemed to everyone else she and Eddie were on the same page, but she did not trust him. He still was not telling everything he knew. She was certain of it and had to tread carefully with everyone around because Nick and Ty were ready to pounce on him at the first chance.

The main thing, though, was Eddie thought he had her trust. She would have to play the situation carefully over the next few days until he showed his cards. And to keep things going her way, she had to keep Sandro out of the loop. As Eddie sat across from her, Lizzy realized keeping her cool was going to be a major task.

"What are you thinking, Eddie? Something is off."

"I couldn't agree more. Why so easy? But we can't let the others know, either. So what do we do?"

"I don't know?" she said. "These are my kids we're talking about and as much as I don't want to get emotionally involved..."

"You can't," Eddie finished for Lizzy.

"Exactly! What do I do? Nick can't know we're concerned; he may want to call it all off. He was right, though. Bringing the fight to our house will give us the advantage.

"There is still the question of why Tio wanted us to kill each other?" Lizzy continued.

"That still hasn't been resolved. Funny how it happens just when I'm close to getting my kids."

"I've been thinking about that as well. As far as we're concerned, Lizzy, you killed me and Tio doesn't know any different. But if he really wanted you out of the picture so badly, why hasn't he sent someone else to finish the job. I don't understand."

Eddie had been in the business as long as she had. They both knew when you wanted someone gone you did not give up easily.

"I know. It doesn't make any sense does it," Lizzy thought out loud. "There's definitely something else going on here and we need to find out what."

"It is why we must be prepared for anything to happen," Eddie pointed out. "Nick and Ty need to stay as far back as possible if anything goes down."

"I agree. But I know Nick and it won't be easy. Eddie, do you think Sandro knows something we don't?"

"I've thought about that. I want to say no, but you never know."

"Would you be opposed to taking him out of the equation? Maybe detaining him for a while?"

"He won't like that, Lizzy. But if he is up to something it will be both of our lives at stake. So, how do we detain him without his knowing?"

"Don't worry about that, I have my ways. Gianni will release him if and when we need him, but I think it's best for everyone concerned."

Lizzy reached into her desk drawer and grabbed some sleeping pills. She never used them herself, but they did come in handy.

"Give this to Sandro or mix it in with his food. If he finds out what we're up to he'll freak, but it will make him tired enough to co-operate regardless."

"Just remember, you're the one who gets to deal with him when he wakes up, Lizzy."

"Awe... Are you afraid of your boyfriend?"

"Yea, all right. Whatever lets you get through the night, chicky."

They both left the office knowing what they had to do. Lizzy would tell Nick about Sandro, but he would know nothing of any other worries. But she still had to make sure Gianni knew to release Sandro if anything went wrong. As long as Eddie believed Sandro was out of the picture, it would be fine. Eddie was all too willing to keep Sandro away, she thought as she wrote a quick note and gave it to Gianni with some quick instructions. There were going to be a few more surprises than just the children coming tomorrow. One thing was guaranteed, though, Lizzy had left nothing to chance.

She had something up her sleeve, that not even Gianni or Mina knew about. The night when she was in Marseille after having her drink the bartender had given her another package. It took her a long time to decide what she wanted to do with the information.

In consideration of everyone's safety and the chance for a normal life, she knew she made the right choice.

Lizzy found Nick up in *their* room — he never did seem to go back to his own quarters — and let him know their plan was working. If all went right, they would have the kids back and Sandro would see what Eddie was really like. She didn't like tricking one of her best friends, but there was little choice, but he would be prepared for whatever happened. Also, if she had read all the clues correctly, everything would be settled this weekend and life would have the chance get on as it should have all those years ago.

Lizzy had so many thoughts running through her head; she just wanted a nice warm bath in which to relax. She would need her energy over the next few days so she left Nick sitting on the chair staring at the picture of his children. It was something he had done every chance he got since he found out.

As she ran the water and filled the tub, Lizzy looked forward to letting all her anxiety wash away tonight. She needed to focus her energies and center herself — balance was the key to everything working out. She just hoped her friends were finding their own.

She settled into the warmth of the tub and let the bubbles consume her. The way they caressed her body was heavenly. As she sank into the warmth of the tub, she wasn't surprised to hear the light jiggle of the door handle as it opened. Lizzy allowed herself to close her eyes and be lost; Nick loved to talk to her as she relaxed — he said it was the only time the true Lizzy would come out from hiding.

The hairs on the nape of her neck began to tingle. Something was wrong. Nick would have said something by now. Lizzy discreetly reached under the towel at the edge of the tub and felt her glock. Reassured, she gently wrapped her hand around the cold steel, old habits die hard and hoped Nick was all right in the next room.

The reflection on the tap her only guide, she was not surprised to see who was standing in the doorway. All she could do now was hope he would understand.

The expression 'sitting duck' had a hell of a lot of meaning, Lizzy thought. Her enemy could not get a good angle for a shot, but she would still only have one chance. She carefully aimed from under the towel and gently squeezed the trigger to get a clean shot off. The intruder thumped to the ground like a dropped sack of potatoes. It was a kill shot and she knew it. Her life in the balance, she really did not care.

* * *

Nick had left Lizzy to enjoy her bath alone for a few moments while he went down to grab a couple of cold beers from the fridge. If he was going to intrude on her in the tub, he thought, the least he could do was bring a peace offering.

He enjoyed watching her in those moments; she was so relaxed and carefree. They could talk and catch up. Fill each other in on their lives. There were no boundaries, to their discussion, just much needed open conversations.

As he descended the stairs Sandro and Eddie were having a drink at the kitchen table. After catching a glimpse of Ty and Dani on the terrace, he decided to say a quick good night to his best friends before heading back upstairs.

Sandro joined them outside right behind Nick and the four began discussing the events in the days to come.

"Dani," Nick said, "you need to stay away if anything goes down. If something happens to you, Lizzy will have my ass. Your only job is to distract the kids when needed."

"Sure," she complained as she took a swig of beer, "you guys get to have all the fun while I get to baby sit. Why does this feel like high school all over again?" Dani loved nothing more than to egg Nick on, continuing a decades-old ritual.

"Sandro," Nick continued, "you need to keep out of sight and be back up. Lizzy needs you because you're focused and will get things done. Ty you...."

Everything went still as they heard the gunshot from upstairs. Nick's heart sank.

Before his beer bottle even hit the ground he was racing up the stairs two and three at a time. His heart pounded and dread filled him as he raced. Why did he leave her alone? What could be happening? An eternity passed as he ran down the hall to her room. Upon reaching it, the door was locked. What the hell was going on? He thought. Every second felt like an hour. Who fired the gun? Who was shot?

Nick quickly ran through the options: Gianni and Mina went to town so they weren't there. Dani, Sandro, Ty and he were on the Terrace. There was only one person left. He had thought the two settled their differences... Nick had to find Lizzy and make sure she was all right.

He rammed his shoulder against the door until it gave way under the force. Nothing was going to stop him from getting to Lizzy. She had to be all right, she just had to be.

*   *   *

Lizzy grabbed a towel and quickly wrapped herself without taking the gun off its target. She was sure it was a kill shot, but knew better than to take any chances. She would love to know why the son of a bitch chose that moment to try and kill her. Unfortunately, he could no longer give any answers.

Lizzy made her way around Eddie's sprawled out body in the door way to check if Nick was all right but he was not in the bedroom. As she heard someone com racing towards the door, she backed up and prepared for anything.

MINE

Once this new possible threat realized the door was locked, it would not be long before they broke through. As Nick almost fell through the door, she exhaled without even having realized she was holding her breath.

Nick was relieved as he saw Lizzy wrapped in a towel holding her gun ready to fire. When he saw Eddie on the ground he was glad she always kept a weapon at the ready, even if he couldn't see it.

Sandro pushed past him and assessed the scene. Nick's heart went out to the guy. He would have been inconsolable if it was Lizzy on the floor instead of Eddie.

"What the fuck happened?" Nick asked. "Are you all right?" From the raised eyebrow she gave him, he realized it was a dumb question.

"He's dead," Sandro began, unable to believe what was before him. He didn't understand. "Lizzy you killed him why?"

"Would you rather it was me dead in the bath tub, then?" she said in quick defense. "I was expecting Nick to come in, not to open my eyes and see a reflection of him with a gun aimed at me. Tell me, Sandro, what would you have done? Especially when you consider it was the fourth time since he's been here."

"What are you talking about?" Nick said. "He called a truce."

"Um....no. The other three times he got lucky that one of you always seemed to walk in. I never trusted him. Now you can see why."

"Why didn't you say anything?"

"Yea, because I'd say 'Hey, Nick, Eddie keeps trying to kill me.' All hell would have broken loose. Besides, the less people that knew the better. I needed him to trust me so I could get the information he had."

"Lizzy," Sandro pleaded, "he wouldn't have hurt you."

"Look at the gun, Sandro. Look where he was standing. I was in the tub and he didn't know I was armed. He had every intention of killing me."

As he took in the information with the eye of a professional, he knew she was right. He just did not want to believe it. Eddie had truly meant to kill Lizzy. He had taught her well. Now, he just needed to figure out why his boyfriend would want to kill her.

On top of it, Lizzy asked, "Does he have his cell in his pocket, Sandro? See what it says."

He pulled Eddie's cell from his pocket and scrolled through the messages. He hoped to find nothing but knew better. Pausing at an email from his father, Sandro looked Lizzy in the eyes. He immediately knew they had been double crossed. The million dollar question was why?

"What's the email say?" Lizzy asked.

"Basically, Tio knows everything that's going on," Sandro said, "including when the children are coming. He wanted Eddie to kill you, but frame me for it happening. The funny thing is there is no mention of any money being transferred. So either this was already paid for in full or...."

"Eddie was working both sides."

"If so, then what are we going to do?"

"If you two are done with your own little conversation," Ty interrupted, "do you mind filling the rest of us in?"

"If I'm right Ty," Nick put in his two cents, "they're saying Eddie was working with both Sandro's father and the Cirescos. The only question is why?"

Nick didn't like where this was going, everything was already set in motion and it was too late to change anything.

"Nick, Ty," Lizzy took the lead, "I need *both* of you to know where everything is in the house. Dani, you need to know where the safe room is and stay there with the kids. Nick, show Ty everything; Sandro and I have some planning to do."

"Lizzy, come on. There's got to be another way..."

"Nick, this is going down bad either way. All I know is it ends in the next few days, though. I am going to get our kids back and be done with all of this forever. So you can either help us, or...."

"You already know the answer," Nick did not let her finish her sentence. There was no way he was going to lose his children after just finding them. "Come on, Ty. There's lots you need to see."

Nick left Lizzy and Sandro along to lead Ty and Dani on a tour of the house. The couple had known it before, but the tour showed how the house was truly built for combat.

After Mina and Gianni came home and were filled in. Eddie's body was disposed of and as the night slowly faded into morning, Lizzy figured everything had been accounted for. Everyone knew where they had to be and with only a few hours to spare, they all needed sleep. Unfortunately Nick would only be able to sneak in an hour before heading off to school.

There was just one more thing to do before tucking in. Lizzy reached for her cell phone and sent off a quick message. She had her own backup plan none of them knew about and, for all their sakes, it had to all go smoothly. She had worked hard for the final outcome and was going to make sure it suited her means in the end.

TWENTY-FOUR

NICK HAD TO leave early and Lizzy woke up alone in her room to reflect on the events of the day before. Her concerns about Eddie had been right and Sandro was still in the dark. Lizzy had kept some of the information she gleaned to herself since he was dealing with the loss of his boyfriend. There was something else going on and she was just getting to the bottom of it.

With only a few hours until Nick brought the children home, though, she needed to prepare the house. Lizzy took a moment to check her phone and knew all the pieces were in play; her move was going to happen soon.

She was sure Gianni had already started; he was always more prepared than she. With a target to bring down, Lizzy was golden. But this... getting her children back... it was scaring the shit out of her. Nothing could be left to chance. She had devised a plan to account for every scenario possible, but she was careful not to be overconfident. Being cocky only led to mistakes and there was zero margin for error.

Lizzy put on a pair of fitted yoga pants, combat boots, and a tank top and was ready for action. The more freedom of movement she had, the better.

Next, she strapped on a glock and a few daggers. Lizzy liked to be prepared and had stashed other weapons around the property with ammo concealed in different locations so it would be easy to reload as necessary without any slowdowns. Her need for vengeance was growing by the minute, the fire inside re-ignited as the end neared. Lizzy was finally going to have back what was hers.

As she made her way down the stairs everyone was in the kitchen, but a movement in the office caught her attention. No one should have been in there. Everyone in the house was accounted for, so who was in the office?

Lizzy made eye contact with Gianni to let him know something was up and gave him a quick nod as she made her way down the rest of the stairs. She would have to find out how someone got in undetected. But first, she was going to find out who was in her study, one way or another.

She positioned herself against the wall to listen for movement and made out there were two people. The only other people who might know how to get into the house undetected were the previous owners and they wouldn't be that stupid. Whomever it was, though, Lizzy never liked it when the rules changed.

She eased forward to look through the crack in the door and did not want to believe her eyes. They looked so calm, so relaxed, *so smug*. They were here for a reason and must have assumed the owner would not care if they were there because Mina and Gianni were not even given a second thought.

Lizzy reached for her phone and sent a quick message to Nick. She needed to know if the kids were in school and did not want to risk losing them now.

'r the kidz w/ u'

'yes, in class. watz up?'

'get them out n get here.'

'WTF is going on'

'cirescos here, in house. don't know how.'

'omg. b smrt!'

Since she knew the children were safe with Nick, Lizzy next had to get Gianni's attention to let him know about their visitors. Sending Dani a text message. The Cirescos obviously knew people were in the house, so a phone going off would not surprise them and Lizzy sent a quick text to Dani.

Looking between the hinges of the door, she surveyed their positioning and they had been here before; they were too familiar with the surroundings. New questions came to mind.

She needed to hear what they were saying, but could not get closer without being noticed. It was ate her up inside to have them sitting so close, but she had to remain smart about the situation. Everyone's lives were at stake.

Lizzy tapped into the remote link for her computer accessed the video feed hoping it would get her what she needed. She was thankful to be living in era of computer spyware. *What did people do before this crap anyway?* she thought. She did not like what she heard over the feed.

"He said he would be here well over an hour ago," said Mr. Ciresco. "This better be good."

"Who are we meeting anyway?" his wife inquired. "I was enjoying my trip before you dragged me here."

"Your trip? What a nice way to put it."

"I've worn out my usefulness for you years ago," she said calmly. "You took away everything you ever promised me. For what?"

"You'll see," he sneered at her. "Don't think I've forgotten where you came from or what you left behind. I have people everywhere."

What the hell were they talking about? He apparently did not know the villa had new owners. It was fine by her, but what past could Mrs. Ciresco have left behind? Missing pieces to the puzzle sucked big time. Lizzy was going to be glad when she was out of this shit forever.

Ty had made his way to the opposite door and Lizzy motioned for him to cover her. Sandro and Gianni were at the kitchen door. The only way out for her adopted parents now was through the passage and they would not be fast enough.

Her back against the wall, she checked her glock and felt the daggers strapped against her inner arms for easy access. This needed to be quick and neat, but they were not going to get off easy without giving answers first. Her resolve set, Lizzy opted to take the direct approach and pushed the door open to go inside.

A gun aimed at his head, Ciresco could not believe the apparition before his eyes.

"You're dead," he said. "I put the dirt on your coffin myself."

"Yea, about that, someone fucked up. Where are my kids?"

"How did you find us here?" he asked.

"Find you?" Lizzy spat back. "That's funny. I've spent the last 11 years hunting you down like the animal you are. How did I find you? This is my house, you asshole. You walked right into the lion's den. How does it feel to be caught after so many years?" she asked her nemesis. "Did you actually think you would get away with trying to kill me and taking my children? I trusted you and you took advantage of a young, naive girl. For what!? All you did was abandon and ship the kids from school to school. You're a fucking arms dealer and I trusted you."

"Mimma..." he began.

"It's Lizzy, fuck head. Remember? Lizzy. You know you have a whole lot of people out there more than willing to sell you to the devil. All the people you screwed over. You have enemies everywhere, and your greed and arrogance made me rich along the way. I made more than enough money to look after my kids for the rest of their lives."

"You'll never find them."

"Bullshit!" she spat back. "I already have them. Did you really think I would leave anything to chance where they were concerned? See, you did teach me one thing: to be patient. And trust me I've been very patient. But it ends now!"

"And you," Lizzy turned to her stepmother, "sitting so nice and quiet over there, you don't get off easily either. Your only saving grace was faking my death.

"That's right, asshole, your wife helped fake my death. She just didn't count on my wanting revenge."

Ciresco looked between his wife and Lizzy. His head was spinning with the information. His wife had helped Mimma; had set this whole thing in motion.

"Just answer me one question you ass hole. Why? Why take them from me?"

"Because you, my dear, didn't fit into my plans. You were a liability. *She* had the family she wanted, and you weren't of any further value."

"That's what you got?" she pushed.

Before he could answer further, though, a gunshot rang out from behind Lizzy. Ciresco had been hit square between the eyes and was gone. Her gun still level, Lizzy turned around and was not surprised to see Sandro's uncle had entered the room.

"Tio," she said matter of factly.

"Yes, Bella. It took a while but I finally tracked you down. And Emilia, you are as beautiful as always."

"Santiago, how did you...?. Why are you...?" Mrs. Ciresco sat there unable to believe she was staring at him. It had been over 30 years.

"I take it you two know each other," Lizzy said knowingly. "No wonder he never took you on his trips to Brazil.

"Well Tio or Santiago, whoever the hell you are," she continued, "what the fuck are you doing?"

"Well, Bella, if Eddie hadn't screwed up, we wouldn't be having this conversation right now. But don't worry, it'll be a short one. Once Eddie comes in, he'll make it quick. I promise."

"I hate to break it to you, Tio, but Eddie won't be coming in because he's dead. Can't say I'm sorry he's gone, though. He was an arrogant ass just like you and you're more than welcome to join him. But I have to ask why: after everything you have done, why kill me now?"

"You were what I needed to find the Cirescos. I told you I wanted payment for what he took all those years ago. The funny thing is, the bastard never even knew, did he, Emilia? Did he ever know who you really were before you ran away?"

"You forced me to leave, Santiago. Don't forget that! You made me leave the only thing I ever cared about."

"Yes, my dear. But you see I should have killed you all those years ago instead of letting you live."

Lizzy watched Tio intently, unwilling to believe what he said, but she had been in their world long enough to know you could trust no one. Your spouse least of all.

She needed to keep Tio talking. He was a loose cannon and anything could happen when he was around, but she needed to bide her time. The message she had sent out earlier would end all of it. It just needed to be answered soon or no one would be left alive.

Another shot rang out too fast for even Lizzy to react. It wasn't meant for her, though. Emilia laid there in shock, shot in the gut by Tio.

It was a kill shot, but Santiago had aimed to ensure she would suffer. It seemed to be a pattern: he made his family suffer for his own benefit. She should have known Tio would be the same as Ciresco. They were cut from the same cloth.

"Take the pillow off the couch Emilia and put pressure on it," Lizzy told the woman who had at one time saved her life. Her gun still aimed at Tio, she asked, "Why hire me to kill Eddie and Eddie to kill me. It doesn't make any sense... unless you wanted Sandro to feel pain?"

"Sandro turned his back on his family so he and Eddie could be together. He thought I didn't know, but I knew all along. I owned Eddie. I knew everything they ever did. Even when he left Sandro in Venice to come here with you."

"He left Sandro in Venice." Eddie did one thing right at least, Lizzy thought. She shifted position to get Tio's back to the kitchen door. Ty was in the hallway waiting for an opportunity and Sandro was just itching to get in there. She'd make sure he had his chance. She just needed to keep his father talking for another minute or so.

"So, then," she stalled, "why all the secrets? Why did Emilia leave? What did you keep of hers?"

"Why did she leave? She didn't want the life I offered her. Little did she know she had traded the serpent for the devil himself. She was mine, and I needed to hurt her as much as she hurt me."

"You don't seem like a man that could get hurt. Wait," Lizzy remembered, "the story?"

"Very smart, Bella. Only the mother didn't die. I cast her out in the streets with nothing to her name keeping the only thing she would ever want."

Lizzy looked down to the woman on the floor. As she lay there struggling to survive, Lizzy realized she was Sandro's mother and Santiago had kept their son.

"You know, Tio. That wasn't a very smart thing to do. You should never separate a mother from her child. You see, payback's a bitch."

"Yes, father, it is."

Tio turned to see his son behind him as realization set in. Sandro did not hesitate when he fired the shot that killed his father. He had been behind him and heard the entire story. He finally knew his father had taken him from his mother and caused all the drama in his life.

Tio on the ground beside him, Sandro quickly went to where Emilia was resting knowing there was nothing he could do to save her. He simply hoped to spend their first and last few moments together.

Lizzy gave them some space and left the room to sit on the staircase. All of it had been for what... revenge on one another? All because Santiago didn't like his ex being with his adversary. These kinds of men never learned what is truly important. The money in their pockets is worth more to them than their family.

Lizzy watched from the stairs as Sandro held his mother for the first time in years. The sheer misery of all the lies his father ever told him scarring his face. His mother cradled in his arms, he rocked back and forth like she would have done with him when he was a child.

In empathy for her pain, Mina gave her something to help make her more comfortable.

A commotion came from the front of the house as the door opened. Nick had finally walked in with the children, their faces lost in the glistening sun behind them. They were truly there. All that was left was to explain why the only mother they had ever known lay dying in the other room. Chalk this up as one of those days. Two dead bodies, three teenagers and Nick with the 'what the fuck did I miss' look on his face.

"Sir, this is your house? Are you fricken loaded? Holy....." Tiano didn't even get to finish his sentence. He saw the woman sitting on the steps and knew instantly who it was. Anna and Tori stood speechless as well.

"Mimma?"

As she heard her name from their lips, all the weight of the last decade lifted. They were there, in front of her. After years of waiting her dreams were finally being realized.

"Yes. It's me." She stood up to walk towards her children and tears began to fall from her eyes. She had waited so long for this day. They were here with her. Even better, they knew who she was.

Lizzy drew them all into a hug, never wanting to let go. So many years of searching, so many lives lost. Lizzy looked up at Nick and felt they were a family now. Nothing was going to change that ever again.

"There is something I need to tell you guys....." Lizzy began, but before she could begin her name was being called from the office. She did not want the children to see the horrors of the day, but Lizzy recognized they would need to say goodbye to the only mother they had known. She could not deprive them of that.

"Lizzy," Emilia called out, "please bring them here."

Lizzy needed to be strong for the kids as they entered the room. They would not understand everything going on. She just hoped one day they would.

"Before you guys go in there," she said, "I warn you, it's not nice. There were some problems and there are two men dead. If you can't handle it, I understand. But the woman in the other room is dying and needs to see you before she does." She saw the confusion in her children's eyes and knew there was no way she could protect them.

The triplets walked into the room and saw who they believed was their mother laying on the floor dying. It was more than they should have had to deal with, but they did not seem shocked.

Emilia called her children over to her and, as they sat next to her failing body, told them the truth of Lizzy being their mother, how Mimma had 'died' and everything that had happened. She wanted their forgiveness before she died. It was something only they could give.

She took comfort in Nick's being close beside her. So much had happened that day. But she was glad to finally have back everything lost all those years ago.

"I told them everything in the car on the way here," Nick informed Lizzy. "I wanted them to be prepared. Except I left out the part about being their father. I thought you could do that."

"I will gladly do so as soon as we're done in here."

She stepped away from Nick and made her way to Emilia. Lizzy wanted her to know she forgave her. It was the least she could do... Emilia did help fake her death, after all.

Lizzy was thankful to hear Gianni answering the front door. She knew who it was and they were not a moment too soon.

As her guests walked over to them in her office, she heard a shot go off and everything went black.

There was a commotion and Lizzy heard Nick saying something to her, but could not make it out. She knew she had been shot, but she lost consciousness before she could determine who fired.

TWENTY-FIVE

LIZZY AWOKE TO the beeping of machines, but was unable to open her eyes. Her body was numb all over. Memories of her accident all those years ago flooded her mind and back from when she was in the accident all the panic set in.

She had no idea what was going on or where she was. Her body wanted to move, but was not co-operating with her mind. She began to struggle against the feeling of being trapped when a familiar voice broke through.

"Mom," Tori said excitedly. "It's ok. Relax. I'll get the nurse. Anna, watch her."

"Mom, you're going to be fine," pronounced her other daughter. "Dad's here with us, too. He and Tiano just went to get a coffee and Tori's getting the nurse. Everything will be all right."

They were calling her mom. Nick was there with them, and they knew he was their dad. If she could only move everything would be perfect.

"Anna," Nick's voice broke in, "what's going on?"

"Tori just went to get the nurse. Mom's waking up."

"Lizzy its ok," he consoled her. "I'm here. We're all here. You were shot, but you're fine. Everything is fine. The nurse will come and remove the restraints and tubes in a minute. They just didn't want you waking up and hurting yourself.

"Ciresco shot you," he explained further. "The bastard was still alive, but he's gone now. I made sure of it. Emilia told them everything before she passed. They know the truth. We have our family back. You, me, the kids."

Nick gazed down at his love and brushed the hair off her forehead. He was not going to lose her or ever let her go again. Wherever she was, he would be there with her.

Lizzy was glad Nick was the one to save her life. She had her family and that's what mattered.

When the nurses came in and began to remove everything attached to her, Lizzy began to feel better. She could move her arms and legs and the tube in her throat was gone. Her throat would be sore for a few days, but she was alive. Having her kids with her and the smiles on their faces kept her as close to home as she needed.

Everything removed, the doctor asked everyone to leave, but Lizzy insisted Nick stay. She had so many questions and she was sure he did, as well.

"Well, Lizzy," the doctor began, "you're a very lucky lady. An inch lower and you wouldn't be here right now."

"I'm all right, though, right? I can go home soon with my family?"

"Yes, in a few days."

Nick held onto Lizzy's hand and asked, "Is there anything she will need to do when she goes home, any med's or restraining from activities?"

"Only to take it easy. There's nothing another seven months won't fix."

"Seven months? What are you talking about?" She couldn't be, Lizzy thought. It was not possible, was it?

"You're pregnant, Lizzy. You didn't know?" the doctor asked.

Lizzy and Nick shook their heads in shock.

"Well, you're 10 weeks along and you and the baby are doing great. Don't worry."

"I'm going to be a dad?" Nick asked.

"I'm pregnant!" Lizzy was shocked.

In unison, they looked to each other. Pregnant? It was unbelievable. They had found one another after all these years, gotten their children back, and even had wonderful friends who would help dispose of bodies for them. Now a baby? It would be like starting anew. Now they just had to tell the kids.

"A baby, Lizzy." Nick smiled. "We're going to be parents the right way this time." Although still in shock, he was definitely happy about the news.

"By the way," he suddenly added, "you have some explaining to do to Gianni and everyone back at the house. But, first things first, let's get you there." Having her new partners come to the door must have been a shock for them all, but she knew the right choice had been made.

"Do you think we could hold off telling the kids for a bit?" Lizzy asked. "I'd like them to get used to the other things first."

It was all so much for her to take in. Nick was back, great; she was reunited with her kids, a blessing, and, now, to be pregnant on top of it all, she needed time to adjust.

In all the years spent training there was only one goal in mind. Her mission completed, Lizzy was about to embark on a whole new adventure. Was she ready?

Her heart skipped a beat as the kids walked back into the room once the doctor left. They were really here with her. They had grown up so much.

Seeing their fuzzy pictures on the monitor was one thing, but now that they were beside her, she could not have been happier.

"Mom, don't worry," Tori started, "Dad filled us in on everything. You don't have to worry." As she reached down to squeeze her mother's hand, Tori was happy. When she looked over to her siblings, they knew this was where they belonged.

"Yea," Tiano added, "our other mom, Mrs. Ciresco, explained everything, even how she covered for you so you could live. I'm just glad she did.

"See Anna," he threw in, "I told you everything happens for a reason."

"You told me," she said in mock shock, "I said it all along….."

Her children arguing was music to her ears. Nick might have been giving them shit at the moment, but it was nice. It was what brothers and sisters were supposed to do.

"What are you smiling at?" Nick asked as he sat beside her on the end of the bed.

"This! This is what I waited years for. All of you... in one room... arguing. This is what family is supposed to do."

Nick looked at her like she had grown a second head but, deep down, agreed. They quickly said goodnight to the kids as Gianni picked them up to go home for the night. Nick decided to stay with her because the last time she was pregnant and out of his sight he lost her for 18 years. He was not about to make that mistake again.

The next couple days in the hospital dragged on. The room was like a revolving door with her friends and family constantly checking to make sure Lizzy was safe. Really all she wanted was to go home. She just wanted to be in her own room.

Finally, the doctor gave his blessing on the condition she promised to do nothing for a few weeks and let her go home.

Nick and the kids had come to pick her up and Lizzy was enjoying the ride home with the whole troop. She and Nick still had not told children about the pregnancy... Lizzy was still trying to wrap her mind around it herself. Sure she was still young, but pregnant? Was she even ready for it?

Even though this time Lizzy knew she would have Nick's support, she was afraid to admit she was scared. As they pulled up the driveway the rest of the family was already there to meet her. And, by the look on Gianni and Mina's faces, she knew they definitely had questions.

"You're back," Mina said. "It took you long enough."

"I missed you too, Mina," Lizzy confided while giving her friend a hug. After saying her hellos to everyone, the look on Gianni's face told her it was time to start explaining. This was not going to be the most fun conversation she had ever had. She did not know how to tell them she had done it for all their sakes.

"I know a lot probably happened after I blacked out," Lizzy began, "but please know I did it all for our freedom."

Nick give her hand a gentle squeeze for confidence and she continued, "Years ago, I was handed a card by a gentleman who said if I ever wanted to fix things for good I should give him a call. After I did some research into him I knew it meant giving up the life I knew, but I wasn't ready then. They tried again and offered me immunity from all charges, but I wasn't ready at the time, either, as I still had to find them," she nodded over to the children.

"So why now, then?" Gianni asked. "What made you change your mind?"

Taking a deep breath and looking around the room with her family and friends, Lizzy knew she had made the right choice. They were all going to be free. They could all live their lives in the open with no worries.

"With the triplets finally within reach, I offered to help them bring down Tio and the Cirescos. In return, they had to grant Sandro, Mina, Gianni and I full immunity. We would be free and clear to live our lives.

"They agreed on one condition."

"So," Sandro asked, "what's the catch? What do we have to do now?" He trusted Lizzy would have a good reason for doing what she did.

"We are free and clear. We have taken out the Cirescos along with most of their contacts in the last few years… Santiago was a bonus. Sorry, Sandro, but it had to be done." Lizzy could see the hurt in her friend's eyes, but also the understanding.

"We have to work with them from now on," she continued. "They may call us in when they need someone captured. We just have to live a normal life until they need us."

"So, we're their vigilantes?" Gianni asked. "If they can't get the job done, they call us?"

"Yea, pretty much. They ask that we keep our contact with them to ourselves, but when they need us we must act. Thankfully, I don't think will need most of us anytime soon. Except you, Sandro."

"Why me?" he asked. "What did I do?"

"They want you to help train their task force," Lizzy explained. "One as ruthless as we are. If they can't stop their target, that's when we're called into play.

"Can you handle that?" she asked Sandro. "It was the only way to keep you safe."

"All I have to do is train them and I get to live a normal life," Sandro said, "no questions asked until they need me."

"That's the deal."

Lizzy knew it was a lot to ask her loved ones to process, but she did everything out of love and would protect what was hers. By the looks on their faces, she could tell they understood.

As they talked things through, everyone agreed it was for the best. Tori, Anna and Tiano remained quiet, which made her nervous, but Lizzy knew that it would be an adjustment for all of them.

Nick could tell Lizzy was getting tired. It was still her first day back and she needed to regain her strength. He would make sure she got it.

He picked her up in his arms to take her to their bedroom and asked the kids to follow after a few minutes. He set her down in the middle of the big bed and waited for the kids.

"Hey, Mom, we just wanted to say good night and get some rest," Anna said from just outside the door when they arrived. "We love you."

"I love you guys, as well," Lizzy said. "I never stopped looking for you. Every day you were in my thoughts, and everything I ever did was to find you three and bring you back. But we do have some news for you."

The three looked to one another and Lizzy didn't know if they were ready to hear what was next, but there was no time like the present.

"You guys are going to have a baby sister or brother," she announced. "Your father and I are having a baby."

The reaction she received was not the one she expected. They all piled on the bed beside her like they did when they were little. They were happy. They were going to be a family.

The world knew what she would do to protect what was hers and nothing was ever going to stop her.

Printed in the United States
By Bookmasters